Now and at the Hour

Other novels by Martin Drapkin:

Poor Tom

The Cat Tender

Ten Nobodies (and their somebodies)

Now and at the Hour

Martin Drapkin

Three Towers Press
Milwaukee, Wisconsin

Published by Three Towers Press,
An imprint of HenschelHAUS Publishing, Inc.
Milwaukee, Wisconsin
www.HenschelHAUSbooks.com

ISBN: 978159598-990-1
LCCN: PENDING

Printed in the United States of America

BILLY

POOR KID! Bad luck, a lousy accident like that. Crappy luck. Me, I'm not sure I wouldn't rather be dead than like he is, that is if he's not going to get better. What he thinks, I don't know. The rest of these guys in B Ward, they don't know any better—they've been the way they are all their lives and most have the IQs of babies. What do they know? But Ricky, poor kid, that low-key Doctor Winters said his intelligence is the same as before he got kicked in the head. So Ricky knows what's up. He must.

When that bald black guy rolled him into the ward this morning, I was shocked. The look on his pale face as he lay there on that cart, covered with a white blanket—just ... *scared*. I can't get it out of my mind. His eyes, looking around at all the weirdos. I'd be scared, too, if it were me on that cart, going into a place like this. I mean, it's gotta be a shock for a twelve-year-old guy who just a few months ago was running around doing the usual kid stuff with his friends and going to school and living with his parents and sisters and now, *BOOM!*, he can't walk, can't talk, he's in a ward at a state institution with twenty-nine mentally retarded bizarros, many of them bizzare, with weird looks and weirder behaviors, most of them in diapers and sleeping in cribs, making crazy noises, the place sometimes reeking of piss and shit, and now this is his life. And who the Christ knows for how long?

Damn! I guess you don't know how lucky you are until you see someone like him. Sure, I've felt sorry for myself because of my crappy family life, and when I'm here at the food court at the mall and look around and see parents and kids together, people eating and maybe having fun, I always feel jealous. But I realize how piddling my problems are compared to his. And not just him, but others there too. Buddy, for one. Like Ricky, he's trapped in a useless body but his mind seems fine too. He even has an eye for the ladies, the old lech. But at least Buddy's lived with his situation his whole life, whereas for this kid it's all new and has to be startling, horrible. It *must*.

1

I like to come here after work when I've done a day shift, like today, and sit by myself and have a slice or two of sausage pizza and a big Cherry Coke and watch people for a while before I go home. It's the time of day when the high school kids come to the mall straight from school, and I like to watch the girls in their tight jeans and long hair sitting around stuffing their pretty faces and talking about God-knows-what, just like, not that long ago, I liked to sit with Boyd in the losers' corner of the Thomas Jefferson High School cafeteria and watch girls—in fact, some of the same chicks that I see now a lot at the food court. What *do* they talk about? They're cute and sexy, sweet little bodies, but they could be from another planet for as much as I know them. I wish I could hear what they say, but usually they sit too far away. So I just watch—the way they stand in line at McDonald's and Taco Bell and Sbarro; the way their fingers flutter as they gesture while talking; the way their plucked eyebrows arch and they open their eyes and mouths wide and curl half of their upper lips in contempt or amazement; how they play with their hair, stroking it with one hand or twirling it or rubbing the ends with their fingers; the way they pick up each greasy french fry with a thumb and index finger and dip it into a little white paper thingie of ketchup and slide it between their sweet lips; how their breasts strain against their shirts and sweaters—and store the images in my mind for later.

I watch, but try not to stare. If one of them catches me looking, I immediately turn or lower my head or glance at the open paperback, *Of Mice and Men*, I hold in my left hand for that reason. After that I'm oh-so-cautious about staring at that particular group, at least for a while. I mean, what if one of them should stride over to me, arms crossed and eyes blazing, and snarl, "Hey, weirdo! What are *you* looking at?"

Later I'll go home to my little apartment and happily lock the door behind me and get into my pajama bottoms and gray hoodie and sink into my beat-up beige recliner and cover myself with my dead grandma's blue afghan. I'll turn on my little TV for the company of its light and sound, but probably won't watch much unless maybe it's a western—*Rio Bravo* or one of those. Maybe I'll watch one of my Laurel and Hardy videos. Mostly I like to sip my hot mint tea with honey and read. After a while I'll probably fall asleep in the chair with my book open in my lap, and then sometime during the night I'll wake up and stumble into bed and set my alarm. And then a few hours later it'll be back to work to see how Ricky's doing in his new, sad home.

Anyways.

BUDDY

HELL OF A LIFE, ain't it? I been here for ten years now and seen a lot—some of the saddest cases, pathetic human beings really, and you wonder why they're alive, why they didn't just die in the womb or at birth, and spare all the fuss and bother. Me too, I guess. I'm as pathetic as any, and maybe more than most. The difference between me and the rest of these *residents*, like they call us, is that I know it.

But I gotta think there'll be a better life someday, a life where this damned cerebral palsy ain't my damned fate. Heaven. That's what I think about the moment I wake up and before I fall asleep at night and a lot of the time in-between. How wonderful to be somewhere up there in the sky, not trapped in this no-good old body, just pure spirit, and not have to endure the daily indignities, as you might say, of this life in B Ward. Just peeing's an indignity. If I'm in bed or my wheelchair and gotta pee, I gotta squirm and look uncomfortable and make weird sounds until one of them aides or a nurse notices and then they pull my thing from my pants and stick it in a cold metal urinal and I do what I can and then they take it out and shake the last drops off and stick it back in my pants. Here I am, a fifty-four-year-old man and they're almost all young women and they're holding my dingus and helping me pee and going, "Good boy, Buddy." Good *boy*! I'm quite sure that kind of bulltwinkie don't happen in heaven.

Sometimes I feel so down I wish I could put an end to it all, but I can't even do that. I mean, I can't exactly shoot or cut myself or overdose. Maybe I could somehow tip over my damn wheelchair and hope for a fatal head injury, but with my luck I'd live and just have a throbbing headache and a big old lump on my stupid head, like I did once about three years ago when my wheelchair tipped over, and be worse off yet—probably end up even more of a drooling fool than I am now. So I guess I just gotta hang around and hope God'll take me sooner rather than later.

Of course, it ain't all hell. The one good thing about living in a place like this is there's a lot of women around, and I get to look at 'em every day. They ain't *all* so great to look at, but some are—particularly this new aide that started a couple months ago, Mary Lou. What a rack! I like it when she's here. And others too—that little dark-haired nurse Randi, for one. I like to see them and listen to 'em talk and laugh and smell their perfume when they take care of me. And even though it's embarrassing when one of them women helps me pee, I gotta admit there's also something sort of nice about it—some cute young thing holding my ding-dong in her soft little hand. I don't know. Maybe I'm just a twisted old fart who don't deserve to live.

These other poor guys on B Ward ain't no better off than me, though most of 'em don't know no better neither. Gramps for example. Here he's a seventy-two-year-old Down syndrome guy—the oldest one in the state, Randi said—who sits in a chair all day holding a pair of tattered cloth dolls in them scrawny arms—his "babies," some of the aides call them—and making bad faces at doctors and the head nurse and such and holding hands with his best friend, Timmy. Gramps used to be able to walk, they say, a long time back, but no more. Timmy's all twisted up and spastic, a shrunken pathetic dwarf who lives to sit next to his beloved Gramps day after day. Then there's Larry the Whacker, like Billy calls him, whose pathetic moans and groans, including his trademark "Wah-GOO! Wah-GOO!" we have to hear most every day during after-lunch naptime and other times. And old Dino the blind guy, whose head is maybe three times normal size, legs paralyzed, and who spends his days listening for and laughing like a crazy madman at sneezes, throat-clearings, and other such wonders. And that grumpy Arnie, always wearing his stars-and-stripes hard hat and day after day paging through them catalogs people bring him. And Davey, scooting around on the floor and cleaning wheelchair wheels and crib legs with a white washcloth like he does. What a crew! And that's just some of us.

And now this poor new kid that came yesterday, Ricky. B Ward's the freak house that he steps into. He ain't no more retarded than I am, I heard Doc Winters say, just brain damaged from a football accident so his body don't work no more, can't walk or talk. I imagine he's scared here. I guess there's no other place for a kid like him than here, though it sure as hell don't seem like *this* crazy place is the best. You wonder what's going through that guy's head, being in a place like this and seeing all these bizarros. Me included.

Hell of a life!

RICKY

I CAN'T BELIEVE what's happened to me. It's been at least a few months now, I think, since that day of my accident, maybe more, and I still can't believe it. Every day I ask myself if God's punishing me for something I did. What'd I do to deserve this? Why me? I can't think of anything I did that was so bad. Okay, I cheated on two math tests at school last semester and I read my sister Chelsea's diary, but that doesn't seem so terrible that I should be punished like this. If God's mad at me for stuff as dumb as that, then I gotta think He's not as great as everyone says. What sins did I do that were so bad? I mean, I went to confession the best I could, and even told about the math tests, and confessed about whatever other little things I'd done that I shouldn't have, and did whatever penances they said—the Hail Mary and Our Father and stuff.

This is like some nightmare that I can't wake up from. I want to wake up from it and be in my bedroom with all my stuff, and it's just another day and I get out of bed and get dressed and get ready for school, like most days, then go to school and see my friends, and goof off after school or play ball or walk Riley, and do my homework, and stuff like that. A bad nightmare, and then you wake up and shake it off and it's over and you just go ahead with your everyday life and forget about the dream. But this bad dream just keeps going.

I don't even know where I am. I was in that hospital—it must have been a hospital—for a while, but I don't even know how long that was for. It was definitely weeks, but maybe it was months. I don't know. Being there was scary enough, but then they loaded me in an ambulance and brought me here—yesterday, that was—and I don't know what kind of place this is. All I know is that it's weird. There're all these guys in brown metal cribs, and some of them are little kids but most of them are older and some look like adults. Some sit up in chairs, but a lot of them are just in these cribs most of the time. And a lot of them make these strange sounds, like animals or something, or they grunt or scream

5

out things that don't make sense. And some of them *look* so weird too. There's this one guy, his arms and legs are drawn up and bent at crazy angles and it looks like they're that way all the time because he never straightens them out. He just lies there in his crib like that all the time I've seen him, and his bed is right next to mine. And then there's this other guy a few beds away, he has the biggest head I've ever seen. It's just *huge!* He has this big muscular chest and shoulders, like a linebacker, but his legs are just real short and shriveled and they never move, and every once in a while he yells out something like, "Hey-kay-kay! *YEAH!* Hey-kay-kay." Weird! And then there's this other guy who mostly looks like a normal guy but he wears this construction hard hat with stars and stripes like an American flag and he spends most of his time looking at some kind of catalog, as far as I can tell. Then there's this little kid who scoots on his back across the floor, pushing off with his feet, and usually carries around a white rag or cloth of some kind in one hand.

The scariest thing is not knowing when I'm going to get better. I have to think I'm going to get better, be able to walk again and talk, but I don't know when. I know I got hurt pretty bad in that touch football game. I remember that I fell down when I was chasing Brandon and then Jeff accidentally kicked me in the side of the head, pretty hard, and my back too, and I remember that it hurt real bad, but I don't remember much after that. I know Jeff didn't do it on purpose, so I don't blame him. It was just one of those things that happen, just an accident. Or maybe God wanted it to happen because I did something wrong. I really don't know. Either way, though, I guess I got hurt pretty bad. But when am I going to be able to walk and talk and stuff again? Maybe it just takes a long time to heal, but it sure is scary not knowing. I wish someone'd tell me that kind of stuff. No one does. If I at least had an *idea* when I'd be better, I think I could get through this nightmare easier. And it *is* a nightmare.

One of the guys here keeps staring at me. He's kinda interesting—an older guy with gray hair and these real watery blue eyes and he sits in a sort of battered brown wheelchair, always slumped over like he can't hold himself up, like he's really weak. His mouth hangs open a little and he drools from one corner. He doesn't sleep in a crib like most of the people here. He has a regular bed, but with these metal rails that go up and down, like in that hospital. Anyway, I'm lying here in this crib—they put me in a *crib,* like a *baby*—and I see this old guy on the other side of the room sitting in his chair, near a TV, slumped over, just looking right at me with these big blue eyes. I don't know if he understands anything at all. But then I think he must cause when our eyes met he looked right at me and held his gaze, but not rude, and I just had the feeling that he knew something about me. He doesn't scare me, like some of the other people in this place. He seems nice.

So far I only know one person's name. He's one of the guys who works here, I guess, because he fed me my breakfast and, later, lunch and before he did said, "Hey, Ricky. I'm Billy Malsavage. Nice to meet you." Then he picked up my hand and shook it. That was nice. He seems kinda young, but nice. I wish I could have lifted my hand myself. I can lift it just a little bit, but it's a major effort. I wish I knew other people's names.

It's funny that they have this place decorated with cutouts of chicks and rabbits and stuff like that for Easter.

Oh, God, I wish someone would tell me what kind of place this is and how long I'm gonna be here. I wish someone'd tell me when I'm going to get better. I wish I knew what I did to deserve this.

BILLY

CHRISTY REMINDS ME of Mary Lou. She has a serious set of bazooms inside that green waitress uniform and the same big dark eyes. She's shorter than Mary Lou, though. I've been coming here to Junior's for breakfast for two years now and she's almost always the same—friendly and nice, and not just to me but to all the early morning breakfasters hunched over their eggs or pancakes and shlurping coffee. "Oh, *hi!*" she always says, even at 5:45 a.m., an ungodly hour. "How ya *doin'*? Coffee, hon?" I love that "hon," even though she says it to everyone, not just me. She's the main reason I like this greasy spoon—her and big Junior, the owner and cook, with his flattop haircut and bulging biceps and blue *USMC* tattoo on his right arm and his black tooth. But mostly Christy. Sometimes I wonder if she's really in such a good mood all the time or just puts it on to get bigger tips. Doesn't matter. I like to be around her either way. In fact, I sort of love her. I think I do. At least she's the only female I even think about being with, if I were so inclined, which I'm not. Not as of now, anyway.

I like to sit at the very end of the counter nearest the kitchen and eat my two eggs over easy and bacon, not too crisp, and buttered white toast with strawberry jelly, soaking up the egg yolk with my toast, and sip black coffee and watch Christy and listen to her kid around with her customers— mostly truck drivers and carpenters and construction guys and such who start their days early. It's warm in Junior's and I can just sit there on my usual red-plastic-covered stool and watch pretty Christy—blond ponytail swinging, sweet little body inside that green uniform, her cute slightly-pockmarked face—taking orders and bringing guys their food and refilling their cups and giving them their checks and taking their money and smiling and thanking them and telling them to have a nice day. Now and again Junior comes out of the kitchen to ask guys how they like their breakfasts, and when they say "Good" or just nod their heads when their mouths are full his reply is always the same: "*Out*standing!"

Junior surprised me a little bit last week. One of the customers, a short and chubby guy with one squinty eye, was talking with some other guys about the war in Vietnam and was saying how those four students who were shot and killed by the National Guard last year, in May, at some college in Ohio, deserved what they got. "A bunch of spoiled rich kids who don't love their country," the guy called the protestors. For some reason, I expected that Junior would agree with the chubby guy, would at least nod his head. But no. He just stared at the man for maybe thirty seconds, with a neutral facial expression, and didn't say anything, and then just turned to walk back to the kitchen. I wondered what that was all about.

I remember I started coming here my sophomore year of high school just to get the hell out of my nutso house and have some place to go before school opened. My wacko parents usually started their screaming matches at about six a.m., *horribly* startling me awake every time—*terrible* feeling, like having a bucket of ice water thrown on you—so I tried to be out of the house before then. They didn't fight *every* day, of course, but since I couldn't predict when it would happen it was best to just get the hell out every day, or most days anyway, and not take any chances. Junior's seemed a good place to go and nobody there seemed to mind my coming in most days, even when I ordered just toast and coffee and nursed that coffee for the better part of an hour, reading a book or sometimes the newspaper. Christy was nice enough to me from the first day I went there and, unlike my mother, I could pretty much expect that she'd be on an even keel, more or less predictable, day after day. She still is, and that's good.

That's why I never mind starting work at 6:30 when I have day shifts, which I usually have. I'm used to being up early. I prefer days to p.m. shifts and certainly to nights. There's more going on, and I like it when the kids are up and around instead of sleeping.

Kids. Strange word for some of them, old as they are, but I guess it describes them mentally. Buddy's definitely not a kid, nor is Gramps, at least in terms of age.

Ricky's a kid though, damn it to hell anyway, and he should be out doing kid stuff instead of where he is, but he had bad luck. *Horrible* luck! He's been on B Ward for a week now, in my group of ten kids, Group One, and I've gotten to know him a little. He doesn't seem as scared as when he first came in, but he must still feel scared a lot. How could he not? *I* would. I like him. I'm glad he's in my group, but I wish I had more time for him.

It's busy during the day, what with feeding breakfast at seven when Destini and that fast-talking Cassie roll the food cart in, then cleaning and dressing everyone, doing baths for two or three kids each day, making beds, constantly changing diapers, hauling bags of dirty or soiled stuff to the laundry chute, putting kids in their various chairs or carts and wheeling them out to the solarium or to church or music, feeding lunch, putting them down for their naps, getting them cleaned up and ready for the p.m. shift, and charting. And, of course, you have to go on breaks and lunch and all. The only down time is after lunch, when the kids nap. Meanwhile, this poor Ricky spends most of his time in bed or in his chair, not doing anything. And when he's in that damned chair, most of the time he's slumped over to one side because he can't even hold himself up. We tie a white cloth thing, a wide dealie that covers most of his chest, around him to hold him up, but even then he slumps over a lot.

I wonder what he thinks, what's going on in his head. I don't know. I can't. I talk to him when I can, tell him some things, but I'm not sure what to say, really, and he can't answer. I can see in his eyes that he understands. Those blue-green eyes are intelligent, and I can tell that he knows what I'm saying. But I can't tell what he thinks or feels because his face doesn't show that, except, of course, he sure as Christ doesn't look happy. And why the Christ should he? His life's been shattered. How would anyone feel in his situation? I can only imagine how I'd feel.

I wish I knew what to do.

I don't know if the other aides or even the nurses feel like I do. They seem to like Ricky and they treat him nice and all, but I can't tell if they feel like I do. They don't show it if so. But maybe their way is right. Maybe it's best just to treat him normal, not get all sympathetic—"Oh, *poor* Ricky!"—so that he doesn't feel worse yet about himself. Not that I do that, I hope. I don't know. As usual in my pathetic life, I don't know my ass from my elbow when it comes to how to relate to my fellow human beings.

One thing that was nice was when Rita was taking down some of the Easter decorations from the wall, the cardboard chicks and bunnies and like that, and she taped one of the bunnies over Ricky's crib. "Here ya go," she said to him, "this guy'll cheer ya up." She's into decorating the place for holidays. Arnie seemed to like it best when she stuck those green cardboard shamrocks all over the place last month.

Linc seems to like Ricky. He's been working here, he said, for about five years—tall, muscular black guy who always wears these tight T-shirts that show off his physique. Pretty quiet guy, though, doesn't talk much to anyone. On weekends when he's on he likes to watch sports on TV in the ward, whatever's in season, and sometimes mutters to himself about it. "Oh, *great* decision," he'll say sarcastically. "Why doesn't he get his wooly head out of his hairy ass for a damn change?" I don't even know what he's talking about. I like it when he sings to himself now and again, though—show tunes mostly, in this deep voice. "Old Man River," he does a lot:

> *Tote dat barge and lift dat bale*
> *Git a little drunk and ya lands in ja-a-i-l...*
>
> *I gits weary and sick of tryin'.*
> *I'm tired of livin', and scared of dyin',*
> *But Ole Man River,*
> *Dat Ole Man River,*
> *He just keeps rollin' along.*

I like that. Even though Ricky's not in his group of kids—he has Group Two—he'll come over to him once in a while and say, "Hey, little man, what's goin' on?"

Anyways.

I guess I'll just finish my damn eggs and bacon and go to work and do what I can—whatever that is.

BUDDY

I LIKE BEING out here in the solarium in the mornings, particularly when it's sunny like today. The warm sun on my face feels good, and I like looking out the windows at the fields and trees, and the birds flying around—particularly the hawks. Sometimes I like watching them squirrels fart around in the tree branches, chasing each other now and again like they do, zipping up and down the tree trunks. Billy put Ricky right next to me, and I hope he likes it out here too. I like it that the leaves'll be on the trees before too damned long, and maybe in a few months there'll be corn growing in a field, them stalks high and green.

I've been watching how them nurses and aides treat Ricky. Oh, they're real nice, yeah, but it seems strange. Mary Lou's nice to him, and Billy is too. It makes me think about how they treat me. They know I ain't retarded, like they ain't, yet there's still this big difference between us, between them and me. They're the people who work here, who come here five days a week to do a job, take care of us feebs, and get paid for it, and I'm one of the guys who lives here in this damned ward for them to care for, probably for my whole useless life. I'll probably die here. I ain't goin' nowhere else, I don't imagine. They talk to me now and again and they're friendly and polite enough —"How ya doin' today, Bud?"—but at the end of their shifts they put on their coats and walk out the door and get in their cars and go home to their lives, and I doubt they give me another thought, and I stay here and then the next bunch comes in for their eight hours and on and on like that, day after day, week after week, year after year. They tell each other stuff about their lives, but they don't tell me nothin'. That ain't to say I don't like 'em a lot, most of them anyway, or look forward to seeing 'em. Billy, Mary Lou, Linc, Randi the randy registered nurse, like Billy calls her—I like 'em and like seeing them when they come to work. But they go home and I stay here.

Same with Ricky. He ain't retarded either. He's brain damaged, they said. He just has a different kind of damage than what I got. Them aides and nurses, they know that about him, I'm sure, and I'm sure they feel sorry for him and all, and they treat him pretty nice, but it seems strange. It's their job to come here to take care of him and me and the rest of these pathetic wrecks, and then they go home to their real lives and their families and dogs and cats and goldfish or whatever, and we stay here in this crazy place. It's home, but it ain't home. It ain't like when I was on the farm. These people can quit the job and be done with this place, but I can't. I don't know. We're all just people, yeah, but our lives are so different. I can't get my mind around it, somehow.

Retarded. I don't like that word. It sounds demeaning, or something. But it's what all the muckety-mucks around here say, and they throw around words like "severely" and "profoundly," and they're smart and got educations and all, so it must be okay.

Mary Lou's funny sometimes. Yesterday, I think it was, she busted a fingernail when she was dishing up a tray and she shook her hand and went, "Oh, *poop*-a-doodle anyway."

I don't know how long this place'll be Ricky's home. Me, I'm sure I'm here until I die and get to go up to heaven but I hope to God, if there is a God, that he ain't the same. It'd be sad if he had to stay here like me.

Billy's the one who takes care of Ricky a lot during day shift. He's just a kid himself almost, started working here right after high school, almost a year or so ago. He's pretty quiet compared with most of them other aides— keeps to himself a lot, don't seem to have a lot of friends. Me, I watch. I noticed that. One thing he does I get a kick out of is he makes Dino laugh. Dino just lies in his crib or sometimes a cart with big wheels, day after day, blind and his legs paralyzed, and listens to the sounds of the ward—the staff talking, the carts and chairs moving around, the televisions and radios, the bizarre sounds of the kids—and when he hears something he likes, like someone making a weird sound, like maybe a loud burp, his face lights up and he lets out this deep belly laugh. Billy, he can make Dino laugh more than anyone else. He does this loud fake sneeze with a big build-up—"Ah-ah-AH-AH-*CHOO*-OO-OO!"—and old Dino just gets the biggest kick out of it. He laughs his huge head off and his big upper body shakes, and after he stops guffawing he almost always goes, "Hey-kay-kay. *Yeah!* HEY-kay-kay!" It's amusing.

Billy put Gramps and Timmy out here, too, in their chairs. I guess they like the solarium too. Old Gramps, he hangs onto them two ragged dolls in the crooks of his skinny arms, and him and Timmy just hold hands most of the time. That's okay. That's nice. And the other aides put some of their kids out here too, and that's nice too—a bunch of us useless feebs just being out here together, quiet and liking the sunshine and looking at the trees and out across them fields. Davey's out here today, scooting around on his back like he does, and carrying around one of them washcloths like he always does to clean the wheelchairs and carts and cribs and such. Jimmy's here, and crazy Zach and Matthew from Group Three, they're here in their chairs today. Every now and again Zach looks up at the ceiling and he gets this strange look on his face and grins like a fool and waves one arm and goes, "*Ah-h-h!* O-O-H!" He's either seeing something that ain't really there or has gas or who the hell knows what. Some of these guys make a noise like that just before they have a seizure, but I don't remember Zach ever having one of them. A lot of guys here have seizures, but it ain't no big deal. They get all stiff and shake real bad for a while and maybe drool, but afterwards they're usually okay. They just sleep. The main thing you hope is that a guy don't crack his stupid head open when it's pounding against the slats of a crib or the floor or whatever before he's done shaking. They don't last long, them seizures, but I suppose a guy could hurt hisself.

Jimmy's some kind of an Indian, I heard Randi say once. He's dark enough, with coppery skin, and he's got these dark eyes and a big ugly nose like this picture my brother showed me once of Chief Sitting Bull. Jimmy don't have a tooth in his head, and the aides keep socks taped to both his hands to keep him from gnawing on them. That's what he does—gnaws things. Or, really, gums things. If he can't gum his hands, he gums whatever's near—mostly washcloths or these quilted diaper pads they stick under everyone's butt to soak up their piss. I don't know what pleasure he gets out of it, but there must be some.

When I look at them fields, it makes me think about growing up on the farm. That seems like a long time ago now. I liked it there, mostly. I was there with my whole family and then, after the old folks died, with just my brother and his wife. They never had no kids. Sitting here in the solarium in the sunny mornings, I think about my brother a lot. Donald took care of me the best he could for as long as he could, him and Amanda, but finally it was too much for them and I had to come here. My brother always calls me by my real name, Albert. That's fine. I miss that there farm. My brother, he comes to see me here when he can, and I like that, but it ain't the same as being home with him and Amanda.

One thing I like is that Donald sometimes brings me Hawaiian shirts. Him and Amanda like to go to Hawaii every few years—something about a big island they got there—and he always gets me a few of them colorful shirts they make. I like ones with green and yellow the best. Billy likes to put them on me pretty much, and I like that. The only problem's I drool a lot—hell, I can't *help* it—and the drool gets on them shirts.

I hope Billy keeps putting Ricky next to me. We can't say nothin' to each other, but it's nice anyway. Maybe I can somehow make him feel better, I don't know. He's away from his home too. I don't know how he feels, and he can't say, but how the hell would *anyone* feel if they was him? I hope he likes sitting out here in the sunlight too. At least, damn it, it's *some*thing.

RICKY

THESE NIGHTS are the worst time. They're long and quiet, it's dark outside and dark in the ward, except for a few little lights, and there's only one aide on—Bernie, I think his name is. Very quiet guy, he is, and calm. I'm stuck in my bed. If I need to pee, I can't just get up and go to the bathroom, like I used to do. I have to either hold it till morning or go in my pants. My *diaper*, that is. God, I cannot believe that I'm wearing a diaper at night! But I'd rather hold it and be uncomfortable than wet myself like a stupid baby.

At least they took me out of a crib after a while and put me in one of those beds like Buddy has, with the metal rails that go up and down, like in that hospital.

I can't even roll over by myself. If they put me on my back to sleep, that's where I stay for hours. If they put me on my side, that's where I stay. At home, I like to start out sleeping on my right side and then after a while roll over onto my left. I don't like to sleep on my back. Sometimes I like to hold onto a pillow. So now I can't even sleep the way I want to, and I can't tell anyone what I like so they can put me on my side, and then move me to my other side after a while. Usually Bernie or whatever other night aide's on will change my position a few times during the night, but it's when *they* want to do it, not necessarily when I want to. And the nights are *so* long! I don't know how much I actually sleep most nights, but it seems like a lot of times I sleep for a while, I don't know how long, and then I wake up and just lie there for a long time and maybe sleep a little more, but maybe not. I don't know. There's no clock, so I never even know what time it is. I wish there was a clock I could see. That'd make me feel better, I think. I'd at least know what time it is. At home when I can't sleep, which is rare, I can read for a while or maybe listen to music. But here I can't do that. I can't do *anything* for myself any more. *Nothing!*

It's discouraging.

I like it better when it's daytime. Billy mostly works then, and then that Mary Lou often comes in after that for the late afternoon and the evening. Sometimes she works days. Mary Lou's *so* pretty. I feel better when it's light out and there're more people around and stuff happening and someone gets me out of this darned bed. I had a kind of rough night last night, and was feeling sorry for myself, and I think I was even crying a little, so it was nice when Billy, right before breakfast, lifted me out of bed before he worked with anyone else and cleaned me up and dressed me, got me out of that stupid diaper and into regular underwear and put me in my chair. There's this little pad, sheepskin or something, they put behind my back when I'm in my chair. "C'mon, kid," Billy said, "time to get your skinny butt out of bed. Only rich farts get to sleep all day, and far as I can see you ain't one." That made me smile.

It's interesting when those two ladies push in that big stainless steel food cart and plug it in to keep the food hot. One's a sorta cute young girl, short, with short blond hair and these big round gold-colored glasses. Destini's her name. I notice that whenever she brings in breakfast or lunch she always looks around for Billy, and smiles when she sees him. She has this kinda crooked smile. The other lady's this big black woman who never shuts up. She's usually talking to Destini or whoever else is around, any aide or a nurse, from the moment she comes into the ward to the moment she leaves. But I can't understand much because she talks so fast. "I tole Shawanda she givin' me gray hairs," she was saying this morning, "and she said, 'Momma, nobody don't care 'bout that 'cause you such a good cook,' and I said, 'Girl, ...'" That's all I could understand because she started going a mile a minute. I like hearing her voice though. She's funny. I really like her. I don't know if she's *trying* to be amusing, but she is.

After breakfast, Billy wheeled me out to that room with big windows on three sides at the end of the ward, which he said was the *solarium*. It was sunny out, so it felt good to sit out there and feel the warmth on my face. That older guy, Buddy, was there already and Billy put my chair right next to his. "Now you keep an eye on this old lecher," he said to me, "and don't let him teach you any nasty habits." Buddy kind of giggled at that, this weird laugh in a deep voice. So he understands things. I wonder what's the matter with him, why he's here.

A few others from the ward were out there too, including this really old guy they call Gramps. He's got the most wrinkles on his face of anyone I've ever seen, and they're deep too. A fly could hike along one of 'em. He carries these two little cloth dolls with him all the time, and every once in a while he turns his head and sort of kisses them, one at a time. Weird! And then once in a while he kinda sings this song that sounds like "Old McDonald." He doesn't say the words, just sounds that are like the words, but the tune is sort of there. I can tell that much. Gramps is always with this other guy—Timmy, I think his name is—who's real little and can't sit still in his chair somehow. They tie him in the chair—a small wooden chair that kind of tilts backward—with a white cloth thing around his chest, like they use on me. Still, he's always twisting around, making these jerky movements like he can't control his body. Maybe he can't. One of his feet is all kinda twisted around and his toes pointing down. Larry was out there too, and talk about *weird!* He sits there with this dumb look on his face, a sort of half smile, and plays with himself a lot. Every once in a while he stares at the ceiling, and kind of smiles, and goes, "Heek, heek, heek." What does *that* mean?

At least Larry can feed himself. I notice he always throws his spoon when he's done eating, and sometimes knocks his empty tray onto the floor. But at least he can feed himself. I wish I could do that.

One guy who's sort of weird, too, is Arnie. I noticed him when I first got here. He's a big guy with dark hair and whiskers and looks like any normal guy on the street, except that he always wears this hard hat, like a construction guy, and it's painted with red and white stripes and on the left side has white stars on blue, like the American flag. He can move his wheelchair by himself real slowly, usually with his feet. He puts one foot in front of the other and digs his heel in and pulls himself forward with it and then the next foot. He spends his time looking at catalogs of some kind, and it's funny how he studies each page from about six inches away. He turns the pages real slowly, not by holding a page between his fingers but by putting his entire right hand, palm down, on a page and then slowly moving it over. Every now and again he kind of giggles, putting his hand to his mouth. He's pretty quiet except when someone tries to get him to do something he doesn't want to do, like go to the bathroom. There's this little room with just a toilet and sink in it, and the aides have to get Arnie to use the toilet. They wheel him there and then they sort of help him out of his wheelchair and onto the toilet. He hates that, for some reason, and makes this loud sound, something like *"O-o-o-w!"* like someone's hurting him. It's kind of scary. Also, once in a while when he's just sitting around, something must bother him because he slams a big fist down on his tray and looks kinda pissed off.

This place is *so* weird! One guy's weirder than the next. I learned that that guy whose arms and legs are all bent at weird angles is Gilbert. I feel sorry for him. I don't know who it is, but someone at the other end of the room now and again makes this sound just like a cat meowing. It's like a freak show in a circus. I guess I don't mind freak shows, but I don't like *living* in one. But how long do I have to live here? That's what I think about all the time, and these nights are when I think about it the most. I wake up in the night and remember where I am and kinda feel like crying. I want *so* badly to be okay and leave here and just go home again, to Mom and Dad and Amy and Chelsea, to be in my own room, to hang around with my friends, go to school, and everything. I want to see Riley and put his green leash on and take him for a walk. I want to be able to talk to other people. I never thought about how nice all that stuff is till I lost it.

Of course, right now I'd be happy if I could just *roll over* on my own.

I'm glad Billy puts me out in that solarium. I like being there. It's strange being there with all these other guys who live here, none of us talking with each other, everyone in their own little world. But it's okay that Billy put me next to Buddy. I like him. He seems nice, but kinda sad. I notice him sometimes sitting in his chair looking out at the sky, real quiet, just staring at the sky. I wonder what he's thinking. I don't know, but for some reason it makes me feel sad too when I see him like that.

BILLY

I CAUGHT the old lech staring at Mary Lou's boobs just before report at shift change time today, and told him so. "Hey, you," I said. "Buddy. Yeah, *you,* you old reprobate. I saw that ugly tongue hanging out. Don't get yourself too excited now, old man, 'cause it ain't gonna do you no good." He just laughed, that semi-wicked deep-voiced laugh, and his face turned a little red. I kid around to make him laugh if I can because the old guy is too damned melancholy. Most days I ask him if he wants to go out in the solarium because I know he likes it there, and he nods, but even then he seems down a lot. I wish I could figure what to do to make him less that way, but don't know what that'd be.

Hell, I like to look too. Mary Lou's endowments are ... right there. On the one hand, I wish she wouldn't wear those distracting low-cut tops so much, but on the other hand, I'm glad she does. She knows I look, but I don't think she cares much. Linc looks too, when he can. Probably lots do. I think she likes to be looked at. The trick is to get a quick eyeful but not stare. When I'm talking to her, when I have to, I try to look right into those big liquidy brown eyes and not at her chest. It's hard sometimes not to look down, particularly when that cleavage beckons, but I try. I read somewhere that women like it when you look in their eyes instead of staring at their bazooms, but what do I know? About women, practically nothing. They're mysteries. I'm ignorant, I admit. Anything I think I know is from books, since my actual experience is practically zippo.

Books are good though. My books are fine. I'm never happier than when I close the door to my apartment each evening and get into my red flannel pajama bottoms and my gray sweatshirt and pull the hood over my head and tie it under my chin, and make my hot mint tea—usually spearmint, sometimes peppermint—with a teaspoonful of honey, and drink from one of my blue teacups that I bought new the second day I lived here, and sink into my recliner to read, like now. I'm by myself in my own little home, and the nutso sad confusing world stays on the other side of my locked door, at least for a while. I read novels mostly, sometimes good stuff and sometimes crap. Lately I've been reading Hemingway, *A Farewell to Arms.* Poor Frederic Henry, losing that nice Catherine Barkley in childbirth. "Don't worry, darling," she murmured before she kicked the bucket. "It's just a dirty trick." Oh, *really?* Well, who played that dirty trick? God? And why? Anyway, next I'm going to read *For Whom the Bell Tolls,* and then re-read some of those Nick Adams stories that I like—maybe "Big Two-Hearted River," parts one and two. Nick said he didn't want to fish in the swamp.

I like to read some Shakespeare too, particularly in winter. I like the tragedies and some of the histories, but not the silly comedies too much. *Macbeth*'s my favorite—those scheming witches. I hated it, though, when the thugs killed Macduff's wife and kid. I like to read parts of *King Lear* now and again, too, even though it makes me sad that poor Cordelia got hanged at the end. *Hamlet*'s okay, but both the prince and his ghost old man are irritating. *Romeo and Juliet,* I can't stand. We had to read it aloud in ninth grade English, for some ridiculous reason, and I had to read the part of Friar Laurence. That was *horrible*—probably the worst experience of my pathetic, misbegotten education. Talk about irritating people, those two horny teenagers in that play causing all that ruckus and then killing themselves for absolutely no good reason. Star-crossed chuckleheads! I liked it a lot better when we studied *Macbeth* in tenth grade. Thank God, we didn't have to read that one aloud. Macbeth's crazy wife croaked herself too, but at least she had more of a reason than those sicko adolescent lovebirds. After we studied that, I started to read some of the other plays on my own in my room at night. It's good to read stuff like that and think about it, but not have to take tests or write essays or read aloud or have class discussions.

I wonder if there really are women like Catherine Barkley. But what do I know? Nothing. While reading *A Farewell*, I imagined talking with Christy like Lieutenant Henry and Miss Barkley did with each other. "Did you enjoy your breakfast, darling?" she'd ask. "Yes," I'd answer. "It was a lovely breakfast and you're a fine, simple waitress." "Oh, darling," she'd say, "we *do* have a fine time here at Junior's, don't we? And you *do* love me truly, don't you, darling?"

I don't mind being alone in the evenings. It's quite okay. Being alone is fine. It's good being by myself and not having to talk to anyone, to deal with anyone's crap. Being alone in my room every night was what helped me cope with my parents' bullshit when I lived at home. Oh, the bullshit of that pair of wackos! The boozing, the screaming, the fighting, my mother's door slammings and crying jags, my father's threatening to leave, their bed-shaking screwing at all hours. For two people who yelled at each other as much as they did, who if you listened to them you'd swear they hated each other's guts, they certainly did it a lot. If I had a dollar for every time their marital bliss woke me in the middle of the night, the old man moaning, "Oh, *baby,* it's good! *Yeah!*" I'd be rich. The best I can say about that pair is that they ignored me most of the time, never paid me much attention one way or another since I was maybe ten. At first that bothered me, but then I liked it. Their apathy made it easy for me to come right home from school and go to my room and close the door behind me and lock it and spend the evening by myself. They didn't care. We rarely talked. If the old man ever had anything to say, it was to yell at me, cuss me out, tell me how stupid I was, how worthless, what a loser. That was always his big line: "Jesus Christ, Billy, I can't *believe* what a fucking *loser* I've raised!" Blah blah.

I'd do my homework, doing the minimum to get by and no more—who cares, anyway?—get a little something to take to my room to eat, grilled cheese on rye a lot, and then just read or maybe watch some TV. I was never interested in music or sports or the other stuff most kids seemed to care about, and never gave a damn about clothes or shoes or partying or drugs or drinking or being popular or cool in any way. From fifth grade on, I just craved being alone as much as possible, except for hanging around now and again with Boyd. Boyd and I were both blessedly uncool in our undistinguished careers at Elmwood Middle School and Jefferson High School. We never cared if the stupid football team won or lost or were all wiped out in a horrible bus-train accident.

When I left home right after high school—the day after graduation, in fact—and moved into my apartment, I did the same thing I'd done at home: ensconced myself in my little cave because that was familiar, comfortable. My little home is good—small and simple: only a few pieces of furniture, all used and cheap; hardly anything on the walls except the three small posters of drawings of Cordelia, Ophelia and Desdemona that I bought at the used bookstore for five bucks apiece; a total of two windows, both small. I have my recliner, my little TV and VCR, my four china blue cups and saucers, my Laurel and Hardy tapes stacked in two piles on a little wooden coffee table I bought at Saint Vinny's, Grandma's blue afghan, my oak bookcase in my bedroom, my bed and stuff—and I'm happy there. *Very* happy there. And never happier than when I come home from work, stopping at the food court first a lot, and close and lock my door behind me. I wish I had *three* locks—industrial-quality tempered-steel deadbolt locks— so I could hear the lovely definitive click of each one snapping shut! Oh, I know I'm like some little old lady—sitting in a soft chair covered with an *afghan*, for God's sake, drinking hot tea, like Grandma. *Tea!* I guess all I need now is a damn *cat* sleeping in my lap. But who cares? I have my own little home, my sanctuary, just mine, no one else's, where I'm safe and quite content. Screw everything and everyone else!

I'm sure if the old man could see my apartment and how I live and what I do for a job he'd think I was an even bigger loser than ever. Maybe he'd be right. I don't think I'm that bad, but when you're a kid and one of your parents, even if he's a gaping asshole, tells you over and over and *over* for years what a *loser* you are, such a major fucking *disappointment*, part of you can't help but believe it. Still, I'd rather be me than that foul-mouthed, self-centered bastard any day. My only legacy from the sonofabitch is that I have a potty mouth too. I'm not exactly proud of it, but I can't somehow help it. I guess he got it from his own father because I recall, when I was little, seeing that ugly old white-haired and big-nosed fart in his kitchen banging his forehead against a cabinet, eyes closed, and softly muttering, "Son of a bitch! Son of a bitch! Son of a *bitch!*" over and over.

What I hated even more, I remember, is how Dad badmouthed women all the time. It was "dumb broads" this, and "silly-assed ditzes" that. He hated women drivers particularly. "Jesus Christ!" he'd growl, "where the *fuck* did that stupid broad learn to drive?" I know my mother hated when he'd talk like that, but for whatever reason she never said much, just looked pained

I remember, growing up, I used to wonder a lot what it would be like to have a nice normal home with somewhat normal parents who didn't scream all the time and drink themselves blind and stuff. I wondered what it'd be like to have a brother or sister that you could talk to about all the bullshit. I don't think much about that stuff now. It's behind me. I've moved on. Screw it!

Anyways.

Ricky must have good parents. He seems like a nice kid from a nice home. Mary Lou told me his parents and sisters visit him fairly often in the evenings, and she said they're nice, but sad. I hope and pray he can get the hell out of B Ward and be back with them as soon as possible.

BUDDY

TODAY'S CHURCH DAY. Every Wednesday is. Billy, when he's working on Wednesdays, wheels me down to the multi-purpose room outside D Ward, and today Ricky's here too, right next to me. I think this is his first time here. The aides always bring Gramps and Timmy too, but I ain't sure that's such a great idea since the old fart don't show proper respect for the occasion. When Father Callahan comes into the room, Gramps always frowns and knits his brow so that them wrinkles on his forehead are even deeper than usual. It's the same pissed-off expression he gets whenever that sourpuss Doctor Winters or one of them other docs, or even Mrs. Hanson, comes into the ward. For some reason, he has a bug up his ass about authority figures. But he likes them cute little nurses and aides, and always tries to impress them, I guess, by sticking his disgusting tongue far up his disgusting nose, which he can do. It's his main skill. I don't imagine they're all that impressed, but maybe I'm wrong.

Father Callahan always has the aides put all our chairs and carts in a big kinda circle in the multi-purpose room. He's at least eighty-years-old, an old man dressed in a white and gold robe, and his bald head is so pink and smooth that the glare off it from them fluorescent lights damn near blinds me. "Bless you all!" he starts out in this deep voice. "God's merciful blessing on each and every one today." Then he puts on a record of "Yes, Jesus Loves Me," with these happy kids singing, which gets on my nerves for some reason. I get irritated at the part that goes, "Little ones to him belong...*they* are weak but *he* is strong." Then Father says that today we're gonna talk about how Jesus loved to go to church. He didn't say what church. He pulls out these big white cards with colorful drawings and holds 'em up, one at a time. The first one shows some pale kid with long brown wavy hair, wearing a white robe with a brown rope tied around his belly, carrying a long wooden walking stick—real serious-looking little guy— walking along a dirt road toward a small white building high on a hill in the distance. Lambs and goats and such along the side of the road are staring

24

big-eyed at him as he passes. As Father holds this up, he tells about it in his deep voice:

> *Jesus went to church each day,*
> *The word of God to hear.*
> *Sometimes the church was far away,*
> *And sometimes it was near.*

The lesson of the whole deal, which goes on for a while, is, I guess, that us feebs should be happy to go to church, such as it is for us, because Jesus liked to do that and to listen to what God had to say. That's fine, I suppose, though I can't get too excited about all them stories Father Callahan always tells about Jesus—all the stuff he did in his life back when, like curing the lepers, and all them wise things he said, and how he loved mankind and died for our sins, and all like that. I mean, I guess I'm glad that because of Jesus I'm forgiven for my sins, but, hell, I never had the chance to sin that much anyway, so what's to forgive? I wish I *could'a* done some sinning, but I didn't when I was younger, livin' on the farm, and I sure as hell can't sin much now.

I remember hearing that envy's a sin, though, and if that's true then there I'm guilty. I'm jealous of people who can do what I can't, which is damn near everything. But what's the other way—to just accept whatever crappy hand God's dealt you and be happy with it and *not* feel envious of anyone else? Ain't it natural I should feel jealous of people who can walk and talk and feed themselves, and get dressed, and go to the bathroom by themselves, and who can take a nice walk around the neighborhood, holding an umbrella in one hand if it's raining? I guess it's holy to not feel envy, but it don't seem natural.

I like it best when Father Callahan tells about heaven. *That* I believe in. He does a pretty good job of describing heaven, telling that it's the reward we get after this here life of toil and grief and that it'll be totally peaceful there and we'll be sitting at the feet of Jesus, who loves us purely, he said, and never know the pain of this earthly existence no more. We'll be reunited, he says, with all our loved ones who passed. Now I don't know about sitting at Jesus's feet, but the rest of it sounds good. Hell, I can't wait! Hell, if I could stand up straight and take a long walk in them fluffy clouds, and not have to be the slumped-over drooling old fool that I am, I'd be the happiest dead guy in the world.

One thing I wish I understood better is when Father talks about the father and the son and the holy ghost, like when he crosses himself and stuff. I guess I understand that God's the father and Jesus is the son, but the ghost part I don't get. Ain't ghosts scary? He should explain that better to us feebs.

Ricky don't look like he's into this whole church deal that much. He's kinda slumped over in his wheelchair, leaning a little to his right, and looks sorta nervous. I notice he looks thinner than when he first came to B Ward, but maybe I'm wrong about that. He pays attention to Father Callahan and his silly drawings, and you can tell he understands everything. I don't know what he thinks of it all. Billy, after a little while, lifts Ricky up and sets him to sitting straighter in his chair. "C'mon, kid," I hear him whisper, "you're in church here. Gotta make a good appearance." He wipes Ricky's nose with a tissue and then turns to me. "Pay attention here, old man," he says real low, so Father Callahan can't hear. "You've got a damned lot to be contrite about, all that lust in your heart. If he offers you confession, grab it. You need it bad. My opinion, you need to do a whole truckload of Hail Marys and Our Fathers and whatever else they have." He looks at Father Callahan and smiles, and then leans down and whispers in my ear. "Me too," he says.

Just then Gramps cuts loose this tremendous fart, which sets him and Timmy both to chuckling. Father Callahan glares at Gramps and frowns, and Gramps could care less, but the nice part of the whole deal is it makes Ricky smile and even laugh just a little. It's the first time I seen him smile since he's been here. Billy notices too, and I can see that he's glad.

RICKY

IT MADE ME SAD to go to that church thing this morning. It made me think of Sunday mornings with my family, at church and then lots of times going out to breakfast at Perkins or Pancake Palace or somewhere, and I wonder if I'll ever do that again. I never thought much about it before my accident, but now I do. Part of me wants to think about it and remember it, even dumb stuff like spreading butter and then pouring maple syrup on my chocolate chip pancakes at breakfast after church and watching the butter melt on the warm pancakes, though you hope the pats of butter on the table aren't too cold because then they take longer to melt and the butter's too hard to spread, and the good taste of hot chocolate after a mouthful of pancakes and syrup, but another part of me doesn't want to think about it too much. It's nice to think about that stuff, but then I look around and here I am.

But I liked some of it. It was funny how mad that priest looked when Gramps cut that huge fart. I liked how his face and the top of his bald head turned red and how pissed off he looked, and it was funny what Gramps did then. He and Timmy both sorta giggled and then Gramps leaned down and kissed his two dolls and laughed some more. He's got this crazy laugh, sort of like, "Hyah, hyah, hyah!" And he doesn't really kiss his dolls, just sort of licks them with the end of his tongue. He's a riot! It was funny yesterday, too, when that nurse with the black curly hair—Randi, I think her name is— came over to Gramps to give him his pill after lunch and, when she got near and was putting the pill in a spoonful of applesauce, he looked right at her, though cross-eyed like he is, and opened his mouth and stuck his tongue out and it went right into his nose, way up there. He was looking right at her, cross-eyed, with his stupid tongue in his nose, and she didn't flinch, just held the spoon near his face and said, "C'mon, get that silly tongue out of there and open your mouth." He kept his tongue in his nose for a little bit but then it slithered out and he opened his mouth and took his pill. I've seen him do that once before, and it's weird. It seems like his tongue is too big for the size of his head, or maybe his head's too small for the size of his tongue. I don't know. But how many guys can stick their tongue in their nose like he can?

What bothered me though was Father Callahan's talk about God and Jesus. He was saying how great God is and how He loves all of us despite our faults and sins and all, which is what I used to hear at church, too, but I kept thinking that if that's true, then why'd He let this happen to me? I keep thinking about that. I wake up every day wondering the same thing: What'd I do to deserve this? If God loves me that much, when's He going to help me get better and get out of here? I want to believe in God and have faith, like I think I did before this happened to me, but I don't know. I think I still have faith, but I'm not sure. I'm not sure how you know if you have faith, like they always say in church we should. I guess you don't think much about stuff like that until something bad happens to you, or maybe to someone you love. I never did before. I just went to church most Sundays and went through the whole ritual and then went home to watch football when that was on or played baseball in the summer or hung out with my friends or did stuff with my family and never thought much about that kind of stuff. I heard what they said, but I never thought about it too much.

I feel angry with God, and I'm sure that's not right. I wonder if it's a sin to be pissed at the Lord. Seems like it must be. But I can't help it. I know you're not supposed to take the Lord's name in vain or believe in any other gods and stuff, but I can't remember if anyone ever talked about feeling angry with God. I feel bad for thinking that way, but that's how I feel. I was feeling that way more and more listening to Father Callahan with his stupid little poems, so I was really glad when Gramps cut that disgusting fart. It sort of improved my mood.

Billy was good too. I liked it when he helped me sit up straight in my chair. I think he got a kick out of Gramps, too, and so did Buddy. I saw him smiling. It was sorta like being in school and some guy cuts one and all the guys laugh. The girls act so horrified, most of them, but all the guys laugh. I don't know why that is. You'd think girls pass gas once in a while too, but maybe not. Maybe their systems are different that way.

I wish I didn't have to think about bathroom stuff so much now, but I do. Now every time I have to go to the bathroom, either way, it's a problem. I can't do anything for myself. People have to help me. I'm going to pray for help with that, to be able to go to the bathroom by myself, because I *hate* being like this. It's horrible, and embarrassing. I hope God'll listen to me, even though I'm mad at Him. I have to think He'll understand how I feel.

I liked it that I got a haircut this morning. These two barber guys come to the ward to shave some of the guys, like Arnie, a couple times a week and they do haircuts too. Billy told me they're brothers, Bob and Eric. Bob's losing his hair, pretty much. I notice that both of them, when they come here, look around for Randi and stare at her if she's here. I guess they think she's cute.

I'm trying to think what my sisters ate when we went out to breakfast on Sundays. I'm pretty sure Amy always ordered French toast and bacon and orange juice, and I remember she'd dip the end of each strip of bacon in syrup before eating it, but I can't remember about Chelsea. I wonder why.

BILLY

YESTERDAY, BEFORE REPORT, I mentioned to Mary Lou that I didn't think Ricky needed to be in diapers at night. "He can control himself until morning," I said. "And I'm damned sure a twelve-year-old kid doesn't like to be in diapers."

She nodded. "Good thought," she said, "I'm gonna mention that in report." I knew she'd do that.

I like going on break with Mary Lou when we work the same shift and she has a different group than ours, which happens now and again, because she doesn't piss and moan all the time like most of these other aides and some of the nurses do. Good Christ, how these whining women go on! Their lazy husbands, their no-good boyfriends, their ungrateful kids, their aches and pains—mostly feet and backs, their money woes, the late child support checks, all the daily chores they say they have to do, how *tired* they are, whatever. God, it never ends! And then they gripe on and on about stuff at work: this one took too long a lunch break yesterday; that one didn't want to switch shifts last week when someone needed to take their kid to the dentist; some other one didn't fold the towels just right or stock the damned carts on night shift; the head nurse, Mrs. Hanson, said this or that or just looked at one of them the wrong way. Jesus H. Christ! They must get *something* out of this constant griping to each other, but I'm damned if I know what. Part of me doesn't want to go on breaks or lunch with them because of their never-ending grousing, day after dreary day, but I know if I didn't go they'd think I was antisocial—which, basically, I am, I admit — and consider me even weirder than they probably do now. But, *damn,* what a downer!

On the other hand, though, I have to admit it's sometimes interesting to hear them talking, some of them anyway, and hear their grievances and sad stories. Sometimes I like hearing them piss and moan about how busy their lives are outside of work and how tired it makes them, because mine isn't busy at all. I get to just park my pathetic ass in a soft chair in my humble apartment and read and not have to please anyone, and that's the life I like just fine. So maybe in a way I'm better off.

All Mary Lou ever complains about is her period and, once in a while, how horny she is. Now and again she'll say that she's "bleeding like a stuck *pig*—yuck-a-doodle, anyway" and "can't *wait* to get off the damn rag." But it seems she's not really *griping* when she says that, like these others do, just observing. She talks about her period the same way she might talk about the weather: "Oh, I just can't *wait* for the darn rain to stop." As to being horny, her complaint's that her boyfriend, Duane, doesn't want to do it as much as she does. "He says he's too tired," I heard her tell Randi once. "I told him he could be on the bottom and I'd do all the work, but he still kept his darned zipper up." Randi nodded and said that she *preferred* being on top. I saw Duane once when he picked Mary Lou up after work—tall, lanky, long-haired guy with one of those gaunt Abraham Lincoln faces and a stringy little goatee and sort of vacant light-blue eyes—and wasn't much impressed. Seems like she could do better, but what do I know? They say love's strange. Maybe he's a magnificent lover when he's not too tired.

I can't even imagine Mary Lou being my girlfriend. Even if I were interested in her that way, I can't imagine that. I mean, I always like to look at her and listen to her talk and laugh and even just walk around the way she does, so healthy and confident and all, but I never have anything particularly clever or interesting to say to her, or, really, to any of these women, and I can't imagine being alone with her on a date or something. I wouldn't know what to say. I suppose I could ask her if she's ever read *A Farewell to Arms* and, if so, if she liked Catherine Barkley. But then what? What do you talk about with women?

Even little Christy. I've never seen her outside of Junior's, never seen her without that tight little green uniform, though I've known her for a couple years now and, I think, sort of love her. Sort of. More and more maybe. Suppose I asked her out and took her to a movie or something. What would we talk about after? I'd have to think up a list of questions in advance: *Tell me, Christy, do you like working at Junior's? Is Junior nice to you? Are most people good tippers, like I am? Are you really in as good a mood as you seem all the time? Did you have a happy childhood? Really, did you? What was that like? Tell me. I'd like to know. How do you get along with your parents now? Do you like to see them?* But probably those are blah questions. Maybe I could ask if the sight and smell of corned beef hash makes her want to puke, like it does me. But maybe that's too personal. I don't know.

What I'd *really* like to talk about with her, I think, is Laurel and Hardy. I want to tell her my favorite films and the scenes I like best, like the one in *Blockheads* where Ollie finds Stan on the grounds of the old soldiers' home twenty years after the end of World War I, where they were soldiers together, sitting in someone else's wheelchair with his right leg folded underneath him, and thinks Stan's lost his leg in the war and wheels him off the grounds to take him home to meet his wife and have dinner—"one of those big thick juicy steaks, *covered* with mushrooms, and those hot biscuits *oozing* with melted butter, and those seven-layer chocolate cakes, *swimming* in whipped cream." And Stan—that sweet, vacant look on his face—asks, in that great English accent, "Any *beans?*" I love that! "Any beans?" A little later Stan says, "Hey, Ollie, remember how *dumb* I used to be. Well, I'm *better* now," just before he allows his friend, still thinking Stan's lost a leg, to carry him the rest of the way to the car.

But what if Christy's never heard of Laurel and Hardy, which is likely—they're not exactly what girls know or care about, I'm sure—and thinks I'm weird for even mentioning them? Then what? Maybe she'd stop calling me "hon."

I wonder if Destini has a boyfriend. She's always friendly, smiling at me and all, when she and Cassie roll the food cart in. I smile back, and say hi, but not much more. Once she said, "How are you today, Billy?"—I didn't even know she knew my name—and I think I said, "Fine." I'd been wondering about *her* name, so before I knew it I heard myself ask, one morning when she was picking up the cart after breakfast, how she got it. She blushed, but told me. "Before my parents met, my father was in love with a woman named Destini. Then he went into the army, and when he got out she was married to someone else. Then he met my Mom and they got married and when she got pregnant with me he asked her if it'd be okay, if they had a girl, to name it after the woman he'd gone with before. She said that'd be okay." I like her soft voice. It's soothing.

Cassie's a stitch. She never shuts up. Her main topic's her three daughters—Shawanda, Tamika and Susie—and the unending grief they cause her. The only problem's that once she gets going you can only understand the beginning and then *maybe* the end of the story, because she talks six miles a minute. This morning she was telling Destini something about Tamika. "I tole that girl to fold all the laundry 'fore I got home or I'd whup her l'il behind, but she started givin' me mouth about all the stuff she had to do, algebra homework and I dunno what-all, and I said 'Listen here, you fold that laundry *first*, girl, and *then* you ... '" and then it went on too fast for me to understand for maybe another three or four minutes straight while they were setting up the food cart, and then I could make out the end of the story, barely: "Oh, man, what a *bummer*!"

Cassie seems to like Gramps and Timmy. "How you gentlemen today?" she'll sometimes say to them. "Still holdin' hands, huh?"

Mary Lou laughed when I told her about Gramps farting. I told her I was glad to see Ricky smile when that happened, and she nodded. "Yup," she said, "The little shit could use some grins." She's right. If Gramps breaking wind made the kid smile, maybe I could tell him some fart jokes or other dumb stuff that twelve-year-olds like. Boyd knows a lot of that, since he's basically a case of arrested development. I'll have to ask him. It would be great to get Ricky to laugh a little. He sure doesn't have much to laugh about as it is.

I think Mary Lou was impressed today. At the end of the shift, I usually volunteer to wheel the full laundry bags over to the laundry chute and lift them up and into the chute. Those bastards are heavy, full of wet diapers and towels and all, and I noticed early on that the women usually struggle to lift them. I'm thin, puny even, but I can lift those bags okay. I've seen Linc do it, and it's nothing for him—he always croons, "Tote dat barge, lift dat bale" when he hoists the laundry bags—but I can do it okay enough. So today, when Mary Lou came in for her p.m., she was watching me lift the bags. I wish I had some actual muscles to show off, but at least it's something.

Anyways.

One thing good I did, I got Ricky a little clock for near his bed—just a simple little electric thing that I got for about eight bucks at Walgreens. I figured where he is, he can't see the ward clock above the nurses' desk and he'd probably like to know what time it is once in a damned while. I know I would if I were him. This one has red digital numbers so he can see it at night. I suppose he could wear a watch, but it's hard for him sometimes to even raise his arm, so he might not always be able to look at it. I think he was glad for the clock. He looked at me like he was.

BUDDY

THAT LARRY gets on my nerves sometimes. After lunch they put us all in bed for naps, and that's usually when he starts with his crazy loud "Wah-GOO! Wah-GOO!" and bouncing on his bed. When Billy's on, he always lets me stay up and sit in my chair to watch TV instead of being in bed, or maybe wheels me out to the solarium if that's what I want. It's a nice quiet time in the ward, but that damn Larry usually ruins it with his frantic whacking off. You'd think he'd get tired of it, but he don't. I don't even know if it works for him. But if he'd at least do it *quieter*, I maybe wouldn't mind so much. And he goes on like that for the longest time too! *No* shame.

Sometimes I just like to watch TV after lunch. We have three of them on the ward, one for each group, and our group's TV is near my bed so I can see it okay when I want to. The aides, them women anyway, like to have soap operas on while they work in the late morning and afternoon, and they look over at the televisions a lot and once in a while stop what they're doing to stare for a few minutes. I watch them shows once in a while too, not 'cause I care about the stories but just to look at them women. They're all thin and healthy and pretty, mostly young, and wear lots of lipstick and mascara and such women stuff like that. Most of the people on them soap operas look like they're pretty well off—nice clothes, jewelry, homes with expensive-looking furniture, and the like. You hardly ever see no poor people or even ordinary working stiffs like the aides here. My favorite parts are the kissing and other sexy stuff. They seem like a passionate lot, them characters, always hugging and kissing and groping each other and tumbling into bed. When they ain't actually screwing, it seems like they're thinking about doing it or remembering it. Today, for example, on *All My Children* some lady with a huge pile of dark wavy hair and big gold hoop earrings—Erica, I think her name is—had a misty flashback to a bedroom scene where her and this tall, skinny but muscular guy with no shirt on are hugging and stuff and he's telling her that he loves her "more than life itself" and she's looking up at his face with big wet brown eyes and then they close their eyes and kiss and go on like that for a while and then he kinda eases her onto the bed and she's lying there on her back, her nice dark hair spread over the pillow, and the camera closes in on just her face and her eyes are still closed, and now her mouth is open a little and she's sort of breathing a little faster. There's all this nice music playing, getting louder, and then they leave them there on that bed and go right to a commercial for a laxative just for women, showing this pretty, slightly heavy black woman in a red jogging suit smiling nice because, apparently, she just took a good dump. It makes you wonder if the women on them soap operas ever have to take stuff to help them go.

Or the commercials are for soap or deodorant or shampoo or toothpaste or stuff to help you lose weight, or for sanitary pads or tampons—Kotex and so on. All this junk for people's bodies, to help them work better or not be so ugly! Well, hell, what good does that stuff do *me?* My body don't work so good anyway, and I'm sure it ain't too appealing. I can't relate to all that romance and sex on them soap operas, of course, but them commercials for laxatives sorta hit home 'cause that's the story of my damned life. These nurses here, they spend most of their time, it seems, either trying to get us to swallow our pills by hiding 'em in a spoonful of applesauce and sticking the spoon into our mouths or shoving suppositories up our asses—*Fleets* something or other. Poor Gramps always squeals real pitiful when they do him. Then when the nurses and aides get together for report at shift change them nurses are always asking, "Did so-and-so come through?" That is, did so-and-so take a crap or not? They're very concerned about us feebs moving our bowels like we should, and they even keep notes about it. Anyway, suppositories are the thing I hate most about my life in this place, having to submit to that particular bulltwinkie indignity every few days. Most of the nurses are nice enough about it. Randi always says, "Sorry, Bud, really sorry. I have to do this now," as she rolls me over on my side in bed and puts on one of them plastic gloves and squeezes some kind of lubricant from a tube and sticks that goddamn thing in me. *Yuck!*

I don't know if they have to do that with Ricky. I ain't seen it if they do. Hopefully, he don't need it. He's sure got enough to put up with without that.

The main thing I care about as to how I look is my hair. Not that I can see it or nothing most of the time, but I like it when the aides comb it straight every day. Billy, in particular, usually rubs a little of this oily stuff in my hair that my brother brought me a few bottles of when I first come here. He's the only one that does that, and he combs it real careful too. I don't know what I'll do when that stuff runs out.

One thing I like is they moved Ricky's bed nearer to mine, I think so he could see the TV easier from his bed. I believe it was Billy's idea, and he mentioned it to Mary Lou and then she brought it up in report one time, like it was her idea, and they agreed that was okay and then they done it.

It'll be great to not have to worry about bowels up in heaven! I'm sure old St. Peter won't be worrying about whether or not useless old Buddy came through.

RICKY

I'M GLAD TO HAVE that little clock by my bed. Billy was really nice to do that for me. This way when I'm up at night, I know what time it is and how much longer until morning. I sort of know that by now anyway by what goes on in the ward. I know that Bernie, the guy that's on most nights, takes his break at 2:30 or so because he announces it to himself a lot: "Two-thirty, boys. Time for break." Bernie talks to himself a lot, mumbling really, and I guess he figures that none of us'll notice or judge him for it, which is probably true. I don't, that's for sure. I'm glad enough at night for the sound of *anyone's* voice. I'd like it if Bernie'd come over and talk to me once in a while, actually talk to me, but he hardly ever does. Even when he turns me over, he doesn't talk. I guess he's one of those strong silent types you hear about.

These nights are always my worst time, but at least now I know when it's getting close to 6:30 and the day shift starts and things get better. On the days Billy's on, most days, he always comes in the ward just a little before his shift starts and comes over to tell me "Good morning kiddo," and then goes over to Buddy to do that, or sometimes Buddy first. I like it when he does that. It makes me feel a little better. I like it that they switched my bed and Gilbert's, so now I'm more near Buddy.

After Billy says hello he has to go to report, when the night aide and the nurses who were on at night and all the aides and nurses coming on for the day shift stand around a little desk at the front of the ward and one of them reads from a book of some kind and they talk about stuff that happened during the night and stuff that's gonna happen that day. Bernie has to talk a little bit about if anything happened during the night, like some guy had a seizure or puked or something, even though he doesn't seem to like talking that much. After the report, all the nurses leave in a group and, I guess, go to the next place for report there and then the aides start getting us ready for breakfast.

Seizures. I heard of them, but never saw one before I came here. Scary! When we were in the solarium the other day this little kid from Group

Three had one. He was lying on the floor on a thick white blanket when all of a sudden he started shaking and jerking around real bad. His face was all kind of tight and his eyes were wide open. It lasted for a minute, or maybe a little longer. Then he stopped and the room stank horribly. I guess the kid messed himself.

Billy always gets me and Buddy ready first. Some of the guys just stay in bed and get fed there, but he always puts us in our chairs for breakfast. I'm glad of that. By the time it's morning, I'm anxious to get out of that bed and to sit up. Usually Billy gets me dressed pretty quickly, which I also like. I sleep in a T-shirt and, now, my underpants, and it feels nice to get pants on and a shirt and my slippers. I'm so glad I don't have to wear those stupid diapers any more. How embarrassing! I don't know why they decided to change that, but I'm glad they did. Now they take me to the bathroom and sit me on the toilet and kinda prop me up so I don't tip over. It's weird to always pee sitting down, like a girl, instead of standing up. But at least it feels more normal to dress like other people do. Billy does the same for Buddy, usually putting on one of his Hawaiian shirts.

He gets Arnie and Davey and Larry up, too, and puts them in their chairs for breakfast. Arnie, I notice, has to have his hard hat on, the one that looks like a flag, whenever he's not in bed. When he's in bed, his hat's always on a little night stand next to him. He's kind of a grouch in the mornings. A lot of times while he's in his chair waiting for the food cart to come he gets this upset look on his face and then pounds his tray real hard with a closed fist. The weird thing is that sometimes after he does that, his mood changes—his face kind of lights up and then he puts one hand to his mouth and giggles like a little girl. Weird!

One thing I like is that Billy puts Buddy and me next to each other for breakfast. Usually he wheels me over near to Buddy's bed, which is near the TV. Usually the *Today* show's on and sometimes I like to see it and know what's going on in the world outside B Ward. My favorite's when Willard tells the weather and then talks about some old geezer whose birthday it is—most often an old codger a hundred years old or even more—and shows their picture, sponsored by Smucker's. Sometimes they have wrinkles deeper than Gramps's. It makes me wonder, sometimes, if I'll ever get to be old like them. If I have to stay like this, not get better than I am now, I'm not sure I want to. I mean, I don't know.

Even though I've lived here for a while now, it's still really weird that I have to be fed all my meals. These ladies, usually Destini and Cassie, who talks so fast all the time, bring in this big stainless steel food cart and plug it in. Billy dishes up a tray for me from the food cart and sits on a plastic chair and puts this white cloth bib around my neck that fastens with a snap—a *bib!*—and feeds me with a spoon. Always a spoon, no forks here. And no knives because there's nothing to cut. For breakfast it's usually some kind of yucky hot cereal—I'm not sure exactly what. I know it's not that good Quaker Oats stuff like Mom fixes, with butter and milk and brown sugar. This cereal doesn't taste horrible exactly, but definitely not great. More sugar on it would help a lot, but how can I let Billy know that? But it's not how it tastes that I care about, it's that someone has to *feed* it to me, like a baby, while I'm wearing a stupid bib! It's ... *humiliating.* Makes me feel so helpless.

God, what I wouldn't give to be able to hold a regular old dumb cheeseburger in my hand and bring it to my mouth and take a bite. Or maybe a slice of pizza with pepperonis, onions, and extra cheese. I always like extra cheese, and light on the tomato sauce. Two things I hate on pizza are green peppers and mushrooms. *Yucko!* Amy likes peppers, but I can't stand them and always take them off if we go out for pizza or order one at home. And Brandon likes stupid mushrooms. I'd love to know that taste of hot cheese and crust and sauce mixed together in my mouth again, but, more than that, just be able to feed myself. *Sheesh!*

Oh, man, every day and night I wonder if I'll ever be able to do what was so ordinary, stuff I never gave a thought to—holding a sandwich or a slice of pizza in my hands and bringing it to my mouth. Or grasping a glass of milk or a can of soda and drinking. Even that weird Larry feeds himself, sitting in a chair with a tray thing attached. His manners stink though, what with his chucking his spoon as far as he can as soon as he's done eating and then sometimes shoving his tray on the floor. Then he immediately goes to playing with himself and singing out "Wah-GOO! Wah-GOO!" or sometimes just "Heek, heek." So in a way he's better off than me, because he can do what I can't.

What if I can never feed myself again? What if I never walk or talk any more? What if I never get better than I am now? What then? What if the way I am now is my life forever? That's what I've been thinking lately, and it's darn scary. I wish I didn't think about that so much, but I do. What if I never leave this place, never get to go home again? What if I never get to go back to school? Up to lately I've been thinking that this is just temporary, that I'd get better, sooner or later anyway. Maybe not right away, but sooner or later. But what if I don't get better? Dear God in heaven, what if I don't ever get better?

Sweet Jesus, what *then*?

BILLY

MAYBE I *WILL* get a cat. That's what I was thinking at the food court after work today, before I came home to watch *Pardon Us* for maybe the thirtieth time. That movie's a riot—Stan and Ollie are in prison for bootlegging during prohibition, trying to sell booze to a cop on the street.

It's never boring to watch girls at the food court, but sometimes being there's a little torturous too. When I see families together, whether it's a mother and her kids or, more rarely, both parents and their kids, and they seem like a normal family that gets along and likes being together, it makes me crazy. Well, not *crazy* exactly, just ... envious. It makes me feel bad sitting there alone, always alone, with my pizza and Cherry Coke, and there're these happy little families together at the mall, eating junk food, mothers wiping their kids' mouths with paper napkins, and later they'll go home and be together. I mean, I know things aren't always what they seem to be—lots of families that look fine at the mall or someplace are actually majorly screwed up, maybe even more than mine, you can't really know—but still. *Still!*

I was watching two women at a table, a mildly pretty bleached blonde with too much green eye shadow and a big-haired redhead with gargantuan gold hoop earrings, and they each had a cute little girl about the same age—four, maybe five—and both women were eating huge pretzels, those big warm soft ones you get there. They each broke their pretzel into big pieces and then dipped the pieces into mustard they squeezed from little packets onto the white paper wrappers the pretzels came in. The redhead delicately dipped the end of each piece of her pretzel into the mustard and gently shook off the excess and then took a little ladylike bite, while the blonde slathered her pieces lengthwise into her mustard and then stuck each whole piece into her gaping mouth, sometimes dripping some of the yellow stuff. *Yuck!* They both wore lipstick and at one point I looked up and the blonde had pretzel crumbs and a dab of mustard on her mouth. The bright yellow of the mustard on those soft coral lips was startling. The redhead looked at her friend and tapped her own lips and the blonde rolled her eyes and licked

41

the mustard and crumbs off with the tip of her sexy pink tongue. Both little girls got a huge kick out of that and giggled. After the four of them left, I noticed that their table was covered with salt.

That's when I decided to maybe get a cat. Just then the idea of going home to my empty little apartment made me feel weird. I definitely don't want to live with anyone else, but maybe a cat would be okay. A cat might be good. Sitting in my recliner watching Laurel and Hardy, drinking my tea and covered with my afghan, I'm thinking a cat would be nice. Maybe it would be nice to have a little furry thing in my lap to stroke, hear it purr maybe, see it sleep. It would be okay to have something to take care of. It would be okay to have a little company, as long as it wasn't actual people. Of course, having a cat in my afghan-covered lap while I sipped my hot mint tea would surely round out my old lady image—turn me, finally, into Grandma, I suppose, though she didn't actually have a cat—but what the hell! Nobody comes here, so no one will know. Just me.

Frederic Henry surely wouldn't sit alone night after night with a sleeping cat on his lap, or Robert Jordan or Nick Adams either, probably. Or Sheriff John T. Chance from *Rio Bravo*, my favorite western— potbellied John Wayne, always capable and in control, barking out orders to everyone. I've seen it on TV at least a half dozen times since it came out maybe ten or eleven years ago. But what the hell! I'm not those guys and never will be. That much I know. No grace under pressure. Maybe the old man's right—I'm a pathetic loser—but so what? Maybe I'm not Lieutenant Henry, but at least I'm not my gaping asshole old man either.

If I get a cat, I'll probably get one from the shelter. There was a story in the paper about how many dogs and cats they have to "put down" there because they can't find homes for them. Crappy deal for them—locked in some cold metal cage hoping and praying in their way that someone'll take them, anyone will do—*please, please, SOMEONE take me! I promise I'll always use the litter box!*—and if not they're killed. Dead forever. Bad luck. Dirty trick. *"Put down!"*—what a nice, sanitary little phrase. *Executed* is more like it. So maybe I can get one of those poor felines.

In my chair at night lately, alone in my little home, like now, for some reason I've been thinking more about work, about the kids. Now I'm comfortable and warm and getting a little sleepy after my tea and watching Stan and Ollie in the warden's office after they've inadvertently broken up a prison break and the warden's congratulating them and saying solemnly, "My boys—and you *are* my boys—I hold in my hands the pardons for both of you. You have saved us from a disaster of *cataclysmic* dimensions. Now go. Begin life anew. Let this episode be just a *hiatus*, to be *obliterated* from your memory," and the guys look at each other quizzically, and you know they don't understand what the hell the warden just said, those big words, and I'm laughing at that scene again, the blank looks on those two magnificent faces, even though I've seen this movie dozens of times, and I'm thinking about what baths I have to do tomorrow and who I'll try to get up and into their chairs for breakfast before sweet little Destini rolls the food cart in.

Destini. Does she maybe like me? I don't know. She smiles at me when she comes in, that toothy little smile.

Tomorrow it's Timmy and Gilbert for baths. I'll get Timmy up for breakfast. He likes to sit in his chair next to Gramps to eat. Timmy's such a spaz, though, I have to be extra careful so he doesn't roll off the bath slab. Maybe I'll use the tub instead. I wonder what Buddy's up to right now. And Ricky. I wonder if there's anything I can do to make his day just a little less tedious—just a *little* less tedious, for Christ's sake. Day after day in that crappy ward, same boring routine, surrounded by all these bizzaros. The other day I noticed Ricky furrowing his brow and kind of tilting his head to listen to Christopher in Group Three making that weird catlike sound. Linc said that Christopher's going blind now, his eyes glazing over. He has a thing called *cri-du-chat* syndrome, cry-of-the-cat. Sounds just like a damn cat, too. Poor little guy.

Gilbert, another poor bastard. Randi said they did some kind of experimental surgery on him, which is why he's so screwed up—his arms and legs permanently bent up and rigid like they are. I remember the first time I saw him naked, when I had to give him a bath the second day on the job. He was lying there on the bath slab, bent up and his eyes all crazy, looking around everywhere, his forehead glistening with sweat, mouth open wide, making little gulping-like sounds. I thought he was just scared of being bathed, but then found out he's like that pretty much all the time. What a life! The weird thing's that Gilbert has a big dingus—not just long, but thick. Where's the justice in *that?* It's sure as hell never gonna do *him* any good, whereas some of us who it might do good, someday, aren't as blessed. Oh, well.

I asked Boyd if he knew any jokes I could tell Ricky, but he didn't. He said the only jokes he knew were too raunchy for the average twelve-year-old, though he knew some of those raunchy jokes when he was eight because his brother, who's both a rummy and a pothead, told him. "Why not tell him some of them knock-knock jokes?" he said.

It's funny. I never used to think about work stuff much after I got home, but lately I have. I don't know why. Ricky keeps coming into my head. I worry that he's getting thinner. He's been on B Ward nearly two months now, and he's not only no better, he looks worse. His skin is paler, I think, and it seems like his hair is different. I noticed that when I gave him his bath a few days ago. Most of the kids we bathe just by lifting them onto this raised ceramic slab in the tub room and wetting them down with a spray hose and lathering them with soap and then rinsing them off. It's quicker than the regular bathtub. But we can use the tub if we want to, and that's what I always do with Ricky. It's more normal for him, I'm sure, less demeaning than to be sprayed with a damned hose, like washing a car. That's not right. Maybe I'll do the same for Timmy tomorrow. Anyway, I was washing his hair, using this greenish shampoo his parents had brought in, Prell, and I was pretty sure his hair felt, I don't know, drier or thinner or something.

Mary Lou said she thought he was getting thinner too. The crap off the food cart isn't exactly gourmet meals, but it should be filling enough. I'm sure he'd prefer more normal food, the kind of junk any kid his age likes. Maybe a burger and a shake or something. Maybe a hot dog. Pizza. At least maybe tomorrow there'll be ice cream for lunch, like sometimes. Usually it's strawberry, in a Dixie cup. I think he likes that.

I was thinking too that Ricky'd maybe like some sunglasses for when he's out in the solarium. Sometimes it's bright as a bitch out there, and he's sitting there kind of squinting. Buddy too. Of course, he spent all those years on the farm and I doubt he had sunglasses then, but now maybe the old fart'd like that.

Anyways.

If I get a cat, I'll have to find out what kind of food to give it and what kind of cat litter to use and all. I don't think they need much, but I'd sure like to do *something* right if I can.

BUDDY

SOMETIMES RAINY DAYS are okay. Billy's off today, but Rita put Ricky and me out in the solarium and we're out here along with the usual guys, just quiet and watching the rain. It's one of them all-day soakers, the sky a dull gray and the trees outside the windows dripping water, like tears. I've noticed that on days like this the guys, for some reason, tend to be calmer, quieter, than on them sunny days. More low-key. Dino's out here on his cart—a bigger one that they just got for him—and of course he can't see nothing, but he don't laugh or even chuckle, just smiles a little, when he hears Randi sneeze three times in a row. Arnie's just staring out the window, his stars-and-stripes hard hat cocked to one side of his head. He has one of his catalogs, but he's not looking at it much. Even that nut case Larry's just sittin' quiet in his chair, chin in one hand and tapping his upper teeth with the fingernail of the index finger on his other hand, looking out the window.

But today I wish it was sunny, not like it is. I feel particularly down today. Maybe it's the weather, I don't know. Maybe just life. Maybe nothing. Hell, I just feel tired of everything, the same shit day after day, trapped in this pathetic body, playing the pissy hand God dealt me. Part of me feels ashamed for feeling sorry for myself as much as I do. At least I'm alive, and should be glad for that. I know that. I do. At least my mind works, and there I'm better off than most of the poor wrecks here. I know that, too. I really do. But right now I ain't glad. Right now, today, I wish I was dead so I can be done with this shit and go to heaven. Looking out at the gray sky and the rain, sitting here quiet with my bizarre roommates, I just want to stop being me, at least the way I am. I want to be something else, a spirit hopefully, or if not that then nothing at all.

I wonder sometimes if there really ain't a heaven and when we're dead we're just dead and that's it. I'm pretty sure there *is* a heaven, where it's always peaceful, like Father Callahan says, and we're free from the lousy burdens of this crappy life, but how do you really know? I mean, I hope that and I think there is, but how do you really *know?* You don't till you're dead. That's a scary damn thought in a way, but in another way maybe it ain't. If you're just dead when you die and you're just nothing forever, no spirit or nothing, then okay. I can live with that. At least you're done with all the bulltwinkie, all them indignities. Free from your useless body. Done with other people sticking your ding-dong in cold metal urinals and shoving them Fleets things up your ass.

Still, I guess there's some things I'd miss if I kicked the bucket. I'd miss being out here on nice days, and sometimes even on days like this, and looking out at them cornfields in the summer. I like seeing them rows of cornstalks. I like seeing the sun and the fields and remembering living on the farm. I like watching the squirrels fartin' around and the birds flying here and there and sittin' on the tree branches for a little while and cocking them little heads from one side to the other and then taking off again. They must have a tough life, always looking around for stuff to eat and worrying about hawks and all like that. One thing I love to watch is them little pickety birds, whatever they are, flying around furiously and pestering the bigger ones, like them hawks, sometimes. I don't know why them hawks don't just turn on the little ones and kick the crap out of 'em, but they don't. At least I never seen them do it. The best thing is to watch them hawks just soaring around like they do, sometimes with their wings spread out and not even flapping much, just sort of floating.

I'd miss seeing my brother when he comes. I'd miss Billy. And I'd definitely miss Mary Lou and her boobs. Seeing them out there and bouncing around is okay. And her laugh, that's just the best thing of all. It's *always* good to hear that girl laugh. It is. It just makes me feel better, somehow. It's amazing in a way to see her just walking around B Ward like she always does, standing up so straight, young and strong and healthy, kinda sexy I guess, just alive, her long shiny brown hair hanging down her back, her round butt in her tight blue jeans, her cleavage there for the whole damned world to see and admire, and she knows that. It seems like she's happy most of the time, smiling, laughing at lots of stuff, talking to us guys and all the aides and nurses, and just liking being herself in the world. Wow! What a thing to be her, Mary Lou. I wonder if she ever feels down like I do so much. If she does, I ain't seen it.

I'd miss the guys too, some of them anyway. I'd miss little Davey, scooting around on his back like he does and cleaning my wheelchair and bed with a white washcloth. He's a pain in the ass sometimes, always underfoot, but cute in a way. He tries hard, you gotta give him that. It's funny how he has them real short little seizures like he does now and again, if that's what they are, where he kinda jerks one arm up and his face goes blank for just a moment. I'd miss Ricky. I like it when Billy puts him and me next to each other out here. That feels good. He just seems like a nice kid, and he's sure as hell had a bad bit of luck, what with his accident and all. Even though I'm just a pathetic old fart, a useless nobody taking up space in this stupid world, I like to think that somehow or another me and him are friends. We can't talk to each other, but maybe just being here, around him, is something. Maybe. I like it, anyway.

I guess I'd miss Gramps, too, and even Timmy. Poor little kid! He's always squirming around in his chair, can't hardly ever sit still, it seems, with his face contorted and his arms and legs flailing around like he can't control them and always slipping down so that the aides have to lift him back up and tie one of them cloth restraints around his chest so he don't fall onto the floor and crack his head open. Seems like the only time he's calm is when he's holding hands with Gramps. And the only time he ever laughs or even smiles is when Gramps does his tricks, like kissing them stupid dolls or sticking his tongue up his nose or singing "Old McDonald" in his bizarre way. I think the happiest I ever seen Timmy was that time old Gramps farted in church and that bald priest got all pissed off.

So what would Timmy do if Gramps kicked the bucket? That could happen, Gramps being as old as he is. What then? The poor little guy would be lonely as hell, I'm sure. His life, such as it is, would be so different. Such as it is. Not much. What would be the point for him of keeping on living? Well, hell, what's the point for *any* of us here? I don't know. I really don't. It ain't like we're contributing nothing to the world. But I know I'd miss Timmy if he wasn't here. Seeing him every day, him and that cross-eyed old fart together, that's nice somehow.

I wouldn't miss Larry though. He's just an irritating pain in the ass.

One thing that brightened up the day, a little anyway, was when Linc sang one of them songs he likes to now and again sing, when he was giving someone a bath. It's a kinda cheery song:

> *I have often walked down this street before,*
> *But the pavement always stayed beneath my feet before.*
> *All at once am I several stories high ...*
> *Knowing I'm ... on the street ... where you live.*

There's a lot more to it, but I can't remember.

I guess I'd feel a little better if Billy was working today. He talks to me more than any of them other aides or the nurses, even when it's just dumb stuff that no one else can hear. Like the other day when he was dressing me, putting on my green and pink Hawaiian shirt, and Randi was walking toward the back of the ward, he stopped for a minute to watch her and then leaned down and whispered, "I tell ya, Bud, that lady has the greatest derriere of the entire damned nursing faculty. Or am I wrong?" I got a kick out of that. Another time, last week I think it was, I was sitting in my wheelchair sort of watching whatever stupid soap opera was on—*Days of Our Lives*, I think it was—with this rich-looking pregnant woman on, and Billy watched with me for a little bit and then said, "Hey, who knocked *her* up? Wasn't you, was it, Bud?" I ain't sure what "knocked her up" means, but it sounded funny when he said it.

RICKY

I HAD A NICE dream last night. I was hanging out with Brandon and Jeff and a couple other guys after school, and we were riding our bikes in the park and watching some kids throwing Frisbees around and Jeff was, as usual, knocking their techniques and saying how lame they were. Then we went to McDonald's and got three of those huge orders of fries that they pour tons of salt on and we were sitting around eating them and drinking sodas and just talking about stupid stuff, the way we always do. Then all of a sudden I stood up in the aisle and made like I was holding a football in my hands and getting ready to punt it. I remember I had this real serious look on my face, totally concentrating on what I was doing. I held the imaginary ball in front of my stomach, took three steps, and pretend-punted it with my right foot. Then I turned to my friends and grinned and said, "Did you guys see *that?* A forty-six-yard punt that pins those losers back on their goal line! *Un*believable!" That's all I remember.

I must have had that dream just before I woke up because it seemed so fresh, so real. Then when I woke up I didn't know where I was for a minute. I thought I was home and turned my head to look at the clock on my bedside stand to see how long I had to sleep yet before I had to get up and get ready for school. But it wasn't there. Then I saw the little clock that Billy gave me, saw the time, and remembered where I was. That was pretty yucko.

Billy told me and Buddy three knock-knock jokes. My favorite was:

> Knock-knock
> *Who's there?*
> Despair
> *Despair who?*
> Despair tire is flat.

Buddy laughed at that one the most too, I think—this deep-voiced laugh he has—and he kinda drools too when he laughs. Billy wiped his mouth with a washcloth.

I wonder if I'll ever see Brandon and those guys again. Mom told me that he and Jeff came to see me when I was in the hospital, but I don't remember. Maybe I wasn't awake. I'd like to see those guys, sure, but in another way I don't. I don't want them to see me the way I am now. If I get better, that's one thing. But not now.

My family's different. I hate for them to see me like this, but I miss them all the time and want to see them. Only it's so hard for all of us. Mom and my sisters, mostly Amy, sometimes cry or at least get all teary when they're here, and that makes me feel terrible. I wish I could tell them it's okay, but I can't. I can't say anything. Dad looks sad too, but I don't remember if he's ever actually cried. When they come to visit, usually in the early evenings, I try the best I can to keep up my spirits and even smile a little, but it's not always easy. Dad wheels me out to the visiting area outside the ward and they all sit on these orange plastic chairs they have there and tell me stuff that's going on in the world, stuff about people we know, things they're doing. Amy always brings me reports about her friends and what they're doing and her school stuff and everything, and I like that. I particularly like it when she talks about this one girl, Jessica, who Amy says everyone hates because she's "so full of herself" and hangs around with the popular girls even though she's not really one of them. "She just thinks she's so cool!" Amy always says. Man, nine years old and she's already so into being popular and cool and all. Chelsea, though, hardly says anything, just sits there quiet. I wish I knew what she was thinking. The weird thing is that when they leave, I'm sort of glad they're gone so I don't have to see them being so sad about me, even though I miss them right away.

One thing that's interesting is whenever my parents visit and then leave, Buddy gives me this look when I come back to the ward. Usually he's in his chair, sitting up but slumped over and his head sort of drooping over to one side. Sometimes he's drooling. Anyway, he gives me this look with those blue eyes, those kinda watery blue eyes, and I feel that he sort of knows what's going on with me and understands my feelings. I'm always glad to see him. I feel tired after I get a visit and it's good just to be quiet when I come back to the ward. It's good to see Buddy, and know that he seems to like me but I don't have to say anything to him. If Billy's on, he always asks if I want to rest and I nod and he puts me in my bed. He knows now that I like to lie on my right side with my extra pillow under my left arm.

I don't like to think about anything too much after my family's left, so I just try to remember nice stuff from the past. One thing I remember is once when we went camping at a state park somewhere, and after my parents and sisters got tired and went to sleep I just stayed up by myself and sat on this little log and watched the campfire. I don't remember how long I did that—may have been minutes, may have been an hour or more—but I remember the crackling sound of the fire, staring at the orange and blue flames, the smell of the pine wood burning in the night air. There was a nice breeze that rustled through the trees. For supper we'd had hamburgers and baked beans and potato chips, the ones with ripples, and I felt full and good. I remember now and again throwing sticks into the fire and watching the sparks in the air, and then seeing each stick catch fire and burn away into nothing. My mind was just empty, I remember, and I had no worries. That was a nice time.

BILLY

SON OF A BITCH, anyway! I wanted to go to Junior's today before work, but overslept. I slept all night in my recliner and never set my damned alarm and just had enough time to get dressed and get my butt out the door to get to work on time. Usually I fall asleep in my chair and then sometime after midnight wake up and stumble into bed and set the clock. I must have been pretty tired. Damn! I really wanted to see little Christy—that cute little pockmarked face, that sweet body in her tight green uniform—and hear, "Coffee, hon?" That's as good as it gets, for me, pathetic as that may be. Damn!

Last night, for some reason, I was thinking about Destini. She keeps smiling at me when she rolls that stainless steel food cart in, and I'm not sure what to do. Should I talk to her? What would I say? We talked a little when I asked about her name, but that's it. I wonder what her mother *really* thought about agreeing to name her Destini, because her old man had once had the hots for a woman with that name. That seems weird. Did her mother resent her later for that? Did she regret agreeing to it? I don't guess it'd be okay to ask her that.

I wish I was off today. Except for wanting to see Christy, I wouldn't mind just staying in my little apartment all day, alone, not having to talk to anyone or do anything, just safe and quiet behind my locked door. Just sit in my chair, sip coffee from one of my blue china cups in the morning, maybe watch a video and take a nap in the afternoon. I'd read some more of *For Whom the Bell Tolls* with Robert Jordan boffing little Maria, snuggled together naked in his sleeping robe in the Spanish mountains, under the pines. "Didst the earth move for thee, rabbit?" he asked. Not talk to anyone. Well, after tomorrow I have two days off.

I wonder if it'll be Maria for whom the bell tolls, like it was for poor Catherine Barkley. I don't imagine Mr. Hemingway would have *another* of his tough guy heroes knock up his beloved and then have her croak tragically, but who knows? The bell tolled for Catherine's baby too, the cord wrapped around its neck. That bell's gonna toll for all of us sooner or later, right? What do you do with your stupid life before then, though? That's the thing. What am *I* doing? Hiding from the world as much as possible, that's what. Being a recluse in a recliner. A reclining recluse. Guys my age are supposed to be doing *something* noteworthy out in the silly world, I guess, preparing for their tedious future—going to some kind of lame college or tech, maybe; getting jobs or getting ready for them so they can make money to buy cars and refrigerators and clothes and houses and TVs and gadgets—never enough, always wanting more and more, more and bigger, new and better; and taking vacations to warm places where they have skinny long-haired babes in skimpy bikinis on lounge chairs next to the pool or on blankets on the beach, rubbing suntan lotion on their legs and bellies and drinking gin and tonics and undoing the backs of their bikini tops when they're lying on their stomachs; and being social, spending time with friends, partying, having amazing sex, or even just mediocre sex; and then at some point finding someone minimally acceptable to pair up with, settle down and play house with, figure out some kind of a silly romantic proposal she'll like and puddle up about, and then plan to get hitched after a while—pretending you care about the color of the napkins or who sits next to who at the wedding reception, and then make babies so that the whole silly cycle starts over again, down through the ages.

And I'm not doing any of that or thinking about it. No more school for me, that's for sure. Enough silly education. Enough annoying teachers. Enough, "Billy, what is the central theme of *Romeo and Juliet?*" or "What is the role of *fate* in the play?" or "Why was Lincoln's Gettysburg Address so significant?" How the Christ would I know *that?* My history teacher, Mr. Quilling, said Lincoln wrote that speech, which we had to memorize for some silly reason, on the back of an envelope in a train. So what? Would it have been a different speech, better or worse, if he'd written it on the finest French stationery with a thousand-dollar fountain pen filled with the purest of inks? Anyway, I feel no ambition right now as to a good job or a career, no idea for being a splash in the world or doing anything worthwhile or making bucks, and no plans to even go out with anyone, much less get married and have kids.

Sweet Christ, the thought of ever living with a woman scares the bejesus out of me—particularly after being with my nutso screaming parents all those years. I'm always jealous of people who're together—families, couples—but I can't see me ever *being* those people. Oh, I think sometimes it'd be nice just to have a girlfriend, like Christy, to do fun stuff with, sex stuff with, now and again, like Robert and Maria, maybe someone to talk with together, like them. "I love thee, little rabbit," I'd say. "Are we not truly one?" "We are so close that neither one can tell that one of us is one and not the other," she'd murmur back while gazing wetly into my eyes. "Can you not feel my heart be your heart?" But then that seems like a fantasy, like imagining yourself to be a war hero or a great athlete or Sheriff John T. Chance—nice to think about, but you know it's not gonna happen because, really, you're just pathetic old nothinghead you, and always will be.

So what do I do? Do I just live the rest of my life alone in a little apartment with my books and my Laurel and Hardy videos and my future cat until someday that bell tolls for me? I don't know. All I know is that I have no other plans right now, no ambitions. Right now, this is what I want and it's all I want. This apartment is where I'm safe, most genuinely me.

Anyways.

Maybe I could be a carpenter. That might be interesting. Father Callahan was talking once about how Jesus was a carpenter, but he never said what he made—cabinets or houses or bookcases or whatever. But, of course, I have no skills there. Or, really, in any damned thing. In wood shop in seventh grade, Boyd had to help me do my lamp project, measuring and chiseling and sawing and all. I would've screwed it up. Boyd did a great job though, I'll say that. The *idea* of being a carpenter, like Jesus was, is appealing, anyway. I like wood. I'd like to make nice oak bookcases, something solid.

I wonder if Christ was any good at carpentry. I imagine he had to give it up when he became famous and gave the Sermon on the Mount and healed the lepers and turned out the money changers and all. There're probably lots of carpenters around, but how many guys can walk on water?

Well, I guess I'll work as an aide, an *institutional* aide, for a while more anyway. It doesn't pay much, but I guess it's okay for now. It's good enough for now. I can do that. In fact, I sort of like it, taking care of these kids. It's a good thing to do, at least for now. At some point, though, I guess I'll have to figure out what else to do.

Whatever I do in my pathetic life, though, I'm always going to have my own oak bookcase. Every day, first thing in the morning, I like to look at my books arranged just so, all of them flush to the edge of each shelf— almost all second-hand paperbacks I got at the used bookstore on Third

Street or sometimes at Saint Vinny's. I usually go to Third Street once or twice a month, usually after payday. You don't have to talk to anyone there, unless you have a question about some book. I have my good stuff, literature-type stuff, on the top two shelves and miscellaneous books, including my Louis L'Amour and Zane Grey westerns and some mysteries on the lower shelves. I have a few hardbacks, maybe twelve total, including a nice *Huckleberry Finn* I bought used for $5.95. Those books and my blue cups and saucers have been my extravagances. Silly maybe, maybe pathetic, but that's my life. Such as it is.

The other day I looked at my worn dark-blue hardcover copy of *Treasure Island* in my bookcase and remembered when I first read it. It must have been in fourth or fifth grade, and I remember I played hooky from school on a nice spring day, warm and just a little windy, and I went to a little park about a mile from our house and parked my bony loser's ass at a green wooden table in a small picnic area at the bottom of a hill. I just stayed there all day and read, and at noon ate the cheese and baloney sandwich I'd made and brought along, wrapped in aluminum foil, and six Oreos. It was a pretty day, the sky blue and those fat, fluffy white clouds floating along. The breeze felt fine. I just sat at that picnic table absorbed in my book, no school crap or other silly hassles. No one came by. Jim Hawkins, Long John Silver, Squire Trelawney, Israel Hands, George Merry—all those greedy limey pirates, so many dying for that shitbird Flint's buried treasure. And, of course, crazy Ben Gunn. Now, *there* was a recluse, though not by choice. The poor guy had been marooned for three years, alone on the island, not seeing anyone, not talking to anyone but himself, totally alone. *Totally* alone, not even a damned cat! Think of that. He'd found the treasure and hidden it in his cave and by the time Hawkins stumbled on him he was half-crazy from loneliness, dreaming of cheese—"toasted, mostly"—and worried sick that Flint's men, particularly Silver, were among the pirates who'd landed on the island. They were, of course.

I didn't see a soul that whole blessed day, thank God. No one came by. That was a much more memorable day for me than any of the forgettable hundreds I wasted at school. No one, thank God, asked me to analyze or critique the book.

I don't know if Ricky'd like *Treasure Island*. Maybe he would. I don't know if kids today like those kind of stories. They should. But do they? What do I know? Not much. He might, though.

BUDDY

BILLY WAS OFF yesterday and again today. I miss him. I like it better when he's here. I hope he's enjoying his time off, whatever the hell he does when he ain't here, but selfishly I like it better when he's around. I wonder what he does on his days off.

This afternoon was story time. After our naps they wheeled a bunch of us out to the multi-purpose room where the lovely Miss Dee Dee read us a couple or three stories—stupid kid stuff about Bunny Foo-Foo and the little engine that could and such crap, since most of us are more or less at that level. Most are less—way less. Miss Dee Dee reads in this soft, whispery voice, pronouncing each word slow and real clear so us feebs can under-stand, I guess. Really, though, she's nice, and nice to look at: short light-brown hair, pale eyes, and this small oval face with one of them cute little upturned noses. She almost always wears these pretty sweaters, usually green or pink or yellow, with little teddy bears or smiling puppies and such on them, like a little girl might wear. She's the calmest person I ever seen, always the same each time, and I wonder if she ever gets real mad. While I was listening to her read today I imagined her having a huge argument with her boyfriend or husband or whoever, all pissed off and screaming and red-faced, her skinny little body all tense, maybe cussing him out, all shrill-like, maybe throwing a book—a children's book, probably—at him. That would be something to see, by gosh. But she never even raises her voice or seems bothered by nothing. Just calm and good-natured, sort of sweet. I can't imagine her getting all upset like Father Callahan did when Gramps farted in church that time.

Gramps seems to like Miss Dee Dee. He apparently don't see her the same way he does the docs or the priest or them other big shots. Him and Timmy just sit quiet, holding hands like always, listening to Dee read her stories, and one time I saw him getting ready to stick that tongue up his ugly old nose. So he must like her. She's a cute young female, which is his type.

Ricky seemed okay too. I noticed he was kinda slumped over to his left when Miss Dee Dee was reading some silly story about a calico kitten with magic powers who helped make sad orphans happy, or some such, but he didn't look bored or nothing. I think he probably likes Miss Dee a little bit. Hell, who wouldn't? I guess he's a little old for them dumb kid stories about magic cats, but I imagine he's happy enough to do something different from the stupid boring routine of B Ward. I know I am.

I think he liked it better, though, when Billy read to him and me, day before yesterday, in the solarium during nap time. That was nice. As soon as Billy got all the kids cleaned up and in their cribs after lunch, he hauled the two of us out there and sat in one of them plastic chairs and read to us for a little while from this book called *Treasure Island*. When he first told us the name I thought he said *Pleasure Island*. But no. Still, that was a good story, what he read so far. That kid Jim Hawkins, he had to deal with all them nasty pirates that kept comin' around and scaring his mother half to death and drinking rum and making threats and waving swords around.

I remember Ricky paid attention and smiled at some parts, like when Black Dog came to the tavern and was talking with Captain Bones, his "old shipmate." Black Dog's a weird name for a guy, but probably that wasn't his real name. Maybe he didn't like his real name, like I ain't that crazy about mine, Albert. Anyway, that was nice, just the three of us out there while everyone else napped. Even crazy Larry must have been asleep, because he wasn't doing his usual thing and *wah-goo*ing all over the damn place.

It was good to just listen to Billy read that story. It got me out of my stupid self for a little while. I liked hearing about old blind Pew, mean bastard, threatening to break Jim's arm and then later getting run down by a horse. I liked that. It made me think I'm better off than that there Pew was, at least in one way. I can see. He could walk and talk, yeah, but he couldn't see nothin' and that turned out to be the end for him.

You wonder what God or St. Peter or whoever says when a nasty jerk like Pew gets up to heaven. "Get the *hell* outta here!" I imagine. "Get your mean blind ass to the other place!" Anyway, *I* can see, and that's good. I can sit in the solarium and look out the window and see them cornfields, the shiny green stalks getting taller in the summer. I can see the sky, the birds, and the squirrels and all that. I can see sweet Mary Lou, and Randi's cute butt. Pew couldn't. So there's that.

When Billy finished reading, he stood up and lifted Ricky up straighter in his chair. "You guys like that?" he asked. I nodded, and I think Ricky did too, a little. "You want to hear some more? Not now, but later sometime?" I nodded again. "Good," he said, "we'll do it soon. Ya know, Bud, you coulda been a pirate. I can see you with a black patch over one eye, swigging rum and singing 'Fifteen Men,' searching for buried treasure and all. Green parrot sitting on your skinny shoulder squawking 'Pieces of eight' and stuff. You definitely have the makings of a gentleman of fortune." I don't know what he meant by that last part, but it sounded funny.

RICKY

I HAD A bloody nose right after breakfast this morning. It just came out of the blue. I was sitting in my chair next to Buddy watching *Today*—I like all those crowds, mostly women, gathered outside the studio holding up signs that tell where they're from and waving their arms and lifting up babies and going "Whoo!" when the cameras are on them—and all of a sudden I felt this sort of itching in my nose and then blood starting dripping down my face, over my mouth, and onto my shirt. When I saw it, I felt scared. I've had a few bloody noses before, once after I picked my nose too hard, I guess, and once when I was playing second base and a ground ball took a bad hop into my face. But this one just started for no reason. I didn't know what to do. I sort of leaned my head back a little. If I could, I would've stuck a handkerchief or something to my nose, but, of course, couldn't. Anyway, Buddy noticed and started squirming around and making these noises, like I've heard him do when he has to pee sometimes, and Billy came over and held a washcloth to my nose and sort of pinched my nostrils together till the bleeding stopped. I don't think there was a lot of blood, not really, but it scared me because I don't know why I had it and also there was nothing I could do for myself. "We're gonna have to charge you for ruining a perfectly wonderful washcloth," Billy kidded afterward. "But don't worry, kid, we'll just deduct it from your allowance."

That yucko bloody nose was bad enough, but what was worse was that a little later, out in the solarium, I just started crying. I was sitting in my chair, looking out the window, and thinking about what happened and remembering that time I got a nosebleed from picking my nose, and I started feeling bad, and all of a sudden I was bawling like a stupid baby. I couldn't help it, and made myself stop as soon as I could. I'm glad Billy or Randi or any of them didn't hear. The dumbest thing is that I remember I was thinking, while I was crying, about picking my nose. I know that's not supposed to be such a polite thing to do, but, of course, everyone does it and it's such a satisfying thing if you can actually get a good-size booger out of there. Then you have to get rid of the booger somehow. If you're by yourself, that's not a problem. You can flick it away or wipe it off under a table or something, or even get a tissue. But if you're around other people, it can be a problem. I remember a few times at school when I held a book up to my face to hide what I was doing and picked and then carefully wiped off the booger under my desk. You just have to be careful when you do that so no one sees—no one who cares, that is. Anyway, I can't pick my nose now, and don't know when I'll be able to again, and even though that's a dumb thing to worry about it got me to crying. I felt ashamed of myself.

I wonder if God doesn't like it when you pick your nose. You'd think that with all the terrible things going on in the world that He wouldn't worry about something that insignificant, but who knows? They say He sees everything that happens, knows everything. So He must know when someone picks their nose, but does He care? I don't know. I'm sure picking your nose isn't even a venial sin, but maybe Jesus and Mary and all just find it offensive. Bad manners. I can't remember all the rules and guidelines about that stuff. I wouldn't mind if He'd get me back to where I could pick my nose again, but probably that's not an okay thing to pray for. I pray to God to help me get better so I can get out of here and go home, but so far He hasn't answered that prayer. I don't know why. Maybe He hasn't had time yet, what with all the wars and floods and stuff in the world, famines and hurricanes and poverty and diseases and all that. Maybe He'll get around to it when He has time.

Speaking of time, I liked it that Miss Dee Dee—I think that's her name—wore that small clock around her neck during story time yesterday. Story time! It's been a long while since I've been in a *story* time. Kindergarten maybe? Jeez! But I liked Miss Dee Dee's little gold-colored clock on a chain around her neck, swinging back and forth as she moved. She reminds me of someone, but I can't think who. Somehow my mind isn't working that great because I'm having trouble remembering little things, details about stuff. I was trying to remember all the posters I have up in my room. I know I have six—at least I'm pretty sure it's six—all sports stuff, mostly football, but I could only remember what four are. What *are* those other two? It bothers me. My favorite poster is one of Johnny Unitas, number nineteen, with that old-time flattop haircut, going back to pass, kinda hunched over for some reason. Anyway, that little clock was kinda cute. I don't know why she doesn't just wear a wristwatch, but it's okay.

Who cares? I couldn't get into those dumb stories though. They're just boring and stupid kid stuff—cute cats with magical powers and stuff.

I liked it better when Billy read *Treasure Island* to me and Buddy. That's a good story. My favorite part so far was when Dr. Livesey told Captain Bones that if he didn't stop drinking he'd die. Just like that. The doctor told it like it was, and wasn't scared of the old pirate. I liked it that the captain was so worried about a guy with one leg and kept going out with his telescope every day to look for the pirates, and then finally they came. Black Dog did first and then that horrible Pew who gave him a piece of paper with the black spot. That was cool. Then a whole bunch of pirates came and Jim Hawkins and his mother had to run out of their house and hide. I want to hear what's gonna happen next. Miss Dee Dee has a nicer voice than Billy's and she's definitely nicer to look at, but I like what he read a lot better. Billy never said who wrote *Treasure Island*, but when I get out of here I'm gonna find out and read that book myself, and maybe some of that guy's other books too. When I get out of here. *If* I do. The black spot. That's cool.

I think Buddy liked that story too. I noticed he smiled and kind of laughed when Billy read about Pew screaming and getting run down by a horse. It's interesting what amuses different people. Buddy has this sort of deep-voiced laugh, but it never goes on for too long. And the poor guy drools most of the time, with little bits of saliva running down his chin. Billy wiped his face with a washcloth at least five times while he was reading to us.

I noticed Linc was staring at Miss Dee Dee in a kind of funny way, almost rude. Then later he was singing that song I've heard him do a few times.

> *Summertime, and the livin' is easy.*
> *Fish are jumpin', and the cotton is high.*

There's more, but I can't remember all the words. I like that song. I like the idea of the fish jumping. I only went fishing a few times with Dad and Uncle Hank, but I'd like to do that more. Well, I probably won't now, but I'd like to.

I don't know why, but for some reason I really wanted a hot fudge sundae during story time. Miss Dee Dee was wearing this pink top with two kittens on it, one of them sleeping with one paw under his chin and the other batting at a ball of yarn or something, and looking at those cats made me think of ice cream. I don't know why. It's weird how your mind works sometimes. I was thinking of a hot fudge sundae and remembering how good the taste is—the cold vanilla ice cream and the dark hot fudge, the warmer the better, mixed up together in your mouth. I always like to start by eating two spoonfuls of just the hot fudge if it's on top and not buried too much under the ice cream, but not too much so that there's still enough to mix up with the ice cream later. And you hope there's some fudge left at the bottom. Someone I know—maybe Jeff or it might be this other guy at school, Pat, who never tucks his shirt in—always eats as much of the fudge as possible right away, before any of the ice cream, but to me that's wrong. Is that Jeff? *Sheesh!* The best thing is to mix it all up on your spoon. Also, I don't like those little nuts on a hot fudge sundae. Amy does. And if there's a cherry on her sundae she always dips it into her fudge first before she eats it. I always save the cherry for last, after my sundae's done, and then eat it. It's weird how different people have such different habits.

I hope I don't get any more of those bloody noses. That was yucko.

BILLY

YOU JUST NEVER KNOW. I was reading the paper this morning at Junior's before work and there was a story about this bad accident on some highway south of town. Traffic was slow and backed up because of construction and some asshole truck driver leans down to pick up a pack of cigarettes from the floor, Lucky Strikes or whatever, and when he sits up he sees that traffic ahead's stopped completely and he tries to stop but can't in time and rams his truck into the back of a Pontiac with three people inside and the truck goes over the top, crushing most of the car. A fifty-eight-year-old woman and her four-year-old granddaughter, Tiffany, were killed instantly and the woman's husband was hurt horribly, his leg all mangled, and it took them more than two hours to cut the poor guy out of the car. It said he was conscious the whole time but in terrible pain—and with his dead wife and dead granddaughter right there *next* to him! Good Christ! The woman was "well-known and much beloved in her community," it said, and had quotes from all these people about what a wonderful person she was, so warm and giving, active in her church, a credit to the community, blah blah, and how her granddaughter was "the apple of her eye." Both of them wiped out, *BOOM!*, just like that, no warning, gone forever because of a stupid dropped pack of cigarettes. Talk about dirty tricks! It makes you wonder how God could let something like that happen. Where's the justice? How's *that* part of some eternal plan? People talk about "God's will" when horrible shit happens, but you have to wonder how something like that could be God's will. What's that all about? Mostly I don't even believe in God, particularly when you read stuff like that, but I'm not sure. I mean, who knows? I think sometimes I'd *like* to believe in God—it must be a comfort to believe there's this all-knowing and kind creator who watches out for everyone somehow—but I don't feel it. Anyway, it's hard to feel sorry for yourself when you read stories like that.

Christy wasn't there. I heard Junior tell one of the guys at the counter, one of the regulars, that she'd called in sick, had a bad case of the flu or some such. The guy asked Junior about her, very interested, so I guess I'm not the only one who notices her. I didn't think I was. All the years I've been going there, I don't think she was ever not there because of being sick, at least not that I know of. She's had days off, but I never heard of her being sick. It kind of startled me to hear Junior say why she wasn't there, but I'm not sure why. Somehow I just sort of assumed she'd always be there and be the same each day, but, really, that's a dumb thing to assume. She's a human being like everyone and gets sick like anyone else. Still, I can't quite imagine my sweet little Christy at home sick with the flu, not in her green uniform but instead a ratty pink bathrobe like my mother's, her face all pale and no makeup, hair uncombed, sweating and feverish, her stomach upset and maybe puking or even having the screaming shits. Poor baby. Maybe I could take care of her, wipe her face with a cool washcloth and cover her with an extra blanket if she got the chills. "Could you make me some tea, hon?" she'd ask in a weak little voice. "Oh, thanks *so* much. I feel a little better now." For some reason, the thought of her sick makes me like her all the more.

I wonder if she lives alone like me or with a boyfriend or whatever. I don't think she's married because she doesn't wear a wedding ring. But I don't know. It's weird that I sort of love Christy and fantasize about her but, really, don't know a damned thing about her and don't know how I ever will.

I think Mrs. Hanson was pissed at me for reading to Buddy and Ricky in the solarium yesterday. She came in there and saw it and didn't say anything, but she kinda looked at me disapprovingly, like some women will, with her nose in the air a little bit. I know that some of the aides think I show favoritism to those two guys, and I guess they think that's wrong. Treat all the residents the same; don't discriminate. I've heard people say that, and that's what they said in training when I started. But screw that! They're *not* the same as the rest. The rest of these poor guys, except maybe for Davey, are severely mentally disabled. Or profoundly, some guys. They're babies, mentally. I love them, but they're babies. Ricky and Buddy aren't. They liked it, I'm sure, when I read *Treasure Island* to them. They seemed to. I think it was nice for them. Dino, what would he know? He likes to hear a sneeze maybe, but that's about it. And Gramps and Timmy? Maybe they like to hear Miss Dee Dee read to them, even though they don't know what the Christ she's saying, and maybe they'd like it if I read to them too, just for the sociability, but they don't understand like Ricky does. Ricky's a normal kid, for God's sake, a normal kid whose poor body got very screwed up in a goddamn stupid football game, and he's here in this crazy place—why, I don't know—and he's *not* like these others, he's different. He *is*! So why not show him favoritism? Why *not* treat him special? Why not treat him *very* special? And Buddy too. And maybe Davey too. Those other guys, they don't mind. Hell, during naptime all Larry wants to do anyway is choke the chicken, pound his pathetic pud. He doesn't care if I read to Ricky or Buddy. None of these guys do. They're mostly sleeping anyway. So what's the damn problem?

Well, maybe there's none. Mrs. Hanson didn't actually *say* anything to me, just kinda looked down her long nose with that dried-prune look she has, the corners of her lips turned down. Who knows why? She hardly ever talks to me, except maybe "Good morning" now and again, but I notice she yaks with the women a lot, the aides and nurses. Mostly dumb stuff, like what she cooked for her family last night and what she's going to make for them tonight, and how her son loves green beans with almonds but her little girl doesn't and her husband likes to eat dinner early, just at six, but she'd prefer to eat a little later, and he still likes fish on Fridays, and on and on in such vein. And, of course, the other broads chime in with their fascinating contributions: "Oh, Jack's the same way. He'd throw a fit if dinner's ten minutes late ..." or "I always like to get green beans fresh. They're better that way ..." Blah blah. Words, words. I guess Mrs. Hanson and I have nothing in common. I eat alone.

Ricky liked this joke I told him the other day: *What did Tarzan say when he saw the elephants coming? ..."Here come the elephants!"* Boyd told me that one once when we were out shooting pool on a Friday night in senior year. I remember we saw this incredible babe that night—huge brown eyes, long straight black hair, black leather jacket, dark coral lipstick, stiletto heels, amazing butt encased in skin-tight blue jeans—who was with her chubby boyfriend who was playing pool with two other guys. Boyd stared at her and whispered, "Man, I'll keep her in mind tonight when I'm home alone with Rosie Palm and her five sisters."

Larry could use some whacking lessons, as far as that goes. His technique is horrible, lying prone on his bed during naptime and grasping his pathetic little doohickey tight in one hand, probably way *too* tight, and just frantically bouncing his body up and down. I could give him lessons—I've had enough practice—but the thing about being severely retarded is that a guy doesn't learn stuff too well. "Look, kid," I'd tell him, "bouncing up and down like an idiot isn't going to get you anywhere." Maybe I'd try to lecture him on proper technique, fruitless though that would be. I don't even know if he's ever made the earth move for himself. I've never checked.

Anyway, I'm *not* going to treat Ricky the same as everyone else in my group. Let Mrs. Hanson write me up or whatever. I could care less. Why should I? As long as they don't fire my ass, screw them. If they don't want me to read to Buddy and Ricky, let them tell me. Dirty looks won't do it.

Looks from women. I've had quite enough of those in my life so far. More than enough. My mother, for one. Bad looks were her specialty, her stock in trade, and I hardly ever knew what she was pissed about. I'd come home from school and she'd be sitting in the living room or at the kitchen table, almost always with her gin and tonic in hand. "Hi, Mom," I'd say, and sometimes she'd answer "Hi" in her usual flat, bored tone, but sometimes wouldn't answer at all, but whether or not she spoke she always gave me that look. Her look. It wasn't, "Oh, hi, I'm *so* glad to see you. How was your *day?*" It was more, "Oh, *you're* here again. Well, now that you're here do you witness how *shitty* my life is? *DO* you? Today and *all* days?" Now that I think of it, I never remember her asking me how my day went, how school was, what I was up to, how I was feeling, what I was thinking. She must have. She was my mother and I was her only child. But I don't recall. Still, she must have. Of course the old man never did either, but from him I didn't expect anything—fat piece of shit. Well, the hell with both of them. So eventually I stopped trying and just said hello, or maybe nothing, and just went up to my room as soon as possible and called it a night. That was okay. That was fine. What do I need them for, anyway? The hell with all those bad looks.

Anyways.

Who knows what women are thinking? Not me. You can't tell. At the food court yesterday I was sort of watching this young couple at a nearby table—cute little pair, both with straight brown hair and *very* white teeth— and he's chowing down some Chinese dish with white rice, sweet and sour chicken I think, very intent on his eating, and she's not eating anything and they're not saying a word to each other. Nothing. While he eats, she's just looking right at his face with her nice gray-green eyes, studying him sort of, with one hand in her lap and the other slowly rubbing the back of her neck. He doesn't look at her at all, just keeps on eating. But I remember thinking that he must know she's watching him. This went on for at least ten minutes. So what was she thinking all that time? What was going on in that pretty head? Was she wondering how he liked his sweet and sour chicken? Maybe, but I doubt it. Was it love? Desire? Worry? Hate? Was she thinking that she'd just love to spend the next fifty or so years with him and have three magnificent healthy children together, two girls and a boy, and live happily ever after and invite her parents over for dinner on Sundays? Was she just hoping to screw his brains out that night? Did she maybe want to cut his gonads off? Was she thinking how completely and totally *bored* she was with a pathetic loser like him? Who knows? I wonder if he knew, or even wondered. Or cared.

When he was done eating he stood up, took his tray to a trash can, tilted the tray to empty his paper plate and cup and plastic fork and knife and napkin into the can, put the empty tray on top of some other trays stacked on the flat top of the trash can, walked back to the table and just stood there, still not looking at the girl. She sat there for a few moments, perfectly still, staring up at his face, and then slowly stood up and they walked away together, not touching. The whole time I watched those two, they didn't say a word to each other. Not one word. Nothing. She had a cute little behind, walking away. I'll say that.

Still, I wonder sometimes how my mother's doing.

Poor Ricky. He was upset when he had that bloody nose. I don't know what that was all about. It worries me.

BUDDY

THAT LITTLE RANDI must have a cold or something. She was sniffling and sneezing all day yesterday, and kept blowing her nose, and once I heard her say to one of them other nurses, "Christ, I feel like warmed-over shit!" Too bad, but at least her sneezing made old Dino laugh. Her misery was his joy.

I thought she looked tired, too, and I was right because later I heard her telling Mary Lou that her husband'd kept her up half the night snoring and farting. "Damn it to hell, anyway," she said, "I finally fall asleep and he starts grunting and snoring and wakes me up, so I push him a little and then he stops and ten minutes later starts up again. 'God*damn* it, Norm,' I yell, 'shut the fuck up! I have to get up at 5:30 in the goddamn morning.' I try to pinch his nose together, nothing works. Finally, I have to knee him in the nuts, so he screams and goes, 'Hey, what the *fuck?* Oh, you bitch!' But it worked. Christ almighty!" She's cute, sure, but, my *God*, what a mouth!

Billy finished reading *Treasure Island* to me and Ricky yesterday. I really liked it. I was glad that guy Long John Silver got away at the end because I didn't want him to hang or nothin'. I thought that's what'd happen. All them other pirates died one way or another, except for the three drunks that got left behind on the island. *Marooned.* Long John was a bad guy, I guess, one of them scoundrel types, but you had to sort of like him. I liked it too when Ben Gunn scared them pirates when they were hunting for the treasure by singing "Fifteen Men" and yelling about some guy named Darby McGraw. "Darby McGraw! Darby McGraw! Fetch aft the rum, Darby." I liked that. I don't know what "aft" means, but I liked it. All them tough-talking pirates were scared of dead Captain Flint, except Silver. He figured out it was Ben's voice singing and yelling that stuff, not Flint's ghost. It was scary that Flint killed them six guys years before when they buried the treasure and then laid their bodies out so their skeletons would be pointers to where the treasure was. Not a very nice guy. I wonder if stuff like that really happened in them olden days.

Long John said that Flint's face was blue. I wonder why. Maybe he had a bad cold or something.

I hope Billy reads more books like that to me and Ricky. Or anything, really. It's a good way to pass the time. It's better than just sitting on my stupid butt doing nothing, feeling sorry for myself or thinking about going to heaven all the time. I like thinking about heaven, though, now and again. That'll be good. When I'm done with this body, they can use it for a skeleton pointer if they want. Or donate it to science. Or toss the damn thing out the window. Whatever. I don't care. Damned little use it's been to me, so if someone can use it for anything, go ahead. What do I care? In heaven, you don't have to worry no more about your body and how it feels or whether it works too good. You're rid of it at last. No more indignities. You're just a spirit, like them pirates were afraid of Captain Flint's spirit, and you got no more worries.

I wonder if Ricky thinks about that, heaven. His body was fine, and now it ain't. He had that football accident, and his body went to hell in a handbasket—whatever that means. My brother used to say that. My body'll never get better, but maybe Ricky's will. I don't know. I never heard Doc Winters or them nurses say anything about that one way or another. But what if he don't? What if he stays the way he is and has to stay in this place the rest of his life, like me and Davey and Arnie and the rest of us feebs? He's been here a while now, and I don't see him getting no better. In fact, I see him getting skinnier and I don't think he looks as healthy even as when he first came. I've noticed that for a while. So I wonder if he thinks that way, and if he does I wonder if he thinks about how good it'd be to go to heaven instead of being like we are now.

Of course, I don't know if he believes in heaven, like I do, or believes in God, or what he thinks about. Him and me, we can't exactly talk with each other. I wish we could. I wish I could tell him things—tell him that I like him being here, even though I'm sad he's here and wish he wasn't here and could be home instead, and that I like it when it's just the three of us, him and me and Billy, reading and all. I'd like to tell him stuff like that, so maybe he don't feel so alone.

Sometimes at night I hear Ricky crying to himself a little in his bed. Not much, not bawling or nothing, just a little bit. I wonder what's bothering him. I wish I could ask, so I could help him. But I can't. God, I wish I could, but I can't. All I can do is hope that weird Bernie or whoever's on hears him and helps him a little.

Bernie, strange as he is, he's kind. He's been here long as I have, always on nights, always talking to himself. My favorite's when he goes, "Well, boys, time for a smoke, ain't it?" just before he takes a break. Or, right before the day shift aides come in for report, he nods and says to himself, "Got through another one, right? Well, good enough." He always says goodbye to me before he leaves—"I'll see ya later, Buddy. Right?"— and now I notice he does the same to Ricky. That's fine.

I hope that foul-mouthed little Randi feels better soon. It must be terrible to feel like warmed-over shit.

RICKY

NIGHTS HAVE BEEN tough lately. I haven't been able to sleep well. I don't know why. For a while I was sleeping okay here at night—never great, but okay—but for the last week or so it's been hard. I don't know why. Jeez! I sort of fall asleep after a while and then wake up and look at my clock to see how long until morning and then I'm up for a while more. Sometimes I fall asleep again, but most times not. Sometimes then, later, I'm not even sure if I was asleep or not. I wish I could move around in my bed to get into more comfortable positions so I could sleep better. Maybe that'd help.

When I'm up at night now and can't sleep I like to think about sports stuff, fantasizing about playing football, mostly, and sometimes baseball. Last night I was thinking about being a running back—lining up in the backfield, looking over the defense before the snap, getting the handoff from the quarterback and securing it in both arms and watching my blockers to see where the hole is. It's third down, three yards to go for a first down. I see that the right tackle's sealed the defensive end to the inside and the tight end's tied up with the strong side linebacker, so I make a quick move and dash to my right. The cornerback's coming hard so I hunch over and cradle the ball tight and head for the first down marker on the sideline. I just reach it before he shoves me out of bounds with both hands. I fall down on my butt then turn quickly to see the ref raise his right arm straight up and then point toward their goal with all five fingers stiff and straight. First down! *Yes!* One of my teammates, a big O-lineman, grabs my hand and pulls me to my feet. "Way to go!" he says, patting me on the butt. I nod and trot back to the huddle. "Ready to go again, big guy?" my quarterback asks. "Let's do it," I say. "This time right down the freakin' middle."

If it's baseball, I imagine playing second base, my favorite position. There's one out, a runner leading off on first, and a right-handed batter. The pitcher works him to a three-one count and then the guy hits a hard grounder to the shortstop. Possible double play! I dash to the bag and see the shortstop scoop it up and toss it to me underhand. I catch it with my

71

ungloved hand just as I step on the base and jump to avoid the sliding runner and in an incredibly smooth motion pivot and zing the ball to the first baseman, who's in his stretch with his glove extended. *Perfect* throw! Got him! *Yes!* As I trot to the dugout our catcher comes out onto the infield and high-fives me. "Good play, big guy," he says. I nod and smile. "Thanks," I say humbly. "Thanks a lot."

Thinking about stuff like that makes me feel a little better till morning comes. But I don't like to think about playing ball with actual guys I know, like Jeff or Brandon or those guys. If I think about doing that, I feel too sad. After all, they're still out there playing and doing the things we used to do before my accident. So I just imagine playing with people I don't know— average faces, no one specific. That way I can think more about my techniques in particular situations, like just where to play in the infield with a certain number of outs and runners on base or not, or how to square up for a bunt, or if the quarterback calls a pass play who I'm supposed to block.

I wonder if Linc or Billy played sports. Linc's pretty big and looks strong. He looks like he could have been a tight end or a linebacker or something in high school. Billy's not big—in fact he's pretty skinny—but I've seen him lift those big laundry bags around. I think maybe he *likes* lifting them and carrying them to that laundry chute and tossing them in, to impress the women who work here.

The other thing I do at night now is pray. I've been kind of mad at God for my situation here, and still am, and probably that's not right, but then it occurred to me that maybe I should be asking Him for help more too. Maybe He has a reason that I don't know for why I'm here, for why my body is so screwed up now. I don't know. I mean, how does anyone know why God does what He does, why things happen? I wonder about that. The priests say we can't know God's ways, they're mysterious, and we have to have faith. Faith's the thing. So I thought maybe I should start praying to get better, asking God to take pity on me. I want to get my life back and stop making my family sad. So I pray every night when they put me to bed, and when I can't sleep and wake up in the night I pray again. I can't remember any particular prayer to ask God to help me, other than the Hail Mary or Our Father, so I just pray what I can think of. *Dear God, let it be okay with me. Let me walk again and talk and just be normal again. Let me go home to my parents, my family, and our dog. Let me go back to school, like other kids, and just be normal again. Let my family be okay. Don't let them be too sad about me. I'll be a good person. Really, I will. I promise.*

I'll do everything I'm supposed to do. I'll follow the Ten Commandments and all. Please, dear God, sweet Mary, take pity on me and help me. Please, please, please. That's what I pray for, over and over.

I hope my praying works.

What's embarrassing is that sometimes at night I just start crying. I can't help myself. I wish I could. I'm lying there thinking about stuff, maybe feeling lonely and helpless, maybe feeling a little sorry for myself, and all of a sudden I puddle up and start crying. *Sheesh!* If Bernie's working and he hears me, he'll come over to my bed and ask what's wrong. As if I could tell him. He'll ask if I want a drink of water, and I'll usually nod yes, and he'll do what he can to make me more comfortable. I appreciate that, but I hate for him or anyone to think I'm a baby.

When I have a bad night, I always hope that Billy's on in the morning. Usually he tells me now when he's gonna be working. Like if he's working one day he'll come up to me before he leaves and say something like, "Gotta go now, kid. I'll see you tomorrow morning." Or if he's off for a day or more he'll tell me just when he's coming back: "See ya Wednesday, kid." A lot of times Buddy's with me when Billy leaves and he lets us both know when he'll see us again. It's funny when he calls Buddy "old man." One time when he left he said to Buddy, "Keep your powder dry, old man." That was funny, though I didn't know what it meant. I can't speak for Buddy, and he can't for himself, but I imagine he likes to know when Billy'll be back next too. It's good to know stuff like that.

And I like it when Mary Lou's on in the evenings. She's so nice, and so pretty, too. She jokes around a lot with the other aides and nurses and stuff, and I like that, but it's not the same as when Billy's on. The only thing I don't like that Mary Lou does is talk bad about her boyfriend. A couple days ago she was telling one of the nurses, Colleen, that she was mad at her boyfriend, Duane, because he didn't call her when he was supposed to. "I don't mind that he's basically a dork," she said, "but I will not tolerate being with an *inconsiderate* dork." I don't think she should criticize her boyfriend in public like that. I mean, he probably takes her to the movies and stuff and buys her popcorn and something to drink and kisses her good night.

Billy told me and Buddy that he's thinking of bringing in some videos for us to watch. "You're gonna have to wait to see what they are," he said. "All I can guarantee is that you'll have some smiles."

BILLY

I'M GLAD I got a cat. It took me a while to get around to it, but I finally did. I went to the animal shelter yesterday, the first of my two days off, and it was as bad as I imagined—all these pathetic dogs and cats in little metal cages, some of them looking up at you with big hopeful eyes but some just sitting there quiet and still, looking depressed. Or scared. There was a gray rabbit too, all by itself in a cage, looking around and twitching its nose. Some of the dogs and cats were strays and some'd been given up by their owners for whatever feeble reasons. Their fates are out of their hands, and you wonder if they know what's up. I told the chubby young woman there, *Sheila* by her name tag, what I wanted and she led me back to the cat area and said to look around. There were at least a dozen poor felines—young and old, big and little, furry and less furry—in cages stacked three high. One caught my eye, a small mostly orange and part white guy with green eyes. He was in a middle cage and as soon as I saw him he stood up and put his face to the mesh and looked directly at me—looked right into my eyes with his light-green ones. I asked Sheila about him and she said he was a stray someone found in a garage, maybe six months old, and they'd named him Twinkle. "He's a sweetie," she said in one of those sing-song high-pitched voices some women have. "*Very* affectionate. He'd *love* a good home."

I had to answer a bunch of stupid questions about where I lived and what I did and if I'd had pets before and if I understood about vet care and shots, and blah blah, and had to sign a paper agreeing to be a responsible pet owner, and wrote a check, and little Twinkle was mine. Twinkle. I decided right there at the shelter to change that stupid name as soon as possible. What kind of self-respecting boy's named *Twinkle*? I asked Sheila about cat food and litter boxes, and found out I could buy most of that stuff right there.

My cat checked out his new home right away, running from corner to corner to sniff everything. It didn't take him long, my apartment being as pitifully tiny as a person's abode can be. Still, it's bigger than that damn cage. I set up his food and water bowls in the corner of the kitchen and his litter box in the far corner of the living room, and showed him that, and pretty quick he seemed content. After a bit he jumped onto my recliner and took a nap, curled nicely into himself with his furry little chin resting on his front paws. I just looked at him while he slept, glad to have another creature in my home—just not a human being—and as I stared he opened one green eye for a moment and looked directly at me and then went back to sleep. In that moment I decided on his new name: Stanley. It occurred to me that my Mr. Twinkle looked like Stan Laurel, my hero—same sweet and vacant facial expression, same light eyes. I could almost hear him asking, "Any beans?"

My dilemma was that Stan honed in on my recliner and jumped up on it and was right at home. I didn't want to move him but I wanted to sit there. My idea all along had been that my cat would sleep on my afghan-covered lap while I sat in my chair and read, so what to do? Finally, I decided to try picking him up and sitting down and setting him on my lap. But that didn't work. He looked a little startled, scared, and jumped down. So I picked him up and put him back in the chair and let him have the damned thing. A little later I went to sleep and put Stanley on the bed with me. He jumped down again right away, so I gave up. But when I woke up this morning there he was, curled up against my feet, sound asleep. I liked that a lot. Then, better yet, when I sat down in my recliner for my morning coffee. the little shit jumped into my lap and stayed there.

It wasn't Maria for whom the bell tolled. It was Robert Jordan. I finished the book last week, but I keep thinking about it. They blew up the bridge at the end and were getting away when Jordan's horse falls on him and breaks his leg. He tells Pablo and Pilar and all of them to take off, but Maria wants to stay. It takes a while and he has to sweet-talk her with a lot of silliness about how they're really one person and always will be no matter what, blah blah, but finally he persuades her to go and his friends all leave and then he's alone with a broken left leg and his submachine gun and the fascist cavalry approaching. "He could feel his heart beating against the pine needle floor of the forest." He'll hold them off the best he can to buy time for his amigos—grace under pressure again; dying for a noble, though lost, cause. Now he's going to shoot one of the fascist guys, Lieutenant Berrendo, before he himself goes under. So *more* corpses. Lovely!

So Jordan's done and poor Maria, little rabbit, has to go on alone. They found each other and made love under the pines and almost got away to have their life together, to go to Madrid and maybe later to Montana, and *BOOM!* his gray horse gets hit by a tank shell explosion and that's it. He's "mucked," as he says. But what if that shell had hit six feet further away? *Four* feet? Then maybe they get away and have a life together, making the earth move truly for each other in nice soft beds for many years, decades even, instead of whatever they had in their few days. What about that? Just another dirty trick, right?

Too many dirty tricks. I see them every day in B Ward, and sometimes I'm weary of it. Too much heartache. Too many people mucked—not just Ricky but the rest of those poor guys, most of whom were mucked since their starts—mucked before they were even born, many of them. Mucked in the womb. Mucked by bad genes or fucked-up chromosomes, like Gramps. Mucked *being* born, some of them, maybe with the cord wrapped around their neck like Catherine Barkley's baby. Thank God most of them don't know the difference.

Anyways.

I want to read something light before any more Hemingway—something where no one young dies. No more noble lost causes or true love while war rages. No more grace under pressure and no more death. I need a farewell to arms, for a while anyway. Maybe I'll go back to the Hardy boys or something mindless. Something light. Dashiell Hammett maybe, *The Maltese Falcon* with the incomparable Casper Gutman. Maybe Louis L'Amour westerns, like *Hondo*. John Wayne was in the movie version. Hondo inadvertently kills some shitbird cowboy and then gets the hots for his homely widow, who falls for him, too, and then says her husband was an asshole anyway. She's glad her husband croaked, and glad to be with the guy who croaked him! Wow! It was too bad the Apaches killed Hondo's dog, Sam, though. That was ugly. Maybe I'll read *Huckleberry Finn* again, or at least parts of it. I always like that book, except for when that annoying Tom Sawyer shows up at the end, at the Phelps farm, and sort of takes over.

I told Buddy and Ricky I'd bring in some videos, but didn't say what. Laurel and Hardy, they are. I don't know if they'll like that, but I think they will. I sure hope so.

BUDDY

MY AUNT IRENE kicked the bucket. She was eighty-six years old and had one of them strokes. My brother told me when he came to visit yesterday. "I don't know if you remember her too well, Albert, but she was a wonderful woman. Not beautiful, exactly—face like a fish, sort of—but good-natured most of the time. Good cook, too. Oh, Albert, I recall her pot roasts with boiled potatoes and them little sliced onions, ya know, and of course her deep-dish apple pie. Amanda always envied her baking, ya know. 'Oh, Donald,' she'd say, 'your aunt makes the best pies of anyone. *Perfect* crust!' The funeral was good, lots of people from her church ..." And so on.

I don't remember my aunt too well, and it musta been ten or eleven years since I seen her. She sure as hell never came to see me here, and I don't remember getting a damn Christmas card or birthday card or nothin' like that either. The one thing I remember about her is she was all the time talking about spaghetti dinners they did at her church and how it irritated her that some people, and I recall she named names, *cut* their spaghetti instead of twirling it around their forks to eat it. That bugged the hell out of her. Still, I guess I'm sorry she's gone. I hope she had an okay life. I'm sure them pot roasts with the potatoes and tiny onions made people happy.

I wonder if I'll see her again in heaven. Most likely when you get there you see all your dead relatives, whether you liked them much or not. I think Father Callahan said we'd see them. But do you have to spend *eternity* with them? I don't know. It would be too bad if you had to spend eternity with someone you weren't crazy about or even couldn't stand, just on account of they were your aunt or cousin or like that. I wonder if being a good cook gets you into heaven. "Oh, Irene," Saint Peter'll maybe say, "*you're* the one that made all them lovely deep-dish apple pies. Come right in!" Who knows? I guess if I see her there I'll be glad enough. Maybe I'll ask her why she never even sent me a card all them years, but then again in heaven most likely we won't worry about that kind of petty stuff. Our little grudges and snits hopefully don't matter no more.

I hope I get to see Ricky in heaven. I always dream of walking around in them clouds, my legs and the rest of me working just fine, normal, like everyone else, and it would be nice to take that walk with him—both of us guys standing straight as brooms, strolling around up there like kings, talking and laughing, waving at people we know and shouting hello. "How ya doin'? Hey, nice to *see* you!" Me not all bent over and drooling like some damned baby. Oh, that'd be fine. Of course, I hope it's a long time before Ricky gets there. I don't know when I will, maybe sooner or maybe later, hopefully sooner, but I'm sure I'll be there way before he is. I'll keep a cloud warm for him.

Both of us, me and Ricky, liked that movie Billy brought in for us and showed on that TV that's on a cart they roll in and out that you can show videos on. I hadn't seen those guys in the movie, Laurel and Hardy, for years. I have in mind that they were on TV on Saturday mornings years ago, when I was back on the farm. I forgot how funny they are, always getting themselves into trouble 'cause they're so dumb. That one we watched was funny. *Pardon Us*, it was called. The two guys go to prison for selling beer illegal, and when they get there the prison officer asks the skinny guy his name. "Stanley Laurel," he says. "Say *'sir'* when you address *me!*" the guy yells at him. "Now what's your name?" "*Sir* Stanley Laurel," the skinny guy answers, smiling stupidly.

The best thing was it made Ricky happy. A lot of it made him smile and giggle, particularly when the skinny guy looks into the camera and screws up his face and cries like he does all the time, blubbering like a little kid. Oh, that's *so* funny. It was funny when he had to get a bad tooth pulled at the prison and he cried before he went into the dentist's office to get it out and the fat guy tried to comfort him and then the dentist made a mistake and pulled the fat guy's tooth instead and then, when he found out it was the wrong guy, pulled the skinny guy's tooth too.

Seeing them two guys again made me remember that what I liked was they were best friends, always hanging around together and doing stuff, no matter what crazy things happened to them. That's nice. I remember it made me think how good it must be to have someone like that, a friend who you could be with no matter what. Oh, they had their words and squabbles and all, and things were always falling on their heads, but they always stuck together.

Billy didn't get to watch much of it with us. Pretty soon after the movie started, we heard this loud shriek from Gramps and then heard him yell "BA-A-A BOH!" like he does—his version of *"Bad boy!"* I believe. Billy looked up, over toward Gramps's bed, and said, "Oh, boy. That crazy Dino's stripping the old fart's sheets again. Jesus Christ!" I've seen that. Gramps's crib is right flush against a wall and Dino's right next to him, with just the head of his crib against that same wall. Dino can reach through the slats of his crib and then through the slats of Gramps's crib and now and again he gets a notion to do that and pull off all of Gramps's sheets and blankets, even when the old geezer is lying right in bed. Dino's so strong, with them big arms and shoulders and chest, and he can do that easy. I seen him. He gets this determined look on his face and his big forehead gets all wrinkled with concentration and he pulls and pulls till he tugs them sheets and blankets right through the slats into his own crib and then chucks them over the other side onto the floor. There's Gramps lying on his back on the bare green mattress, all red-faced and pissed, screamin' his old fool head off. I don't know why Dino does it—just something to do, I guess.

I've seen Dino strip his own bed now and again, too. First, he reaches under his head and rips his pillow from there and tosses that out of the crib, then he flings the blanket out, and then he reaches under him and works on his sheets, first one side and then the other, till they're all untucked, and then there they go, tossed over the side to join the heap on the floor. Twice that I know of he even took it into his head to undo his diaper and chuck *that* out of his crib. Them diapers are held together with two sets of strings on each side. He somehow unties the strings and pulls the diaper from under his ridiculous little ass and *zing!* Just takes a notion to clean house, sort of. One of them times his diaper was full, so when he flung it poop went flying. I was watching, and it was somethin' to see. The weird thing was that his poop was bright *green* and kinda loose. It was a bizarre deal to see that green crap splattered on the wall and floor and all, and there's blind huge-head Dino lyin' there bare-assed in his crib, his useless little legs spread out and that big muscular chest heaving from all his effort.

Anyway, Billy had to go over and comfort Gramps and re-make his bed. He said something to him, I couldn't hear what, and put Gramps in his chair before he did the bed, and the old fart was still pissed. He looked over at Dino and yelled at him again: "BA-A-A *BOH!*" Billy gave the old man his two dolls and put them secure into the crooks of Gramps's elbows. Then he lifted Timmy out of his crib and tied him into his little chair and put that chair next to Gramps. Pretty quick the two of them were holding hands, and Gramps was a little calmer. Then Billy fake-sneezed a few times for Dino, to get him back on track, I guess.

While me and Ricky were watching the TV, every time one of us laughed I heard this little weak titter from the floor. Finally, I looked down and saw it was Davey, on his back, holding one of them white washcloths and polishing the wheels of my chair. He was looking at the TV, Laurel and Hardy, and every time we laughed, he did too. I ain't sure if he understood what was going on or was just going along with the crowd by laughing, but either way it was kind of touching. I almost didn't notice him down there on the floor by himself, doing his pathetic little cleaning job, but there he was, trying to get some attention a little bit.

Just before Billy got back to us I looked over at Gramps and Timmy, still sitting together next to Gramps's bed, still holding hands. That's so weird, but nice, I guess. It kinda reminds of the fat guy and the skinny guy. Not that they hold hands, at least not that I seen.

RICKY

MARY LOU WAS in sort of a bad mood last night. I can't remember seeing her in a mood like that before. She started out okay when she first came in, but then right after dinner she and Rita were putting Arnie on the toilet and he got all upset—I could hear him yelling *"WOO!"*—and they had to wrestle with him and I guess he pulled her hair and then it got worse. "That little *shit!*" I heard her tell one of the nurses. "He grabbed my left boob and wouldn't let go. Hurts like hell. I'm sure the big doofus bruised it too. *Damn* it anyway!" After that she was pissy. She didn't talk much or laugh like she usually does and I could just tell that she was upset. At least I'm glad I knew why she was in a mood because otherwise I might have thought she was mad at me for some reason. I don't know what I could do that'd make her feel like that, but who knows? Sometimes you can aggravate people and they won't tell you what you did. I remember one time Amy had two of her silly giggly friends over and they were all up in her room talking and I came home from school and was passing by and I said something to them, I don't even remember what, and Amy wouldn't even talk to me for a day or so after that. When I asked her why she was mad, she wouldn't tell me, just stuck her nose in the air and looked sour.

I don't know what Arnie's problem is about going to the bathroom. He gets upset a lot when they try to put him on the pot. At least he can do that and doesn't have to wear a diaper like so many of these guys. Like I used to. Maybe he just doesn't like it when women put him on the toilet. Maybe he's embarrassed. Who knows?

As for me, I'm glad I can use the toilet again instead of being in a diaper or using a bedpan. Of course, it's still weird that I have to be wheeled in my chair to the bathroom and someone has to lift me from the chair onto the toilet seat and tie me on so that I don't fall over. Then they leave me alone for a few minutes and I do what I can before they come back and then someone has to wipe me and pull my pants up and lift me back into my chair and wheel me back, to bed or wherever. I can't even flush the stupid toilet myself! Sheesh! That's so embarrassing, because then someone else is looking at your business. You never think about stuff like being able to go to the bathroom by yourself until you can't do that anymore. I used to get mad at my sisters in the mornings before school because they took so long in the bathroom, blow-drying their hair and all, and I had to wait and wait to get in. Finally I could get in and do what I needed to do, with a little privacy. I never once thought how lucky I was that I could do something as simple as going to the bathroom, taking care of myself. Now I'd give anything if I could do that again. Maybe I'll be able to do that again. I hope so. I really hope so. But more and more, I doubt it.

I hope Arnie didn't hurt Mary Lou's left boob too much. Maybe she'll be in a better mood tonight, if she's on.

I liked that movie Billy showed us. It was *so* funny! I never heard of those two guys before, Laurel and Hardy, but I love them. Particularly Laurel. When Hardy scolded him and he started looking into the camera and crying like he did, I thought I'd fall out of my chair. And I liked those black hats they wore—*derbies,* Billy said. I wish I had one of those. There were a lot of really funny parts. I liked it when all the prisoners were in a school class and they sang, "Good morning to you, good morning to you, good morning dear *playmates*, good morning to you." Just like in kindergarten. Then the teacher asked Laurel how many times three goes into nine and he screwed up his face and thought hard for a minute and then said, "Three times ... with two left over." Hardy put a fat hand over his mouth and giggled and the teacher asked him what was wrong. "There's only *one* left over," he said, his belly jiggling. I wish I could have asked Billy what Laurel's accent was. I think it's English, but not sure. I hope we get to see more of their movies sometime.

What was fun, too, was when Billy, once he got back from helping Gramps after that crazy Dino tore off all the sheets and stuff in his crib, would mouth the words that the guys on the screen were saying. I remember one time when Hardy turned to Laurel when they first got to the prison and said, kinda pissed off, "Well, here's *another* nice mess you've gotten me into!" and Billy looked at Buddy and me and said that line at the same time, soundlessly. He even kind of puffed himself up like the fat guy, Hardy. God, that was funny. Billy must know that movie pretty well.

I wonder if those two guys, Laurel and Hardy, are still alive. I don't know how long ago that show was made but it was one of those old-time black-and-white movies, so probably a long time ago. I wish Billy would tell about all that stuff, but then again how would he know what I'm curious about? Or what Buddy's curious about. He can talk to us, but we can't talk to him. If I could even write out a message on a stupid yellow pad or something, that'd be good.

One thing Billy told me and Buddy is he got a cat and named it *Stan* after the skinny guy. That's so nice. He said the cat sort of looks like Laurel. Buddy did that weird laugh he does when Billy said that. I didn't think what he said was funny, though it was interesting. I wonder where Billy lives and who he lives with. He never says anything about that. I know he's not that old, so maybe he still lives at home. I wonder if he has a girlfriend or anything. It's frustrating to have all these questions in my head and not be able to ask them. I don't think he cares about sports much because I never see him watching baseball when a game's on and I never hear him talk about sports with the other aides, like Linc. Linc likes to watch sports and comment on stuff, I notice. I liked when he said once, "Oh sweet lord, that is *such* horse-twinkie! My damn cocker spaniel could do a better job of calling balls and strikes than *that* ignorant chucklehead." Come to think of it, I don't see Billy talking much with any of the other people who work here. He must be shy or something.

Poor Davey! While Buddy and I were watching the movie he was on his back on the floor watching too, I guess, though I'm not sure he could see the screen too well, and making his little noises. Finally, Billy went and got the little chair Davey sits in and put him in it and then he watched the rest of it with us. He laughed now and again when Buddy or I did, or both of us did. I think he did that just to be part of the fun, not because he understood the movie. Still, it was okay for him to be there. That's fine.

It would've been nice to have popcorn while we were watching the movie. On the other hand, I guess I don't want popcorn if I can't eat it myself, if someone has to *feed* it to me. That wouldn't be right. The thing about popcorn in the movies is that it's so great to hold the box in your left hand, maybe resting it on one leg, and reach into it with your right hand and get a handful and stick it into your mouth and it doesn't even matter if you dribble lots of kernels onto the floor. Nobody yells at you for that. It's part of the deal. I like butter on popcorn, the more the better—even when it's that artificial stuff. I remember that Jeff hates butter but likes lots of salt, just like he does on french fries. He's so weird about salt, just pours it all over everything he can.

One thing that's irritating at the movies is when you buy a big tub and the popcorn on top is fine, big popped pieces, and then you eat some and get down a way and you find out that it's mostly those little broken-up kernels. I hate that! Sometimes then you have to go to the lobby and complain and usually they give you a new box. And they *should*.

BILLY

I CAN'T BELIEVE IT! I saw Christy at the food court this afternoon and she didn't recognize me. I'm not sure she actually *saw* me, but, if she did, she didn't let on. I was sitting at one of my favorite tables, a little two-seater next to one of those big fake fluted columns and a fat potted plant—nice spot to maintain a low profile and watch girls sitting together at the bigger tables, stuffing their sweet faces—stuffing my own face with my usual sausage pizza and sipping Cherry Coke, when I saw her come in with some short greasy-looking dude with an ugly scruffy little beard and a black leather jacket with silver buckles. My darling was wearing a ratty-looking khaki army surplus jacket and tight worn blue jeans and her pretty blond hair was down. I'd never seen it like that; she always has it in a ponytail at Junior's. Sweet Jesus, her little butt—those twin orbs—looked cute in those jeans! She and the greaser got stuff at McDonald's and sat at a table far enough away that I couldn't hear them, though I could see them fine. The ugly bozo was, I believe, eating a Big Mac and talking to my baby nonstop all the while—chewing with his miserable mouth *full*, for God's sake!—and dribbling that horrible orangish sauce, whatever it is, onto that pathetic beard. Worse, she was practically falling off her chair laughing the whole time. I think I just stared, not caring if Christy noticed, but she didn't. Once, she looked in my direction for a moment. But if she recognized me, she didn't give any indication. I don't know what was so damned *amusing* about the sawed-off shitbird, but sweet little Christy certainly seemed to get a kick out of the him.

Screw it, I thought. The hell with both of them, and the hell with this stupid food court with its silly chatty little long-haired beauties fluttering their hands and playing with their hair and dipping their fries into ketchup and going on and on about God-knows-what. Why keep torturing myself? Why? Plus, the food is terrible. The pizza tastes like cardboard any more and the Coke seems more watered-down all the time. And not only that, but just then I wanted to get home to Stanley. The poor orange guy was alone all day while I was at work, and then, like a jerk, I go to the stupid food court and he's alone even longer. Not fair to him.

So it's better here, sunk deep into my beat-up beige recliner, with my cat. When I walked in the door, Stan looked up at me like he'd never seen me before, a bit startled. Then he must have recognized me—"Oh yeah, *you!* I remember now."—because he raised his tail high and yawned and sauntered away, bored or indifferent. It was good to see him. I put my tea water on and changed into my red pajama bottoms and gray sweatshirt and pulled the hood up over my head and tied it tight under my chin. When the tea'd steeped I stirred in my spoonful of honey and turned on the TV with the sound low and sat in my chair and covered myself with my afghan. I started to read more from my book, *Huckleberry Finn*, but fell asleep before I'd even finished the tea. I'm not reading the whole thing but like to re-read my favorite chapters now and again; I'd chosen "We Ambuscade the A-rabs" because I like Huck's reaction to Tom Sawyer's romantic imagination: "I reckon he believed in the A-rabs and the elephants, but as for me I think different. It had all the marks of a Sunday-school." When I woke up Stan was fast asleep in my lap, between the opened book resting spine-up on my knees and my belly. It was nice.

It's nice to be in my own place feeling warm and comfortable and sleepy and safe. Just me and Stan. The bullshit of the world stays outside our door. *Our* door. Feeling this way, and reading *Huck Finn*, puts me in mind of maybe the nicest time in my life, when I was a kid and stayed at my grandparents' house. I was six or seven and had the mumps or something, and for some reason my parents shipped me off for a week or so to my mother's parents. That was fine. My grandparents lived in the lower flat of a red brick two-story on the east side of town. They had just one bedroom, a big one with faded greenish wallpaper with yellow and red flowers and their big brass bed. I remember dark wood doors and window frames. There was a little alcove in one corner of that bedroom, with the walls on three sides and a sloping ceiling where there was a staircase from the front door of the house to the upper flat. The alcove was just wide enough for a single bed plus a couple of feet on one side, and that's where my sick little ass was parked.

That was a heavenly week. I stayed in my pajamas the whole time, mostly reading and resting. There was a little table with a brass lamp next to my bed and the yellow glow from that lamp bounced off the close walls and the sloped ceiling of my little cave, making it cozy and mine. My nutso parents had at least remembered to send along my cardboard box of comic books, and I remember just lying under a thick green comforter in that bed all week, my head resting on two pillows, reading them. Grandma fed me soup in blue china bowls, chicken mostly, and I remember crumbling saltines into my soup. She kept the crackers in a big tin box to keep them fresh. I ate breakfast and lunch at a tray table next to the bed, and dinner at the oilcloth-covered kitchen table with Grandpa and Grandma. Brown and white checks, that oilcloth was.

Grandpa was gone at work during the day. I don't remember what he did. I don't even remember him that much at all. He died when I was eight. They never said what he died of. It must have been some kind of a secret. Anyway, it was peaceful there in the days, just me and Grandma. I'd be reading in bed and she'd be cooking or doing her housework and sometimes talking on the phone, and now and again she'd bring me a cup of Lipton's tea. I remember there was a heavy rectangular glass container full of sugar cubes on the kitchen table, with a thick glass cover, and I'd put two cubes in my tea and stir it in. I liked the sound and feel of the cubes against the spoon and the sides of the cup until they melted.

I remember, too, they had a small wooden built-in bookcase in their living room, with glass doors and little round silver handles. There were four shelves, and on the second one from the top was an old set of the works of Mark Twain, in hardcover. Dark-green books, maybe six or seven total—*The Adventures of Tom Sawyer, Innocents Abroad, Life on the Mississippi, A Connecticut Yankee in King Arthur's Court, The Adventures of Huckleberry Finn*, others I can't recall. I looked at those books every time I went there, taking them off the shelf one at a time and feeling the pebbly surface of the hard green covers and looking at the gold-colored titles on the spine and front cover and admiring the interesting typeface on the smooth pages and looking at all the illustrations, and when I was a little older I read parts of them when I could. I don't know what happened to that set of books after my grandma died. I really wish I had them.

At night sometimes I'd wake up a little and hear Grandpa snoring lightly. I was in my bed in my alcove, snug under my comforter, and Grandma and Grandpa were in their brass bed a few feet away. That was good. That was comforting. I recall that I hated going home at the end of that week.

As pathetic as it seems, I've often deliberately thought about that time in my life before going to sleep. I still do. I remember I did that a lot when I was living at home with my wacko parents, particularly when they'd had one of their psycho screaming matches. I'd lie in bed in the dark, usually on my left side facing the wall, and think back to that week with my grandparents, trying to remember the feelings I had of being small and taken care of; being secure, safe. I remember my grandmother quietly moving around the flat, the smell of chicken soup cooking, my little walled-in corner of their bedroom and my bed and the brass lamp. It's helped me fall asleep, lots of times. Pathetic? Maybe. But still.

And now every time I pull my white afghan over myself I get to remember Grandma. The weird thing is that sometimes I think she's watching over me somehow, looking out. Maybe that's crazy, but sometimes I feel that. It's an okay feeling.

Anyways.

I'm not going to go to Junior's either for a while. The hell with that. Maybe later. Not now. Screw it! Who needs the aggravation? I'm just going to get up each day and get ready for work and eat something—Cheerios I like, or Frosted Flakes, or I can make my own damned eggs over easy, maybe not as good as Junior but good enough—and be with Stanley until I have to leave, feed him, spend some time with him, and then come home right after work. I'll see Christy some other time maybe, down the road. Not now. *"Coffee, hon?"* my ass! For a while anyway, I think I need a farewell to Junior's and the mall, both. There'll be other days. I'm sure Stan'll appreciate it.

Frosted Flakes. I remember once I was eating them for breakfast and pouring on sugar and the old man yelled at me. "What the hell are you *doing,* for Chrissake? What kind of MORON puts sugar on Frosted Flakes? They're *coated* with the shit! Jesus H. Christ, Billy, what the hell's the *matter* with you?"

The main thing now is I want to bring in more videos for Ricky and Buddy. They loved Stan and Ollie yesterday, and it got Ricky to laugh a little bit. So at least *that* worked. Both of them laughed, and Davey too. That little shit wanted to get in on the party, squealing from the floor like he does, on his back, so I put him in his chair and he at least made out like he was into it, laughing when Buddy did and doing that thing he does with his left arm raised and sort of trembling. Who knows if he understood any of the movie, but he had some fun too.

I wish I could have just sat and watched with them, but I suspect long-nosed Mrs. Hanson wouldn't like that. So I had to set them up and get the show going and then be up and around doing my work, or looking like I was. Plus, I had to take care of the other kids. That madman Dino'd ripped Gramps's sheets out from under him again, and of course the old fart had a fit. I sat him in his chair and gave him his dolls and brought Timmy over and told Gramps to just go with the flow, play it as it lays. He gave me one of his cross-eyed looks and kissed both tattered dolls, so I guess he was okay and hopefully he appreciated the advice. I'm thinking those dolls are looking a little worn, and maybe he needs some new ones for Christmas or maybe his birthday, whenever that is. Larry was looking happy, lying on his back on his bed with one leg crossed over the other and tapping his teeth with his right index fingernail, a half-assed smile on his face, so maybe he actually got off. "Did the earth move for you, kiddo?" I asked. Arnie was awake on his bed too, with his hard hat next to him, looking sour. I heard he grabbed one of Mary Lou's boobs.

Maybe I'll show them movies more on the weekends, when the muckety-mucks aren't around. I'm going to have to go through my collection and decide which one to bring in next. Maybe *Swiss Miss* or *A Chump at Oxford*. Maybe *Blockheads* or *Sons of the Desert*. I bet Ricky'd like that one. He'd like the part where Stan eats the wax fruit at Ollie's house, swallowing hard with each bite, and Ollie's henpecking wife discovers it and says, "So *you're* the one who's been eating all my fruit!" I want him to have some laughs again, and Buddy too. Next time I'll set Davey up with them. Maybe some others too. We'll make it a regular old Group One party. Who knows? Maybe even Arnie'd like a party. Maybe I'll see if I can give the guys some pudding, in those little plastic containers you get at the store. I'm sure they'd like that.

The only thing is it seems it's getting tougher for Ricky to sit up in his chair for long. I noticed when he and Buddy were watching *Pardon Us* that Ricky was slumping over and his color wasn't so great. He laughed a little at the funny parts, yeah, but he just didn't look good. He looks thinner than ever too. He seems to be eating okay, and I don't know if he's losing weight, but ... I don't know, it worries me. Maybe I'm wrong. Maybe I'll talk with Mary Lou, see what she thinks. I'll have to be sure to look into her big eyes when I do, not down at that pleasant cleavage.

Anyways.

BUDDY

THEY TOOK RICKY to the hospital last night—not the regular hospital, that little one they got over in Building One. I was there once for a few days about three years ago when my chair fell over and I cracked my stupid head on the floor. It wasn't bad. I had a lump on my dumb head and a headache for a while, but so what? It's Ricky I'm thinking about here, not me. He'd been crying and sort of moaning on and off all day yesterday, and I noticed he didn't want to eat his lunch or dinner neither. Billy wasn't on. Ricky, he didn't look good to me—more pale than ever, somehow—and the nurses kept checking him. Just before bedtime, Doc Winters came in and him and a couple of them nurses looked at Ricky and the doctor poked at him and felt his pulse and listened to his chest with that black thing that hangs around his neck, and I don't know what all else he did, and then he left and a little later that bald black guy with a cart came in and lifted Ricky out of his bed and onto the cart and covered him with one of them white blankets and strapped him in and then he was gone. Just like that.

At least Bernie, after report, thought to let me know what was up. He musta noticed I was awake because he came up to my bed and just stood there for a minute and scratched his head. "Well, Buddy," he said, "they took Ricky to that there hospital in Building One. He's sick, you know, trouble breathing they said." He paused. "Hope he's okay, right?"

I didn't sleep much the rest of the night. I couldn't. A lot of stuff goes through a guy's head. Is he gonna be okay? Is he suffering a lot? Is he scared? Will he come back here again? Is he gonna die? What if Ricky dies in that hospital? What about that? What if he never comes back and I never see him again? What then? Poor kid, he's just twelve and now *this* happens to him! What if he never comes back here again and me and him never sit together in the solarium with Gramps and Timmy and Zach and them other guys, all of us in our chairs or carts, looking out at the fields and trees now that it's full summer, just a bunch of quiet feebs together? What if him and me never get to sit together again at naptime or whenever and listen to Billy read to us, or watch one of them Laurel and Hardy movies, or go to church

90

or story time with that nice little Miss Dee Dee, with her clock hanging around her neck, or stuff like that? What about that?

It's weird to think that someone you know who's your friend, like Ricky, who you see every day, could be here where you both live one minute and then be gone the next, and you don't know if you ain't gonna see him again. It's weird that stuff like that can change so quick, maybe forever. In the years I been here, that's happened a few times. I remember this blind kid named Russell who was in Group Two. His parents brought him all these stuffed animals that filled his crib, dogs and pigs and cows and such. He was here for three or four years and one day they took him to that hospital, I never knew why, and he never came back and I didn't even know he'd died until a few weeks later when they put a new kid in his crib and I heard Randi talking about where Russell's family buried him. It's weird.

All night I worried about Ricky, and felt bad for him. I felt bad for me, too. I don't know if that's right, but it's how I feel. I feel bad because what if I don't see Ricky again, at least in this here stupid life? If he don't come back here, I'll miss him a lot. If he got better and could go home, though, that'd be different. That'd be great. But I don't want to sit around feeling sorry for myself. I've done plenty of *that* in my stupid life, that's for sure. What does it get you anyway? Ricky's the one who's sick now, not me. *He's* the one suffering now, not me. My time will come, I'm sure, just like everyone's, but it ain't here now. Still, I can't help feeling sorry for myself, thinking that Ricky's in that damned hospital in Building One and maybe not ever coming back from there no more.

Well, what if he dies there? What then? I don't know how sick he is, but what if he dies? It don't seem like that's possible—he's just a kid. But what if he dies? That wouldn't be fair. I'll say a prayer to God that he don't die, that he comes back to B Ward. I hope God'll listen to a nobody like me, a useless old fart who never did nothing God or no one could be proud of. You wouldn't think God'd let Ricky die, what with all he's been through, but who knows? Who knows why God does what He does, why He lets someone like Ricky have that accident like he did and then go through all the crap of being in the ward and then maybe die alone in Building One? It just ain't right.

Well, if he does then I hope I see him later in heaven. I don't know when that'll be, but I hope it happens. Both him and me'll be free then of our stupid useless bodies, and I always think about us two guys standing up and taking a walk in them nice clouds, him and me, proud as anyone—

91

Mary Lou or anyone—and done with all the bullshit, all the indignities of this life. All the goddamn daily indignities. I always figured I'd get up there first, but I don't know. Jesus! It'd be weird if after all my years of being the way I am, useless and broken-down and all these kids like Billy and Mary Lou having to take care of me, that Ricky goes first and here I stay. And for how long?

That's what I thought about all night, on and off, in my bed. I must have slept some, but I don't know how much.

When Billy came in this morning, Bernie told him what happened. I could see in his face he was worried. At report they talked about Ricky and I heard the night nurse, Dawn her name is, saying how they were worried about his breathing, something about his pulse, tests they had to do, lungs or something, and like that. She used some words I couldn't understand. Dawn has these weird thin eyebrows, they look like they're not real, like they're painted on her face. She has a temper, too. I seen her get pissed and red-faced at the dumbest things, like if some aide forgets to chart some stupid thing.

I could see that Billy stayed worried most of the morning. He got me up first, as usual, and put one of my Hawaiian shirts on me, though for some reason I didn't feel like wearing it, and set me up in my chair. "I tell ya, old man," he whispered, "life sucks sometimes, eh?" He patted my shoulder. *"Damn!"* he said. After he'd fed breakfast to everyone in the group and they'd pushed the food cart out, he asked me if I wanted to go to the solarium. I nodded, and he set me up there, in my usual spot.

It's been a long darn morning out here in the solarium. I've just been staring out the window at them fields, the gray sky, and thinking about things—about being with my brother and Amanda on the farm, about Ricky, about them three drunk pirate guys that got left behind on Treasure Island, about Mary Lou and how pretty she is, and stuff like that. Actually, I wish I hadn't nodded when Billy asked me if I wanted to be out here. I wish I'd just spent the morning back in the ward watching TV, them talk shows and soap operas and all, so I wouldn't have to think so much about things. I think after lunch I'm just gonna lie in bed and nap, so hopefully my stupid brain slows down a little.

One thing I been thinking out here this morning is if Ricky dies, if that happens, maybe it'd be okay. Me, I been the way I am, trapped in this stupid no-good body, for all these years, so damned long, and I hate it every day and every day I long for it to end, to be done with this bullshit, and hopefully go to heaven. So if Ricky has to be the same way he is now for years yet, like I've been, then, damn it, maybe it's better to go. I don't know. That's a horrible thing to even think, that it could be better for someone you love to be dead than alive, at least alive a certain way, but that's what I'm thinking. I'd hate for Ricky to die, for his life to be done, to lose him. But, hell, I don't want him to suffer for years and years to come neither.

Well, it's up to God, I guess, either way. I suppose God's got reasons for stuff He does. Damned if I understand it all, though

RICKY

I'M SCARED. I really am. I don't like this place. I want to go back to the ward. I don't know the people here and don't know what to expect. They seem nice enough, the nurses they have here, but I don't know them. It's lonely here, and I'm scared.

At least I can breathe a little better now. I was so scared before they brought me here night before last, when I couldn't breathe so good. God, that was scary. The worst thing was not being able to take a deep breath. *Sheesh!* It seems like it's been harder and harder to get a good breath for a while now, maybe a couple of weeks, especially when I'm in bed at night. When I'm sitting up in my chair it's better, a little better anyway, but being in bed's been tough, especially when I was on my back. There were times like that, when I was in bed on my back, that I could hardly get a breath at all. Then when you try to get a full breath and you can't, that's all you can think about, and you worry about it, and you keep sort of trying to do it, but you can't, and pretty soon you kind of panic and feel all nervous and sweaty and flushed and your heart beats faster, and you don't know what to do. You want to get up and move around, stand up straight, do *something*, but can't. I just have to hope that someone notices I'm in trouble and helps me, somehow. But if it goes on for a while and I'm feeling that I can't do anything to help myself and nobody's noticing that I'm in trouble, and I can't yell or anything, then I feel even more panicky and I wonder if I'm going to die. When you can't breathe like you want to, you start thinking you're going to die. I did, anyway. God, it's the scariest feeling.

I remember wishing I was home in my bedroom, so if I was having trouble Mom would hear me and come help. Even if I were like I am now, can't talk or yell out or stuff, she'd know and come. Or Dad. Somehow parents, particularly mothers, know when a kid's in trouble. Not always, probably, but a lot of the time. But here that's hard. Some of the aides and nurses here and in B Ward are better than others. Some of 'em seem to spend a lot of time watching TV or talking to each other or just farting around, but not all of them.

Mary Lou, in the evenings, talks a lot to the nurses and other aides, but at least she seems aware of stuff with me and the other guys and she checks on me pretty often. She doesn't read to me and stuff, like Billy does, but she checks on me. Billy doesn't talk much to anyone, except sometimes to Linc or to Mary Lou when she comes in and he's on. He and Destini kinda smile at each other at breakfast and lunch, but I don't see that they talk. During report I notice he hardly ever says anything. Pretty quiet guy. He talks to me and Buddy and some of the other guys more than he does to any of the aides or nurses.

Man, I miss him, and Buddy too.

Billy, the last week or so, noticed I was in trouble, I think, because he asked me what was up. That was good of him. I remember one night I was having a lot of trouble getting a deep breath and Bernie wasn't on and the lady who was on, I don't know her name, didn't come around to change my position as much, and when Billy came around in the morning he saw right away that I didn't look good. "Headache?" he asked. I shook my head. "Stomachache?" No. "Want a drink of water? ... Need to go to the bathroom?" I shook my head. He felt my forehead and messed up my hair. "Want to get up?" he asked. I nodded, and he got me into my chair and put one of those thingies around me to keep me from slumping over. It was easier to breathe then, and I felt a little better.

I wish Billy'd been on that night I couldn't breathe and they brought me here. That would have made me feel less scared. Or at least Mary Lou. Wendy was working the p.m., and she's pretty but kind of a spacehead. I think she's shy, too. She always walks around with her head down, sort of looking at the floor. Billy would have helped me more, or at least would've noticed I was in trouble and got me some help sooner. I wish he'd come see me in this place. I don't know if they'll let him do that. They told me Mom and Dad are coming later to see me, so that's good. I'll be glad to see them, but I hope I don't cry. It's harder to breathe okay when I cry, and I don't want to upset them.

I wish they'd tell me what's the matter with me, why I'm having this trouble. Maybe I've got a bad cold or something, and after it goes away I'll feel better. I don't know. The thing is, my nose isn't running or anything and I never had a sore throat like I usually get at first when I have a cold. And when I had colds, I never had all this trouble getting breaths. So I don't know. I'm scared. That much I know.

If I could tell someone how I feel and the trouble I'm in, that would be better.

In bed at night, I've been praying to get better, to be able to breathe better. I've also been silently saying the Hail Mary over and over. I know that's one of our main prayers. *Hail Mary full of grace, the Lord is with thee. Blessed art thou among women and blessed is the fruit of thy womb, Jesus. Holy Mary, Mother of God, pray for us sinners now and at the hour of our death. Amen.* Over and over like that, and it's made me feel better, at least for a while. Somehow it makes me feel more calm. I don't know if God or Jesus or Mary hears my prayers. I think they do. They always said at church that all prayers are heard. But either way, just saying the old words makes me feel better. The words are familiar. How many times have I gone to confession and told the priest I'd done this or that sin—pretty minor stuff but sins anyway, I guess, like lying about some dumb thing or another seven times since my last confession or not respecting my parents or not saying my prayers—and was told to say five Hail Marys or a few Our Fathers as my penance. And sometimes I just say prayers I make up. *Sweet Jesus, help me get better. I'll be a good person, I'll do anything you want me to, but help me get better. Help me breathe better. Make it so I can go home and be with my family and my dog and see my friends and go to school. Just help me be normal again, dear Jesus. Please, Holy Mary. I don't have to play ball anymore, if that's the way it is. That's okay. But please let me just go home and be able to walk again and talk. Please! Dear God, forgive me for my sins. I'm sorry, Holy Mary, if I did anything I shouldn't have. Pray for me. Help me, please. Please!*

I still wonder sometimes what I did, what sins or whatever, to be in this place. Why am I being punished, if I'm being punished? I don't even know. Maybe I can't know, and should just have faith, and not worry. Leave everything in God's hands. I don't know. It's confusing sometimes.

What would be nice is to watch some more Laurel and Hardy. They have a television here in my room, and I'm glad of that. In one way it's nice to have a room of my own, not be in a big noisy ward, but on the other hand it's lonely. I like to have the television on as much as they'll let me, but I don't like all the stuff that's on. The *Today* show's okay, but the soap operas during the day, they're so dumb! In B Ward, it's okay to sit around with Buddy and watch them 'cause he always gets a kick out of them and laughs at some of the stuff—that weird laugh he has. He always seems to like watching the pretty women on the soap operas and sometimes he laughs at things that aren't even funny, like when two people are kissing or having an argument or something. He even gets a kick out of commercials for stupid things like deodorant and women's stuff, like Kotex or bras. But here, by myself, I don't like the soaps at all. They're just dumb. So are the talk shows. I wish they'd just show movies, like westerns or war movies or, better yet, comedies.

The thing that's good is that they crank up the part of my bed that's under my head most of the time. I don't have to sleep flat. That makes it a little easier to breathe. During the day, they crank it up even more, so that I'm sort of sitting up.

I wonder if I'm going to have to stay here now or if I'll get to go back to B Ward. Nobody ever tells me anything, which is really frustrating. They're taking care of me here, but it's lonely too. It would be weird if I never saw Buddy again, or Davey and Gramps and Timmy and those guys. As weird as it is there, with Larry being like he is—"Wah-GOO! Wah-GOO!" all the time—and Dino laughing at people sneezing and pissing Gramps off all the time by stripping his sheets from under him and guys making weird sounds all the time, I've kind of gotten used to it.

BILLY

WHEN BERNIE TOLD ME yesterday morning about Ricky going to the hospital in Building One, my heart near stopped. God*damn!* I thought. Son of a *bitch*, anyway. This isn't right.

At report that weird Dawn told about how he'd been having breathing problems and Doctor Winters wanted him to get some tests and be watched close in the hospital for a while and she threw around some nursing bullshit that none of the rest of us, or at least me, knew about—words like *pulmonary* and *intubation*. I heard that Dawn's screwing one of the dentists here, either McCabe or the other guy, I forget his name. On break a few months ago, someone said that she, Dawn, wants this guy to leave his wife and marry her but she read somewhere that dentists have a high suicide rate and she can't deal with that because her brother committed suicide when she was seventeen, so she's not sure about it, and blah blah. Hell, if I was married to her, with those bizarre eyebrows and her moods and all, I'd probably think about offing myself whether or not I was a dentist.

I felt like a zombie all morning. I got Buddy dressed and fed him first and put him in the solarium after breakfast. He looked worried too. I told him that I'd check on Ricky and let him know. He looked up at me with those watery blue eyes and nodded. I touched his shoulder and rubbed it a little. Pretty bony.

After lunch I asked Mrs. Hanson, while she was looking at a chart, if she'd heard anything. "They're doing some tests," she said, not looking up at me. "They need to find out what's causing his breathing difficulties. That's *all* I know, Billy." I was going to ask the witch if there was any problem with me going to see Ricky in Building One, but decided not to. What if she said no? I don't remember my old man ever giving me any good advice, but I remember him hissing to my mother once, during one of their many arguments, "Listen, bitch, don't ask me any questions you might not like the answer to." I remember that one. That was good. So I decided just to go there next day after my shift and see the kid, after he'd rested a little, and let the chips fall where they may.

The nurse at the hospital, Consuela—cute little smoky-eyed Hispanic thing with this sexy cleft on the bulb of her upturned nose—asked me who I was but didn't give me any shit. "Nice of you to come," she said. "His parents are in there with him now, but you can wait."

I sat in the little lobby, and after about half an hour two nice-looking people walked out of one of the rooms down the hall and out the front door of the building. The woman was looking straight ahead. Her eyes were wet and she was doing one of these trembling chin deals I've seen my mother do so many times over the years. *Too* many times. After they left, I waited a minute and then went to the room they'd come out of and peeked in. Ricky was lying on his bed, eyes closed. His color didn't look that great. He was hooked up to an IV. I sat down in the orange plastic chair next to his bed, quietly, and waited. After a few minutes he opened his eyes and saw me sitting there and sort of smiled. "How ya doin', kid?" I asked. "Feeling better?" He nodded, just a little. I could see he was scared or worried or something, but he looked glad to see me. Then I didn't know what to say. "I saw your parents leaving," I finally said. "They seem nice. You must be glad they came, huh?" He nodded again, and I saw a tear in the corner of his left eye. Just a little one. I still didn't know what to say.

After a while I said, "Well, Arnie was in a mood today. The barbers came to do haircuts and he wouldn't take his hard hat off. 'C'mon, Arnie,' Bob said, 'you have to take that silly thing off.' He tried to take it off his head and Arnie kinda yelled like he does—'*Oo-o-o-w*'—and knocked Bob's hand away. 'The hell with you then,' Bob said. 'Stay ugly. See if I care.'" Ricky smiled. So I told him more ward news: that Larry threw his spoon after breakfast and it hit Zach in the back of the head, and he should have seen Zach's face: he thought the sky was falling. And then Dino decided to toss his diaper and sheets out of his crib. Fortunately, the diaper wasn't full. "At least he didn't go for Gramps's bed." I said. "You know how Gramps gets when Dino goes after his sheet and pillow, right? Then, later, Gramps was in his chair by the tub room, with Timmy, and Doctor Winters came in. 'Morning, Gramps,' he said. 'How's the world looking today?' Well, Gramps gave Doc his famous cross-eyed pissed-off look and then gave Timmy a nod, as if to say, 'I guess I showed *him*, eh?' Then a little later Mrs. Hanson was bringing a tour of nursing students through and Gramps sees this cute little thing with a light-brown pixie haircut, wearing a pretty green sweater, and he looks right at her and of course up his nose goes that big ugly tongue. 'Ugh!' she goes. 'Omi*god!*' Then Gramps tongued those two ragged dolls he's always has with him." Ricky chuckled at that. I noticed he was slumped over to his right side so I stood and straightened him up the best I could.

"Hey," I said, "I have a joke. Ready?

Knock-knock
Who's there?
Utch
Utch who?
Gesundheit."

I asked him if he wanted to watch TV and he shook his head. I didn't know what more to say. I felt a little helpless, wished I knew what to do. "Listen, kid," I said after a bit, "you're gonna be okay. They're going to get you feeling better here. Then when you get back we're gonna watch some movies, you and me and the old man, and we'll maybe get some of the other guys, too. I have one called *Swiss Miss* you'll like. Stan and Ollie are mousetrap salesmen and there's this scene with them moving a piano on a suspension bridge in the mountains and then there's a gorilla ... oh, wait'll you see the end of it. As soon as you get back, it's the first one we'll watch. Promise. Okay?" He nodded, and his face brightened just a little.

I told him I'd come see him again tomorrow and maybe bring something to read to him. "Is that okay?" He nodded. "Listen, kiddo," I said. "Hang in there. I know this is tough. But they're gonna get you better here." He looked up at me. "Would you like some pudding? Maybe they'll let me bring you some, in one of those little plastic container dealies. Chocolate, okay?" He nodded again.

Before going home, I took a walk in the park I like, the one where I played hooky. They have a nice pond there. I saw this white goose all alone at one end of the pond, the north end, and remembered seeing him there once before, maybe a month or six weeks ago, alone then too. There was a nice old lady walking a dog, one of those little yippy things with beady eyes, and when she saw me looking at the goose she told me it lost its mate last spring when a fox burst out of the woods and croaked it, and it apparently doesn't have social skills with other geese and just hangs around all the time, always alone. *Damn!* Maybe that's okay now, in late summer, but what about when the weather turns cold? The dog's name was Alice. I didn't get the old lady's name.

At home now, sipping my peppermint tea, I'm wondering why dentists have a high suicide rate. That seems strange, if it's true. Is it that they hate poking into people's mouths all the time—bad breath, yellow teeth, scummy tongues, rotten gums and all? Are they depressed because people don't floss? Is it that they're causing pain all the time, so people hate coming to them? It's weird. I'm thinking if a person hates being a dentist and doesn't like going to work every day and doing what they do—drilling cavities and filling them and doing crowns and giving advice about good dental health, thinking about molars and bicuspids and incisors and what-all—if it's something that gets tedious and boring yet they do it day after day, week after week, year after year, and make a load of money and have a nice house and a boat and a country club membership and season tickets to football games and symphonies, but they hate doing what they do, hate coming to work every day so much they think about doing themselves in, that's sad. Or is it that people who tend to be depressed and maybe suicidal in the first place become, for whatever reason, dentists? Maybe that's it.

If there's something about *being* a dentist that depresses people and makes them want to be dead, then why the Christ don't they just stop being dentists and do something else—be a carpenter maybe, or a certified public accountant or a plumbing contractor? Or an advertising guy, like my asshole old man. Well, I guess if you go to dental school for however long that is, and you commit to being a dentist, and then you get set up and buy all that equipment, the chairs and drills and spit sinks and all, and hire a hygienist— preferably a chatty one to distract people, just as long as she doesn't lecture about flossing too much—and you start making money, and you get married and have kids, and buy a nice house and a luxury car with heated leather seats and take vacations to Cancun, and you have this status job and people call you Doctor Whatever, and the money keeps rolling in, and you have all these patients with bad teeth, cavities and needing crowns and hideous root canals, or just the ones who come in for their routine cleanings and a free toothbrush and a thingie of floss, and you're going to annual dental conferences and staying in nice hotels and hanging around the bar with all the other dentists and hoping to get lucky what with the little wifey far away, I imagine it's hard to make a change. You're sort of locked in.

But if you feel locked in and despise what you're doing, hate the tedium, and think about being dead—that's your way out—it must be a terrible way to be. My God, to go on like that for year after tedious year until finally you can put down your silly drills and retire, and then you have to try to find some way to fill your empty time until you fall apart and eventually tip over, golf or bingo or shuffleboard or whatever—that is, if you don't cash yourself in first. Damn!

I asked Stan why he thought Dawn wanted McCabe or the other guy to leave his wife and marry her. "Do you think she really loves him? Or does she mostly just want to be married to a guy who makes bucks and has 'doctor' in front of his last name?" But he didn't answer, just looked at me blankly and yawned. The topic bored him.

"You'll never contemplate suicide, will you, kid?" I asked him. No. My little orange man's happy with what he has and doesn't want more and isn't depressed by his lot in life. He'll last for as long as he can and all he wants and needs is what he has now: a simple, quiet, warm place to live; some food, and I don't think he cares if it's the same cat food crap day after day; a fairly clean litter box; and his little comforts, including my lap. He likes watching birds out the window, and tenses and twitches when he sees them, though I imagine the glass barrier frustrates him. Maybe he'd appreciate some companionship of his own kind, but that's about it. That's his little life, and then somewhere down the road that life will end. Stan won't accomplish anything in this world, unless he catches a mouse or two, and his life will be little noted nor long remembered by anyone but me.

Is there some kind of paradise for animals, like there supposedly is for people? Or when Stan gasps out his last little feline breath, is that it? End of story? Yes. I think so now. You can't say for sure, but I think so. I think now that's it for all of us—fur, feathers, fins, none of the above, whatever. I'm not going to give Stanley any false hope because I'm sure, pretty sure anyway, it's all just silly fairy tales. Sorry, kid. Our hearts beat and we draw breath for a while and we eat and sleep and do whatever it is we've arranged to do, day after day, whatever we can, for however long, and then at some point down the line, sooner or later, our used-up hearts stop pumping blood to our tired brains and we tip over and that's it. That's just it. Nothing more. End of story. No sins, no heaven or hell, no great reward or fearful punishment. No paradise. No hellfire. No Santa Claus checking his list to see who's naughty or nice. Sorry! That's it.

So, Dawn, you little no-eyebrowed schemer, if you want to marry McCabe or the other guy, go ahead. Screw his brains out, and throw in some obligatory panting and moaning. Tell him he's the most *incredible* lover you've *ever* had. Give that poor death-obsessed dentist some good memories and then guilt-trip the rich bastard into marrying you. There's no sin in any of it, manipulative as it may be. What the hell's the difference? Really. What does it matter? I hope the two of you have a long, happy life together. I hope you're lucky and neither of you nor any of your future kids get kicked in the head in a touch football game or plowed into by some careless truck driver reaching down to pick up his Lucky Strikes, or gets otherwise mucked. I wish you both success and great happiness in life, and may the earth move often for both of you under the sweet-smelling pines or in some cheap motel near the highway or wherever.

Let's just hope and pray that he doesn't get out of sorts and croak himself before his allotted term expires naturally.

Anyways.

What about me? I hope to be lucky and not have dirty tricks happen, not get mucked, at least too badly, and hope I can stay here in my little home, in my beige recliner, with my Stanley, for as long as we can last. But I don't know what to do in my life if I'm fortunate enough to *not* tip over for a good while yet. I know for sure I don't want to be a dentist or marry one, and I don't want to be a certified public accountant or a plumbing contractor. Maybe a carpenter, like Jesus, except that I'd be a miserable failure. I don't know what I want besides what I have.

Well, what I *want* is for Ricky to get out of that lonely damned hospital room and back to his own bed in B Ward, where Mary Lou and I can check on him and watch out for him a little and he can hear Linc sing "Old Man River." That's what.

BUDDY

BILLY TOLD ME he went to see Ricky in that hospital there and said he looked a little better but not all that great. He said he looked kinda pale and they had him hooked up to one of them IVs, which worried him. "I just hope they take good care of him so he can get his skinny little butt back here as soon as possible," he said.

That was yesterday, and then this afternoon, just after shift change, they *did* bring him back, on that usual cart they use, covered with a white blanket. I was in my chair near the front desk, just hanging around like I do, and that same guy that took him to the hospital, that bald black guy, rolled him in and him and Randi lifted Ricky from the cart into his bed. Randi cranked up the head of the bed so he was sitting up more. The black guy patted Ricky's shoulder and leaned down and looked at his face and said, "Take it easy, young man. Now you hang in there, okay?" That was nice.

They let Ricky rest, and after a little bit I wheeled myself over next to his bed, slow like I do. I just wanted to be next to him for a while, give him some company. It ain't like I had nowhere else to be, anyway. He did look a little better to me than before he went to Building One, but still not great. I noticed he was still pretty pale. When he saw me, he kinda smiled. I wish he would've given me a big grin, but whatever smile he could do, that's okay. I was glad to see him.

We stayed there like that until supper, which just got over. That little Randi had to work a double shift and she checked on Ricky now and again. She seemed to be in a pretty good mood and didn't look tired or nothing, so I guess her husband, Norm, didn't keep her up snoring and farting and all. Or maybe she'd made him sleep on the couch. Or maybe he'd got tired of her kicking him while he slept and left. Who knows?

Sometimes I think it'd be nice if them aides and nurses would tell me stuff about themselves, their lives outside work. That'd be interesting because I never get to know that stuff unless I happen to hear them talking. It'd be nice, for example, if Randi'd come over to me first thing after report each day and tell me what's up with her. "Well, Buddy," she might say, "last night me and Norm had this huge fight. I threw a pan at the asshole and it bounced off his damned head and he bled like a pig. Then we made up and screwed like bunnies." Stuff like that. I'd like that because it'd make me feel not so different from her and the rest of 'em—not just some pathetic feeb who lives here day after day and is just, I don't know, different from her and them other people who come here to work. I mean, yeah, I'm just me, drooling old Buddy with cerebral palsy, but we're all just people. Ain't we? They can do all these things I can't, and they leave here after work to go to their normal lives outside this place, but we're all just people. I'd like it if Randi and Mary Lou and Linc and the rest of 'em would tell me about stuff they do outside of here, and what they think about, even if it was just stupid everyday stuff, like, "I filled up my car with gas this morning, Bud, and bought a Three Musketeers bar and a large coffee with sugar and half-and-half at the gas station." I'd like that.

Even Billy. He talks to me and Ricky more than anyone else here, but hardly ever about personal stuff. He told us he got a cat and what he named it, but that's about it. I wonder why. I think he's shy in a way, but I don't know. I just wish I knew more about his life, and what he likes to do and stuff like that. I bet he has a girlfriend, since he seems to like looking at the women they got here. I do, too, far as that goes. Not that it does me no good.

I'm glad Ricky's back here and okay. I was worried he'd die over there and I'd never see him again. I been worried about that ever since he went there, however many days ago that was. I missed him. I did. Now I hope he just stays here and don't have to go to that damned hospital no more. Me and him, we can just hang around and watch TV or be in the solarium, and Billy'll read more stories to us and put on them funny movies—he says there's a lot more he has—and it'll be good. On the other hand, I don't want Ricky to have to stay in this damn place no longer than he has to. I want him to get better and go home and be normal and not have to live in a stupid crazy place like this with all these weirdos, me included. So I don't know. I don't think that's gonna happen, though. I hope I'm wrong.

Mary Lou's on tonight and she's been nice to Ricky. She's always nice enough but tonight she's particularly good, smiling and laughing and spending time with Ricky. She fed us together, him first, and took as much time as she could with him. She looks good! She's wearing this tight little purple top I seen before, that shows a lot of cleavage. I hope Ricky appreciates that as much as I do. When she got close to feed me, I could smell her hair—some nice shampoo she uses, probably that she learned about from them commercials during the soap operas. She also has this flowery-smelling perfume all the time. So, hell, if a person has to be fed by someone else, I'm glad it's her. I've noticed lately that Linc's been looking at Mary Lou close when she moves around the ward and jokes around and laughs like she does all the time. Hell, a person can't hardly blame him.

RICKY

IT'S GOOD TO BE back here, I guess. It's definitely better than that stupid hospital place. I still don't feel all that great, though. I feel like I could just stay in bed and sleep for maybe a year. Mary Lou's gonna feed me dinner pretty soon, and maybe after that I'll just go to sleep.

What's the matter with me, anyway?

It was good, in a weird way, to see the guys again. Buddy came over soon after I got back yesterday and just kinda parked himself next to my bed, and it was nice to see him. I missed him. Then, a little later, Davey scooted over on his back and squealed like he does, and I could hear Larry going "Wah-GOO" and Arnie going "O-o-w" and pounding his tray like he does. I liked hearing those guys, weird as they are. Mary Lou fed me and Buddy together, and then the two of us watched TV for a while. There was a baseball game on, Yankees and Red Sox, but I wasn't too interested. What's the point, really, of watching these guys do what they do—fielding grounders and zinging the ball to first, going for double plays, trying to guess what the pitcher's going to throw next, getting signs from the coaches and manager, trying to advance guys on the bases, laying down a good bunt, talking with the other guys on the bench, maybe stealing a base when you can? Sheesh! I can't relate to that much any more. I used to like ball on TV, but not now. I almost can't even relate so well any more to ordinary people who just walk around and brush their own teeth and put on their shoes and socks every day, or people who take a pack of gum from a pocket and unwrap a piece and stick it their mouth and crumble up the wrapper and toss it in a wastebasket and then chew their gum like it was the most ordinary thing in the world, you don't even think about it. That's what Mary Lou does a lot while she works, chews gum. Wrigley's Spearmint.

Then this morning I was glad to see Billy. I guess he didn't know I was back from that stupid hospital, because he looked startled at first when he saw me and then happy. He came right over to my bed before report and rubbed my head first and then my shoulder. "Damn!" he said. "You're a sight for sore eyes, kid. Welcome ho ... welcome back."

He almost said "home." It's weird that this place sort of *is* my home now. I don't think about going home as much as I did, because the longer I'm here the more unreal going home even seems. Oh, I still think about our house a lot, and my room with my posters on the walls, and about my family all the time, and Riley, but it just seems more like, I don't know, a dream that I'll ever go home again and for my life to be what it was. I always still pray that I'll get better and I do my routine prayers, my Hail Marys and Our Fathers, mainly, but ... I don't know. Maybe it's best just not to think about it too much. But how do you do that? Anyway, as weird as this place, B Ward, is, it's where I am now and in a bizarre way that's okay. I've grown so used to guys like Gramps and Timmy, and Davey moving along the floor like he does, and Dino's big laugh, and even Arnie pounding his tray and looking at his catalogs all day long and stuff. And Buddy. I can't believe how glad I was to see him when I got back. I almost felt like crying for a little bit. It's weird because Buddy and I've never said a word to each other, not one word, yet I feel like we're almost brothers or something. Or he's my uncle.

The best thing then was that during naptime Billy showed another Laurel and Hardy video. It was the one he'd told me about when he came to see me in the hospital, *Swiss Miss*. Like he'd said, the guys were mousetrap salesmen and came to a village in Switzerland because they figured that since they make a lot of cheese in that country there'd be more mice. My favorite part was when Stan and Ollie are working in this hotel because they couldn't pay for their dinner, and they're outside plucking chickens and this Saint Bernard is sitting there watching them. He's a mountain rescue dog and he's got this container of brandy strapped around his neck. Laurel wants the brandy but the dog won't let him have it, barking at him when he tries to get it or swatting his hand away with a big paw. Then Stan gets an idea. He takes the basket of white chicken feathers that he's plucked and tosses the feathers in the air so it looks like it's snowing and then he lies on the ground and lets the falling feathers cover him. "HELP!" he cries. "*Help!* I'm *free*zing!" Pretty soon the dog comes over and lies on top of Laurel to keep him warm, and, while he does that, Stan unstraps the brandy container and drinks it all. That was *so* funny. I laughed and so did Buddy, and Davey too. Billy'd set him up in his chair next to us, and Arnie also. I think Arnie kind of liked being there. He never laughed or smiled or anything, but he didn't have one of his fits either. That's something, I guess.

The other part I liked was when Stan and Ollie were moving a piano across a suspension bridge over this gorge. The piano gets stuck in the slats and they're trying to lift it out when this ape—Billy said it was a *gorilla*—comes out of a shack at the other end of the bridge, and the guys freak out and try to get away and the bridge starts swaying and spinning and the gorilla and the piano fall into the gorge. Then, at the end of the movie, Stan and Ollie are leaving the village and they see the ape, wrapped in bandages and on crutches. The guys run away and the gorilla winds up and chucks one of his crutches at them and it clunks them and knocks them both down. That cracked me up!

Even Linc came over and watched with us for a while, and he seemed to get a kick out of the movie. "Oh, yeah," he said. "*Them* guys." I don't think I've ever seen him watch anything except sports.

The only problem is that when I laugh sometimes I get out of breath and sometimes cough and it's hard to breathe for a few minutes. That's scary. When I was in that hospital, Consuela told me to try breathing through my nose instead of my mouth sometimes, to breathe in slowly. So I try that now, and maybe it helps. I'm not sure. I think it helps me get a fuller breath, at least sometimes. Still, that's hard. I still get scared when I can't take a deep breath. I wish I could stop thinking about that so much when it happens, because all it does is make me more anxious. But I can't help it.

Billy stuck around for a while after shift change. He just sat with me and Buddy and Davey next to my bed, kinda spacing out, while Mary Lou took care of Jimmy and Gilbert and those guys. Davey fell asleep in his chair after a bit, with his head slumped over to one side and his mouth open, so Billy carried him back to his bed. I was feeling tired too. I can't believe how tired I get any more. I have about as much energy as one of those hundred-year-old people that Willard talks about on the *Today* show. At least tonight I'll probably sleep okay. I hope I can.

BILLY

I GUESS I HAVE the resolve of a turnip. I wasn't going to visit Christy for a good while after seeing her and that greasy asshole at the mall, but here I am. I didn't think about coming here until I woke up this morning to get ready for work, but while I was combing my hair, staring at my pasty reflection in the mirror, that sweet little pockmarked face came into my mind. Jesus! Driving to Junior's, I was afraid maybe she wouldn't be there, that it's her day off or she'd be sick again or some damn thing, but no. She's here, same Christy as ever. "Oh, *hi!*" she said when she saw me, my bony butt parked on my usual red-plastic-covered corner stool. "I haven't seen *you* for a while. How *are* ya?" I don't even remember what I said back—probably "Good" or something equally brilliant—but she just looked at me and sort of chuckled and after a moment asked, "Coffee, hon?" I nodded. *Hon!*

The weird thing is that after a few minutes it occurred to me that one of the good things about being at Junior's isn't just Christy, lovely as that always is, but also sitting at the counter with the regulars, shlurping my coffee and eating my bacon and eggs just like them. I like that. I noticed there was another guy about four seats down doing what I do—soaking up his egg yolks with his buttered toast. Three guys wearing greasy sweatshirts and black Taylor Construction baseball caps, guys about my age or maybe a little older, were talking sports. Disgustingly, one of them was chowing down corned beef hash. I *hate* corned beef hash—the smell of it, the look of it, the idea of it. "All these jig hot dogs do any more is slam dunk, for Chrissakes," that guy said. "No one has a goddamned midrange jump shot any more. It's like a lost freakin' art." I don't know what he meant by that, but it sounded authoritative. Then Junior came out of the kitchen, tattooed biceps bulging, and asked the three guys how their breakfasts were. Two of them nodded and mumbled something, I couldn't hear what, and the third guy, the corned beef hash guy, said, "Hey, man, every day's a holiday and every meal's a feast."

Junior furrowed his brow and pursed his lips. "*Out*standing," he said after a moment, nodding his big head. "An admirable perspective."

My other problem with the guy who said about every meal being a feast is that he keeps looking at my baby as she moves around the restaurant, bringing people their food and refilling their coffee and taking their money. I believe he's staring at her rear end. I guess if I were any kind of a man I'd stand up and tell him to mind his own business and show some manners and keep his damned eyes to himself and then, if he gave me any lip, challenge him to step outside where we'd settle it like real men. That's if I were any kind of a man. That's probably what Robert Jordan would do. Or John Wayne. Of course, I, too, stare at Christy's lovely behind—that sweet little thing swishing around. My oh my.

Anyways.

I'm glad Ricky's back from that damned hospital. I was happy to see him yesterday. For some reason, after I saw him in that place I had the feeling he wouldn't get back to the ward so quick. I was worried, and still am. I guess I'll keep worrying. I was all set to visit him again in the hospital yesterday, before I knew he was back, and maybe get to see that little Consuela with her cute nose, too.

I'm glad, too, that Ricky got such a kick out of *Swiss Miss* yesterday, particularly the part where Stan takes the dog's brandy and gets drunk. Stan's one of those happy drunks. Whenever he gets drunk, like he did in that part, he's silly and funny and laughs a lot. The best was in *Blotto*, when he stole his wife's bottle of booze and he and Ollie got plastered in a bar somewhere and had an immense laughing jag. Happy drunks they were, at least until Laurel's wife shows up with a shotgun. But I can't laugh too much at that. I've seen drunks that weren't so happy. My mother, for one. I don't recall her ever laughing and carrying on like Stan Laurel when she'd had a snootful. Oh no. She's more of a sloppy, self-pitying, whining drunk. More of a vomiting and passing out type of drunk. I don't want to think about it. I hope she's okay.

I don't know what I want to think about. Right now, here in this greasy spoon, eating my two eggs over easy and my not-too-crisp bacon and buttered toast with strawberry jelly, sipping my black coffee, I'm happy enough to just be here with the morning guys and little Christy. I don't need to think about much. One thing I'm thinking is how I don't like seeing the yellow and the reddish colors mixed together from where I dip my buttered and strawberry-jellied toast into the egg yolks. They mix together in an unpleasant, maybe even disgusting, manner.

I'm thinking too, for some weird reason, about Dino—his strange life. He's locked inside that bizarre body—oversized hydrocephalic head, huge shoulders and arms and chest, paralyzed below the middle of his back because of his spina bifida—blind and profoundly disabled. The boundaries of his little world are the smells and sounds of the ward, especially his favorite body function noises, and being handled and moved around by aides and nurses. He spends his tedious waking hours lying in his crib or cart and now and again someone like me comes along and sticks spoonsful of food to his lips or changes his diaper or runs a wet washcloth over his face and body or lifts him and carries him somewhere, like to the tub room, which isn't easy because he's so damned top-heavy—quite unbalanced. It's hard to change his sheets with him on the mattress; you have to move him to one side, spread out the sheet and tuck it in while you're holding him up with one hand, and then move him to the made side and then do the other.

I try to remember to say something to him when I feed him or whatever—"Hey, Dino, what's going on, man?"—thinking that it'd be nice for the poor guy to know who the hell's dealing with him now, but I notice that not everyone does that. Most of the nurses just stick a spoonful of applesauce with a pill into his mouth and then walk away without talking to him, or turn him over and give him a suppository and then walk away.

So here's this bizarre guy eking out his useless days in B Ward, having an okay time of it probably, what with enjoying the sneezes and nose-blowings and Larry's wah-gooing and all, and now and again asserting himself by stripping his bed or Gramps's, but he doesn't exactly have a lot of say-so about living his life, and you wonder what's going on inside that oversized cranium. Hard to say.

What's weird about changing Dino's diaper is that he often has bright green poop due to some med they have the poor guy on.

I wonder if Dino gets headaches because his head is so huge, with all that built-up fluid. Sometimes he gets quiet for a while, and maybe that's why. Or maybe he's in some other kind of pain. But how would anyone know?

What a life!

BUDDY

THAT FATHER CALLAHAN gets on my nerves sometimes, mostly when he talks about stuff that I don't know what the hell he means. "Your faith must be strong enough to help you bear this cross." What cross? I ain't even sure who he was talking to. He looked at me for a second, but then he looked at Ricky and then at Davey and then Jimmy. Jimmy sure as hell don't know what that means. All he does day after day is chews on his sock -covered hands, gums them really, and I don't think he knows the difference between being at a church service like this or being stranded on a desert island, like that crazy Ben Gunn. He's in a world of his own. I don't even know why they bring him or some of these other guys, like Zach or Gilbert, to church. It ain't like they get nothing out of it. I guess they figure it'd be good for Father Callahan to mumble some nice words over them, a blessing or whatever like he does. I suppose that's okay.

Of course, Father don't mumble. He's got this loud, deep voice that booms across the damned room and sometimes it gives me a headache. I like Miss Dee Dee's soft little voice better, but I suppose he's okay. Actually, I got a headache now. I woke up with it and it won't go away. When Billy's on he can tell sometimes that I have a headache, I guess from the way I look. I must look sick some way or another. More than once he's looked at me when he starts his shift or whenever and said, "Feeling poorly, Bud?" Then he goes over his list. *"Stomachache?... Headache?"* I shake my head till he gets to the problem and then nod. That works okay. Then he gets one of them nurses to give me a couple of them aspirins. Anyway, Father Callahan's going on and on today's made my headache worse and I guess I'll just have to live with it since Billy ain't on.

I wonder if he means the cross of being a feeb. That's the cross us guys have in common, I guess. I don't know what faith means exactly, at least the way he says it, or how that helps a guy bear his cross. I have faith most of the time that I'll go to heaven after I kick the bucket, but mostly I feel that way because I figure that'll be my just reward after this lifetime of crap. Also, I figure I should go to heaven 'cause I ain't sinned much. The

113

reason I never sinned much is I didn't have the chance, not because I wouldn't've did it if I could've, but still. I don't know if that's the kind of faith Father Callahan means.

He always now and again says stuff like what he said about faith and your cross, and it's confusing sometimes. I remember one time he said, "The kingdom of God is within." Now what the hell does *that* mean? I understand the kingdom of God, I guess—it's probably like the kingdom of England, only bigger—but what does he mean it's "within"? Within what? If that stuff is confusing to me, it must be total nonsense to a guy like Arnie. Or Larry. Course, they don't bring Larry to these church services because he'd disrupt things what with going "Wah-GOO" all the time like he does and playing with himself constantly. His manners are horrible in general, and sure as hell not fit for *church*—even if church is just the multi-purpose room. I don't know if Davey understands too much stuff either. He has cerebral palsy like me, but I don't know if he's retarded or not. I don't think he is, but I don't know. Our bodies are so screwed up you can't tell. I wish I could say, "Excuse me, Father Callahan. Could you explain what you just said means?"

I'm sure Ricky understands most of it. I imagine he went to church before his accident, being from a good family and all, so he probably heard a lot of this before and knows that stuff about faith and the kingdom of God and all like that. Maybe I'm wrong. At least he seemed to be listening to Father Callahan most of the time, and I noticed he brightened up a little bit when the old man did that prayer he always does at the end, the one about our father who art in heaven. He must like that one. Me too. I like the way it sounds. I like the part that goes, "Give us this day our daily bread."

We don't get bread every day here, but I wish we did. I like bread and butter a lot, and when I lived on the farm with my brother my favorite thing was when there was gravy with the meat and I'd sop up that gravy with a piece of bread and eat it. Even after I couldn't feed myself no more, my brother remembered I liked that and did it for me. I really miss that. I guess we don't get daily bread because some of the guys probably have a hard time chewing bread enough. You can't just swallow bread without chewing it at least a little bit, on account of you'd probably choke or something.

One funny thing about that prayer's the part about "forgive us our trespasses as we forgive them that trespass against us." Amanda always used to go on and on about trespassers on our property, so I knew that word, and she wanted my brother to put up a sign that said to people not to trespass, but he didn't want to because he thought it wasn't friendly. I don't remember who won that one. The thing she hated most was deer hunters who trespassed. I remember that. She liked them deer, I guess, and didn't want no one shooting them on the farm. So when I first heard that prayer I remember thinking I'm okay on this one, since I never trespassed anywhere in my entire stupid useless life. I never had the damn chance. So nothing to forgive. And I think even though Amanda didn't like trespassers, I'm pretty sure she woulda forgiven any guys who trespassed against her because basically she has a kind heart. Some stuff irritates her, like if someone comes into the house with muddy shoes, but that ain't much.

I'm surprised they let Gramps come to the church service anymore after that time he farted and then laughed about it. But I guess Father Callahan forgave him, like a good Christian, and said it was okay for him to come. He didn't fart or nothing this time, but he did kiss his babies a little when the thing started and Father Callahan said, like he always does, "God's merciful blessing on each and every one today." But after a little bit both Gramps and Timmy fell asleep in their chairs and stayed asleep during the whole damned service. They kept holding hands while they slept.

I wonder if Father don't like it when guys fall asleep in church. Hard to tell. He's a nice enough old man, I guess, but he now and again gives out these pissed-off looks if someone makes a noise while he's talking or even if one of his silly cards with them drawings falls off the wall, or stuff like that. He ain't the most patient guy in the world. Now that I think of it, he don't even smile that much either—at least not a real sort of smile. He always does this kind of a fake smile whenever he mentions Jesus. Like a few minutes ago he said, "Jesus died on the cross because he so loved mankind," and then, like always, looked at me and Davey and some of the other guys, one at a time, and his blue eyes kind of shined and he did this little smile, very warm and all gentle and loving. I guess he really likes Jesus, and wants us to like him too. Or, for some reason, we're supposed to smile also at the thought of Jesus dying for us on that cross there. That don't sound to me like a very good way to die. I remember hearing they nailed his hands to the thing. That's gotta hurt! *Ouch!* Plus, the way Father said it made me think Jesus *chose* to be on that cross for mankind. I always figured someone stuck him there, not that it was his idea in the first place. But maybe I'm wrong. I never quite got all the details of that whole deal.

I wonder if Father Callahan'd laugh if he sat in the ward with me and Ricky and the guys and watched *Swiss Miss* or one of them shows. You wonder if he'd loosen up and laugh at dumb stuff like Laurel and Hardy on a bridge with a monkey, just sitting around with us guys, or if he only gets excited about Jesus and the kingdom of God and stuff like that. I wonder if he'd be amused sitting quiet in the solarium watching them little birds flying around pestering the bigger ones, the hawks and like that, the way they do. Them birds are part of God's kingdom, ain't they? They sure seem to have their little spats though.

RICKY

I'M NOT GOING to get better. Maybe sometime I'll leave this place and go home, but I'm never going to get better. I'm never going to walk again or talk and I'll never dress myself or feed myself or go back to school. I know that now. I feel it. I had a bad accident and I'm not going to get better from it. That's just the way it is. I hate it—*hate* it!—but that's just the way it is.

I'll never get to do stuff I want to do, things that other people do, ordinary things that people do. I'll never finish middle school or go to high school and I'll never play sports like I've always done, and never just get to hang out with my friends and be a normal kid. I'll never go out with girls and fool around with them the way guys talk about. Bummer! I'll never go to college and go to football games on Saturdays and live in a dorm. I'll never get married and have kids of my own and a job and a house and a nice car and all that stuff, like other people. I'll never even get to hold a cheeseburger in my hands and eat it myself. *Jeez!*

I don't know what I wanted to do for a job when I grew up. Of course, my dream was to play baseball in the bigs, second base or shortstop, but I always knew the chances weren't great—nice to fantasize about, but not likely to happen. Maybe a research scientist or a science teacher. Fishing guide, maybe. I don't know. I never went fishing much, though I liked going the few times I did, but the idea of being a fishing guide always appealed to me—sitting in a boat and casting and reeling the fish in and all like that, and giving people advice about how to catch more fish, or bigger fish, and wearing one of those hats with lures and stuff stuck to it. I guess I'd have to learn about the different kinds of fish and lures and bait and stuff first. I imagine it's complicated. Now it doesn't matter. It's not going to happen. I know that now. I'm not going to have any kind of normal life, however long I live.

I don't know how long that'll be. Sometimes I feel like I don't want to go on like this, helpless like I am and other people having to take care of me. But other times I want to keep going as long as possible, no matter what I'm like. If I die, whenever that is, I'm pretty sure I'll go to heaven. Death'll happen eventually, to me and everyone else, but I'd just as soon it was later instead of earlier. Most of the time I feel that way. Sometimes when I can't breathe so well and can't get a full breath and can't let anyone know I need help, and no one notices I'm in trouble, I feel desperate and so scared that I'm not all that sure I want to go on.

And I just don't like the idea of people having to take care of me for the rest of my life. I don't like having to be taken care of and I don't want people to have to spend their time doing it. Like my family. If I get to leave and go home, my parents and sisters are going to have to take care of me like Billy and Mary Lou and those guys here do. That's their job, though. But my family, that's something else. I'm sure they'd be okay with taking care of me and wouldn't mind it because they love me and all, but still. It's not what I want. I desperately want to go home to my family, to my own house, to Riley, but I don't want them to have to take care of me and feed me and help me go to the bathroom and clean me up and dress me and undress me and stuff like that for the rest of my life. That's no way to live.

At least I'm alive now. That's good, I guess. I'm glad I'm alive now. I mean, I could have been killed in my accident or killed some other way by now, like some kids have been, in accidents or school shootings and stuff like that. Just the other day there was a thing on the TV news about some kid who was killed on a farm when a tractor he was on fell over somehow. And kids get killed all the time in wars and earthquakes and stuff, or from cancer. You see these starving kids in Africa with flies crawling on their faces. Things like that. Maybe I'll live a long time yet, even if I don't get better. I guess there's something to be said for just being alive. On the other hand, is this any way to live, the way I am now? I don't know. I really don't.

My body's just screwed up. That's the truth about my life. But is my body all there is to me? Is it the *main* thing about me? I don't know. If my body's as broken as it is, and is almost surely gonna stay broken, does that mean *I'm* broken? I wonder about that sometimes. I mean, I think there's more to who I am than just my broken body—my spirit or soul or whatever—but I'm not sure. They always say in church that when you die and you're done with your body, your soul keeps going for eternity. Father Callahan said the same thing. I don't remember exactly what he said, but something like that.

I wish he'd talked about heaven and purgatory and limbo, or whatever. I remember hearing about all that stuff at our church, but I can't remember all the details. I remember that where you go depends on whether you're okay with God for all your sins, if you've done penance. I think that's what they said. One of the places is for babies who died before they were baptized. Or maybe that's what people used to think. I wish I could remember the rules, so I'd know where I stand just in case. I wish I'd paid more attention when they talked about that stuff. If you go to limbo, or maybe it's purgatory, you stay there for a while before you get to go to heaven. Your soul does. Something like that. I don't know for how long—maybe a couple weeks. But I can't remember if there's anything I'm supposed to be doing to get to go right to heaven. I don't know if I have to actually confess or whatever. And how do I do that? Does it have to be to a priest? Or can I just silently say that contrition thing? I was baptized and had my First Communion, so I guess I'm okay there, but what about my sins? Is it just those mortal sins you have to worry about so you can go to heaven, or any kind of smaller sin, a venial one—like cheating on a math test at school?

I can't pay that much attention to everything Father Callahan says, anyway. I'm sure he says important stuff, but in a way he's kind of boring. After a while I just hear him talking, that deep voice, but I don't hear his words. Plus, it's so tiring for me anymore to sit up in my chair for a long time, like during the church service. My back always hurts and my neck hurts, even with that sheepskin thing behind my back, and sometimes I get a headache. Sometimes a bad one. Even Gramps and Timmy fell asleep, the whole thing was so boring. And those fluorescent lights in that room are so bright and they make this little buzzing sound sometimes. Father Callahan has the shiniest bald head of anyone I've ever known, including my Uncle Walt, and it's funny how those white lights reflect off it. I wonder if his head's like that naturally or if he scrubs it and polishes it somehow every day to make it that shiny. Maybe he rubs some kind of polishing stuff into his head each morning, wax or something, to make it shine like it does.

The one thing he told about that I liked was the story about how Peter and his brother, Andrew, were fishermen and they were casting their nets and Jesus came along and told them to be fishers of men, I guess instead of fish. What does that mean? He showed these drawings of Andrew and Peter, wearing this green and yellow hat, and Jesus with his arms stretched out, and it showed the sea and the fishing nets and stuff. I like fishing.

One thing that was interesting was that Father said that Peter's name was Simon originally, but he changed it. He didn't say why. I'm sure someone talked about that in church or Bible school, but I can't remember. Maybe he just didn't like Simon. It *is* kind of a dorky name. I remember my Uncle Hank and Aunt Noreen had a dog named Simon when I was little, a sort of yellow-colored mutt with a short, pointy tail. My cousin Bruce called him Simple Simon because he was so dumb. He used to fall asleep on their couch and then he'd stretch out in his sleep and lose his balance and fall onto the floor. Poor guy.

I don't feel mad at God any more for what happened to me. It's not His fault. It's just something that happened, I think now. I don't think any more that God was mad at me for anything I did and that's why I had my accident. It didn't have anything to do with my sins. At least I don't think it did. Maybe it did, but I don't think so. At least most of the time I don't. Even so, I think I should do confession, somehow, so my soul will go to heaven.

They say that everything happens for a reason but we can't always know those reasons. God has His reasons for stuff that happens, but we don't get to know those. I don't know why not, that's just the way it is. It's like some big mystery. *Mystery*, that's a word they used in church now and again but I was never sure just what they meant when they said it. I don't think they meant like a crime novel. "The mystery of faith," I remember that. I remember there're different types of mysteries they talked about, the sorrowful ones and the glorious ones and the joyful ones and so on, and you're supposed to say different ones as part of the Rosary prayers on different days of the week and on particular holy days. And then each of them has these events that are part of them, like the crucifixion's one of the sorrowful mysteries. That makes sense. The joyful ones are my favorite, I guess.

I vaguely recall someone at our church one Sunday saying that God lets bad stuff happen, even though He doesn't *make* them happen, to keep us humble. If that's true, it worked for me. I'm definitely humble. I don't know if I *could* be more humble. So sometimes I don't want to think about that any more, about why stuff happens. What's the point of thinking about stuff that you can't know about? It doesn't change my ... situation. All I need to do, I guess, is keep saying my prayers and hope for the best—whatever that is.

I'm thinking now that if I pray for anything, I should pray to God to give me the strength or courage or whatever to deal with all this stuff that's happened to me. I don't think it's any use to pray to get better. Plus, there's other stuff to think about. *Breathing*, for one thing. I keep thinking about what Consuela told me, to breathe slowly through my nose and let it out slowly through my mouth. That's a good technique, but I can't just *do* it all the time, I have to *think* about doing it so I can do it the right way. That's what I was doing for a little while there in that church service, inhaling through my nose for a slow five-count and then exhaling through my mouth for the same. I like that.

Arnie was funny during the church service. He sat there the whole time wearing his hard hat, with his whiskers—Billy calls it a "five-o-clock shadow"—and had one of his pissed-off looks, like he was getting ready to pound his tray with his fist like he does. But then every once in a while he rubbed his hands together and hunched over and giggled like a silly little girl for maybe thirty seconds. Then just as quickly, he came out of that and looked all serious and pissed-off again. He went through three or four of those cycles. You wonder what's going on inside his head, why he giggles like that.

I'm glad Mary Lou put me to bed right away when we got back. I was *really* tired. Now that it's getting cooler out, with fall coming, my parents brought over my nice orange comforter for my bed. I like that. It's warm and soft. It's weird that just sitting up in my chair for too long now makes me so tired, but it does. And my back hurts so much too. I like sitting up, usually, because I can breathe better but, man, it takes a lot out of me. *Sheesh!* I used to be able to play ball all day long with my friends, from morning to night in the summer, and now I don't even have the energy to sit in a stupid chair for more than just a little while. Well, that's over now. Done with. I'll never get to play second base again or stand in the batter's box and wait for a good pitch to get wood on—aluminum on—or just sit on the bench with the guys and joke around when we're up to bat, talking about dumb stuff like we always do. Always did. Now I just need to rest and breathe and try to get through one day and then the next day.

That's my dumb life now, I guess. My life is different now than it was, and I'm not going to get better. Okay. I just need to deal with it the best I can.

Mary Lou's nice to me. She's kind of quiet again today, not chattering and joking around as much as she usually does. Yesterday I heard her tell

Rita that her boyfriend, Duane, bought a new motorcycle, a Harley, but didn't talk to her about it first. "I mean, we're not married or anything yet," she said, "but I think he should at least *consult* me before he spends a lot of money like that." Rita agreed but told Mary Lou not to "rag" Duane about it. "Wait'll you get that ring on your finger before you start givin' him shit about money," she said. "Otherwise he's gonna think you're a nag." Rita's married and has a bunch of kids, three or four, so she must know what she's talking about. She's always talking about how tired she is from carting her kids around and cleaning her house and cooking and stuff. "God!" she always says, "I feel like I could sleep for a *week*."

Sometimes I think it'd be nice if Billy and Mary Lou would get married and sort of adopt me and Buddy and maybe Davey, too, and we could all live together in a big house somewhere. They'd take good care of me, like they do now, and we could spend time sitting in the living room, me propped on the couch on some big pillows, covered with my orange comforter, my head elevated, watching TV, and Billy'd read to us and stuff like that. We'd watch every Laurel and Hardy movie and then watch them again, and then other funny stuff too. I don't know what that'd be, but anything to make us laugh a little would be good. Maybe the Three Stooges, stuff like that. I don't know. Stan and Ollie are the best, but I'm sure there're other old-time funny movies too. Billy says he has one he's gonna bring in where Laurel and Hardy join the Foreign Legion so Ollie can forget some woman he's in love with. I'm sure I'll like that, and Buddy will too. That's a nice fantasy, but I wouldn't want to have my own bedroom in a house. I'm too scared any more to sleep alone because of my breathing problem and sleeping troubles at night. If I could sleep through the night and if someone would come along and move me to another position now and again when *I* want that, it might be okay. But that's not the way it is.

BILLY

STAN MUST HAVE a little cold or something. He was sneezing this morning before I left for work, poor guy. He closes his eyes when he sneezes and then afterwards looks kinda startled, like, "Hey, what was *that?*" I love to wake up each morning and there he is at the end of my bed, near my feet, curled up asleep. That's a nice thing. Once or twice a week he gets a notion to gnaw on my feet under my blanket, and the furry dude has sharp goddamn little teeth. Usually he wakes me up when he goes for my feet, but I don't mind much. After years of being jarred awake by my parents' early-morning screaming matches—"Fuck *you*, bitch!" ... "No, fuck YOU, you goddamn *bas*tard!"—being gnawed awake by a little orange cat's no problem at all. It's funny, but when I think back to those times— their morning top-volume arguments, the cursing and name-calling—my heart starts beating faster and my face starts feeling flushed and mouth dry just like the way I felt when those things happened. Even when I'm safe and snug under the covers in my own bed in my own little apartment—my door securely locked, my wacko parents miles away—I still feel that way when I think back to those times. The bad feeling doesn't last as long, of course, and doesn't at all zonk me out for most of the day like it used to, but still.

The worst, I remember, is when I'd be in the middle of a dream and they'd start up with their antics and I'd just be *startled* awake, and for a moment you're not sure where you are or what's going on—is this part of the *dream?*—and then that moment passes and you know all too well it's not a dream. It's a real-life nightmare.

I hate leaving Stan alone when I have to go to work. I don't know if cats mind being alone all day, but I have to think he'd rather have a companion, one of his own kind, than not. Orangutans, I read, are pretty solitary most of their lives, but I never heard that cats are the same. After all, don't cats hang around with each other in the wild, like lions in prides, and tigers and cheetahs and all? I wonder who came up with the word *pride* for a bunch of lions anyway. I guess it's better than saying a *shame* of lions.

Anyways.

I wonder more lately how my mother is, how she's doing. I should call her or something. Even with all the bullshit, I owe her that. The old man, the hell with him. I could care less. But I worry about her. I worry how she's doing, how she's feeling. Even with all the crap over the years, I worry. There were good times, though, at least when I was younger, before the booze and the uppers and downers. I remember when I was seven or eight and we went to a lake somewhere with a nice sandy beach. There was a big blue blanket that we spread on the sand, and my mother, in a bright-red one-piece bathing suit, lay on it most of the afternoon, reading one of those romance novels she likes, except for now and again when she went into the water just to cool off, staying maybe two minutes and then coming back to the blue blanket. I remember what a chickenshit she was about going in the water each time, feeling the temperature with her toes, her arms crossed and shoulders hunched, and then going in just a little way, the water to her knees, and then a little way more, then more, until finally she was in waist-deep, and then she'd slowly lower herself in up to her neck and then swim around a little bit, kind of a half-assed dog paddle, and then come out. It's funny, I can't recall if the old man was with us that day. Maybe he was. He generally didn't like being in the sun, though, except for on the golf course. I remember that about the gaping asshole.

It's weird about the beach. People love going there and hanging around on the sand, but when you watch a movie like *Beau Geste* or some other Foreign Legion movie and you see these poor bastards with their tongues hanging out, tramping around in the desert with heavy uniforms and big boots and those white flat-top hats with the little cloth hanging down the back to cover their necks, wearing black backpacks and carrying those long rifles, trudging up and down one tedious sand dune after another, the sun beating down, guys seeing mirages of oases and hallucinating dark-eyed veiled belly dancers, getting attacked by bearded Arabs on camels, then the sand isn't so appealing somehow. That's why I like *Flying Deuces*, the one I brought in to show Ricky and Buddy later today, or tomorrow: it doesn't take the Foreign Legion too seriously.

Maybe I should've joined the Legion right after high school instead of doing what I'm doing. It would've been a perfect place to forget all the bullshit of my life at home with my nutso parents. That's supposedly why guys joined the Foreign Legion—to forget stuff: women who ditched them, their lives of crime and mayhem, other various failures and disappointments and dashed hopes and tragedies.

I'd write my mother:

Dear Mom,

> *Hope you're well and off the sauce. I'm here in Timbuktu with a bunch of murderers, rapists, and embezzlers. A lot of the guys have been unlucky in love. We get up early each day and drill for hours in the broiling sun. Our sergeant's a psychopathic sadist, but I'm sure he has his good points. The food's horrible—mostly overripe goat and camel meat. Send some chocolate chip cookies when you can. Well, gotta go. We're expecting an attack from the towel-heads any moment. Tell Dad he can kiss my loser's ass.*

Love,

Billy

Then again, I don't think I'd like it much—particularly having to live in a smelly barracks with a bunch of guys who probably don't shower or brush their teeth too regularly, even if what we had in common was that we were all dregs and outcasts. It's better to live by myself in my snug little apartment with my books and my cat, my recliner and hot mint tea. I guess I'm no *Beau Geste* hero, for sure, and never will be. No Robert Jordan.

Poor Robert, alone there at the end, his heart beating against the pine needles for just a few more minutes. And then Frederick Henry walking back to his hotel alone in the rain from the hospital where Catherine Barkley'd just died from childbirth. Dirty tricks. Mucked. Well, maybe everyone's alone at the end. Even when some poor guy is at the end of a long and solid life, dying comfortably and pain-free in bed, morphine dripping into his veins, his wife and kids and grandchildren and whoever else gathered around him, all misty-eyed and holding his hands and telling him they love him, he's still alone.

Still, I suppose a death like that's better than expiring all by yourself. I could have a heart attack in my apartment and tip over and it'd be days, maybe weeks, before anyone knew. Eventually someone'd smell my rotting corpse and call the cops. I'd like to think my mother'd be sad to hear the news of my demise. I'm sure Boyd would come to my little funeral and maybe say a good word. It wouldn't be much of an affair, though. Maybe Mary Lou and Randi would come, maybe Linc. Destini, possibly. I don't know. I don't imagine many would be there. I hope Mrs. Hanson doesn't come. Of course, it would be lovely if Christy were there, weeping uncontrollably, tears streaming down that sweet pockmarked little face. "Oh, GOD!" she'd wail. "He was the love of my *life*, and a great *tipper* too!"

If I do croak, I'd like it if they'd let Buddy come to my funeral. That'd make me happy, and I imagine he'd appreciate being included. But not Ricky. I don't want him to have to go through anything like that. He's got more than enough crap to deal with.

Ricky. When I came in this morning, he looked paler than when I left yesterday. Plus, he didn't seem to have much energy. When I asked him if he wanted to get out of bed and into his chair, he just glanced up at me and didn't nod or shake his head, just sort of looked at me with half-closed eyes. Maybe he was just tired. I asked him again and he shook his head, so I fed him in bed. I got Buddy up in his chair and wheeled him over near Ricky's bed and fed him first and then Ricky. After breakfast, I asked Ricky again if he wanted to get up and this time he nodded, just a little—just a faint little nod. Not much energy. I wheeled both of them out to the solarium, and put Ricky's sunglasses on. Bright as a bitch out there.

I'm gonna read *Of Mice and Men* to the guys. It's pretty short. I think they'll like it, George and poor Lennie and the rabbits and all. I'd like to read *Huck Finn*, because it's so amazing, but I can't figure out how to do that without saying "nigger" all the time. I don't want to say that to Ricky. It's in *Of Mice and Men* too, but just here and there, like when someone's talking about Crooks or even when he's talking about himself. But they use "negro" too, and I could just say that. I guess that's okay."

Now, sitting here in the break room with Rita and Randi and some others of the usual malcontents, I'm thinking that maybe I shouldn't have come here and just let him sitting there. Maybe I should have checked with him to see if he didn't want to go back to bed before lunch. I notice sometimes now he seems to have trouble sitting up for long, sort of slumps over to one side after a while. He always did that, but more now. When Bernie's on I try to remember to check in with him before he leaves, to ask him how Ricky did during the night. But today I forgot. I was paying more attention to Randi's sweet butt than to the kid's welfare, jerk that I am.

126

Well, break's not that long. It *seems* long sometimes, listening to these wailing women, but it's only fifteen minutes. Today one of the aides from D Ward's been griping about Mrs. Hanson, how she didn't follow some rule or routine or whatever when someone'd called in sick yesterday for a p.m. on D Ward and she had to get someone to stay over till eight. Oh, the *unfairness* of it all. Then another one, I don't know her name, went on for a little while about how her ex was supposed to pick up the kids at noon last Saturday but didn't get there until almost 1:30 and lied to her about having car trouble, and how she can always tell when he's lying—his lower lip sags—and she was pissed because she had to miss her nail appointment. Blah, blah. I don't know. I'm thinking that I'm not going to keep coming on these damn breaks. I don't *need* to go on them, usually, but do so my co-workers won't think I'm antisocial. I rarely say a word on a break or lunch, just sit there and listen to the prattle. In a way, I *am* antisocial—not on purpose, that's just who I am. So why be a hypocrite? On the other hand, sometimes I sort of like to hear everyone's sad stories—those female voices going on and on with their various grievances. Sometimes.

Still, I'm feeling I should spend as much time with my kids as I can. I feel I need to do that now.

BUDDY

THIS IS BULLTWINKIE! Yesterday that Rita was helping me pee, holding my thing steady in that damned stainless steel urinal, and just then I had a bad gas pain and couldn't hold still and started squirming, and my leg kinda kicked up and knocked the urinal out of her hand, and it spilled all over my lap and down my pants. Then I had to pass gas, couldn't help myself, and it stunk like hell. At least Rita didn't get mad. She didn't say nothin', just pulled my pants off and threw them in the laundry bag and washed me off and put fresh pants on me. Christ, it was embarrassing. But that's my damned life. Crap like that all the time. It's all bulltwinkie

I'm sick of it.

Then last evening I saw Linc and Mary Lou together in the solarium, joking around, her smiling like she does—all them straight white teeth— and laughing and looking so good in a pair of tight blue jeans, her long hair all shiny, and Linc was smiling too. Then he reached over and rubbed the top of her head and she sort of brushed his hand away and then bumped her hip into his, hard, causing him to stumble sideways a little. They kept on talking and laughing and standing close together for a while. I don't know. I'm glad they like each other and have fun, I guess, but it made me feel a little lonely.

And a little while after that old Gramps had some kind of problem. He was lying in his crib crying like he does now and again, pissing and moaning, and Mary Lou had to get a nurse to look at him. I didn't know then what his problem was, but then later at report they said he was "a little impacted" and they had to "clean out the old fella's drainpipe." Someone asked when was the last time Gramps "came through" and they had to look at his chart to find out.

It must be nice to just get up every day and dress yourself and go to the bathroom and lock the door behind you and relieve yourself and zip up, and then wash your hands with hot water and dry them on a nice fluffy towel, or even just some paper toweling, and go on your way and not give it another thought. I'm sure that's what both Mary Lou and Linc do every day.

And then during the night there was a thunderstorm with a lot of lightning, and this kid Clifford, in Group Two, had a seizure. He's had seizures before, and I recall that at least once before it was also during a thunderstorm. I wonder why. Anyway, every time before he has a seizure he does this weird loud sound, like *"A-a-a-h! O-o-o-h!,"* and raises one arm high and then shakes like a madman for a minute, or maybe more. Sometimes he knocks hard against the side of his crib. Poor kid. In a weird way, it was interesting to listen to, lying in my bed in the middle of the night— the thunder rolling and crashing and poor Clifford at the same time cracking against the slats of his crib. It was like one of them symphonies you hear about. But the poor guy! I seen him once up close during one of them seizures, and it wasn't pretty. His face gets bluish-white and all tight and screwed up, his mouth clamped tight shut, and his whole body is all tense, with his arms and legs pulled in tight like he's trying to protect hisself, and then after it's over he pisses, and sometimes craps his diaper, so the aides have to clean him up and then, finally, he sleeps for hours. They don't even wake him up to feed him or nothing.

At least I don't get them seizures. There's that.

And then Ricky. He worries me. His skin looks terrible anymore, all pasty and kinda dry, and his hair don't seem to stay combed and look neat on his head like it used to, always sort of mussed up. He's got these kinda dark circles under his eyes. And he hardly moves when he's sitting in his chair, always tied with one of them white cloth things around his chest so he don't slump over too far or nothing. Sometimes I think he looks worse now than before he went to that hospital in Building One. Sometimes, I see him just kinda staring out into the room at nothing at all when he's sitting in his chair or when he's in that cart they put him in a lot now, Dino's old cart, or even when he's just lying in his bed. At least he eats when Billy and them feed him, but it don't look like he's enjoying it much—just sort of opens his mouth and lets them put in a spoonful and closes his lips around the spoon, but his face never changes expression. I don't know. He worries me.

I wonder what Ricky'd like to come back as. Me and him and Davey and some of the other guys, too, watched that latest Laurel and Hardy movie Billy showed, and it was funny. That was yesterday, before I made the goddamn urinal spill all over my stupid useless self. The two guys are in Paris and the fat guy, Ollie, is gonna jump in the river with a big stone tied to him, to kill himself because some woman jilted him. The skinny guy,

Stan, asks Ollie what he'd like to come back as and Ollie says a horse. Stan says he'd like to come back as himself. "I always got along *swell* with me," he says. I laughed at that, and Ricky even smiled too, a little. Then some guy comes along and convinces them to join the Foreign Legion instead of jumping in the river. He says that the Legion is where guys go to forget bad stuff, especially women. But then, at the end of the movie, they want to escape the army, so they steal a little airplane and fly away. But of course they don't know how to drive the plane and it crashes. Laurel stumbles out of the wreck looking dazed and stupid and then he hears this harp music and turns to see Ollie, in his Legion uniform and white hat and a little pair of wings, rising up to heaven, waving goodbye as he goes, looking sad. That was *so* funny!

Then the next thing you see is Stan walking by himself along a dirt road, carrying a little bundle at the end of a long stick, and he hears Ollie's voice: "Hey, Stan, look. I'm over here." Stan looks and there's a horse behind a fence, with a mustache and wearing one of those black round hats like them two guys always wore, with holes cut out for the ears. "Well," the horse says in Ollie's voice, kinda scolding, "here's *another* nice mess you've gotten me into!" Stan's so glad to see him and hugs the horse around the neck.

That made me think what I'd like to come back as when I go—if that stuff about coming back is true. Maybe a hawk. I love it how they soar around up there, in those big circles, sometimes not even moving their spread wings much, just kinda floating and tilting first to one side and then the other. Of course, they have to deal with them pesky littler birds, whatever they are, worrying them now and again, dive-bombing them sometimes, but probably the hawks don't care about that too much. Or maybe I could come back as one of them elephants I saw once when I was a kid in a circus that came to the county, and that I used to see, too, in the old Tarzan movies on TV back at the farm. Tarzan'd yell for them elephants when he needed help, that weird yell he always did, and pretty quick a whole bunch of them, including the babies, would come tearing through the jungle toward him, lifting their trunks and flapping them big ears and screaming like anything, and then they'd trample the hell out of whoever Tarzan wanted them to—wild-eyed natives waving them big spears or mean hunters or whatever other bad guys. That'd be good.

Or maybe I'd just like to come back as some normal person, not all screwed up like I've always been—someone who can walk and talk and go take a dump by himself and drive a car and rub Mary Lou's head and stuff. Or maybe even one of them soap opera people, all dressed nice and living in a pretty house and kissing each other all the time. Well, probably not that, though. They seem to have too many problems, what with one thing or another. Someone's all the time jealous about someone else, or suspicious they're foolin' around behind their backs, or they're feuding about some stupid thing, or someone's falling in love with someone they shouldn't, or getting in a car accident, or losing their memory.

Well, I guess that if I come back as a human being, not a bird or an animal or a fish, I want to have a fairly quiet life without a lot of drama stuff, like them soap opera people always seem to have, just as long as I could be a normal person whose body worked okay. I just want to get up in the morning and pee by myself and get dressed and feed myself breakfast and then feed myself lunch and then feed myself supper, eating as much damn bread as I want, dipping it in gravy now and again. And maybe when I felt like it I'd turn on the TV and change the channels all by myself and watch whatever the hell I want to, and turn the damn thing off if nothing good's on. Or maybe I'd pick up the telephone and call my brother or maybe a friend and see if they want to go bowling or go see one of them baseball games. I heard Linc telling Rita how he likes to go to ball games with his buddies, and he said he don't even care that much who wins as long as he can sit on his "fat black ass in the bleachers and eat three or four hot dogs with the works," whatever that means, and "drink a bunch of beers."

I wonder if you really get to choose what you're gonna come back as or if God decides that. Or maybe Jesus. Or maybe some lower-level guy up there whose job that is. Ollie got to come back as a horse, like he wanted, but you wonder if God or someone had to approve that.

It'd be nice, I'm sure, to have friends you like and do stuff with them now and again. That's one of the things I like about them Laurel and Hardy movies, that those guys were friends and always did stuff together and stayed friends no matter what mishaps or tragedies or other bad stuff happened. Or like George and Lennie in that book Billy read part of to us. When Ollie was gonna jump in the river and drown, he told Stan he had to jump in too. But Stan didn't want to. So Ollie says to him, "Do you realize that after I'm gone you'd just go on living by *yourself?* People would *stare* at you and wonder what you are, and I wouldn't be there to tell them. There'd be no one to *protect* you." And then when Ollie did die in that plane wreck there it was sad to see Stan all alone, walking all by himself along that country road, carrying a little bundle on a stick. Then he was so glad to see Ollie again, even if he was a horse.

Another thing I wonder is if you die and go to heaven, like Ollie did, and then you come back as something else, does your soul from who you were when you died stay in heaven or does it go with whoever you come back as, even if it's a horse or a hawk or an elephant or something? I imagine old Father Callahan knows that kinda stuff.

RICKY

IT OCCURRED to me in the middle of last night that I'll probably never shave myself. Yesterday those two barbers who're brothers came in and were shaving guys. Arnie hates them, or at least he hates getting shaved. He pisses and moans and covers his face with his hands, and Bob, the bald brother, gave it right back. "Arnie," he said, "you're giving me a royal headache. Why don't you just be a *man* about this?" That was funny. But I'll never get to shave myself. I'll never have to decide how to do it—electric razor, regular old one with blades, and like that. I'll never put lather on my own face, or aftershave. Oh, well. On the other hand, I'll never have to worry about cutting myself shaving.

Sometimes it seems like my legs aren't even part of me anymore. I can barely move them and they sort of feel like dead weight sometimes, just things hanging down. Like Dino's legs. Yucko! My feet are cold, though, when I can feel them. That's one thing. Thankfully, the aides keep socks on my feet all the time now, even at night, and during the day when I'm not in bed Billy puts on my brown slippers, too. I like that. I can't even remember the last time I even saw my feet, looked at them. I don't even know how my toenails are, if they need to be clipped. I always hated doing that. Oh, well.

I wish Billy'd talk more about his cat, Stan. Once in a while he says something, but I wish he'd tell more. Like a few days ago he was telling me and Buddy how the cat bites his feet through the blankets and that he has sharp teeth, and once it hurt a lot and he jerked his leg under the blanket because it hurt and that sent Stan flying off the bed. He didn't mean to send him flying, but it happened. That was cute, I guess.

Billy talks to me more than anyone else does. I wish he worked every day. That's selfish of me, I know, but that's what I wish. He always tells me "good morning" when he comes in and asks how I'm doing and rubs my head and sometimes my shoulder, and always says goodbye when he leaves and tells me when he'll be here next. I feel better when he's here. Sometimes he tells me funny stuff the other guys do, like about Arnie or Larry or Gramps or even Dino. The other day he said to me and Buddy, "You guys think Dino gets bad headaches, his head being so damned big?' Buddy nodded, but I didn't know. I never thought about that. I suppose he could, though the guy seems to be in a good mood most of the time, always laughing when someone sneezes or burps or something. He's easily amused, I guess. Sneezes are definitely his favorite, and I like it when Billy does that fake sneeze to get Dino to laugh. He does that now and again.

One thing that's interesting is that Billy seems to get embarrassed or something when he swears in front of me. Like the other day he accidentally knocked over some washcloths and towels from a laundry cart and said, "Oh, god*damn* it to hell anyways." Then he saw me looking at him and turned a little red. Like I cared. Like *that's* something that bothers me. Heck, he can swear all day long, as much as I care. The funniest thing was once during naptime when he had to get Larry to stop making so much noise and he came over to me and Buddy and said, "I tell ya, boys, that bozo doesn't know the first thing about whacking. He needs lessons." He looked at me and his face turned a bit red again and he did this stupid little smile, like "Oops!" and looked embarrassed.

God, I feel so weak anymore. I can hardly sit up at all. All I want to do is lie in bed with my head cranked up so I can breathe better. I just like to be there and close my eyes and not think about too much. Just sleep the best I can, if possible. I like to be in the solarium, too, in the sun, but I can't sit up in my chair for very long. Billy and Mary Lou put me in this cart more often now instead of in my chair, and it's good because I can just lie there, on my back with my head raised a little, and it's more comfortable. I don't fall over to one side or another like when I'm in my chair. I think it's one of Dino's old carts, I heard Mary Lou say. It's good. But it makes me feel more helpless too. *Sheesh!*

Mary Lou's cute. While she was doing her work, cleaning guys up, she sang this little song, in a pretty voice, though not too loud:

> *Mish, mish, mish*
> *Fuzzy fish, furry fish*
> *Mish, mish, mish*

A funny thing, too, was she kept scratching her behind when she was working. When she was brushing Gilbert's teeth, I saw her reach behind and give her right cheek a good long scratch. She must've had an itch there. Then a few minutes later when she was near Dino's bed she did it again, and rubbed her butt for about thirty seconds. I wonder what's wrong with her.

I liked *Flying Deuces*. Billy let me stay in bed, thankfully, to watch it. My favorite part was when they decide to leave the army and they're walking out of the fort, carrying their suitcases and smoking these big cigars they stole from the commander's office. They hear this little soldier band playing, and they stop and listen for a little while and then Ollie starts singing the song they're playing: "*Shine on, shine on harvest moon ... .*" He has a really good voice! Stan starts dancing to the song, and then they both dance, doing the same moves at the same time, and the Foreign Legion guys sitting around get a huge kick out of it. Laurel's a *really* good dancer! They're both good. I was surprised.

My other favorite part was later when they're in the jail at the army place, and they're going to execute them in the morning for desertion, and they're sitting around in this cell together and Stan starts fooling around with the bed springs, plucking them one by one, and then he picks it up and examines it and fools around with it some more, and pretty soon he's holding the whole thing upright in his arms, like a harp, and plucking at the springs, his fingers moving real delicately, and it *sounds* just like a harp—a nice tune. Ollie looks at Stan like he's crazy and then looks out at the camera, at us, fat arms crossed and eyes open wide, with this expression like he's saying, "Do you *believe* this? Do you see how *weird* this guy is?" Then Ollie kinda smiles and gets into the whole deal and starts tapping his feet to the music.

Whenever we see one of their movies, I wonder about those two guys. Are they dead now? If so, how'd they die? Which one went first? How old did they live to? Did they have kids? If they're not dead, what are they up to? I wonder if they were good friends in real life, like they were in the movies. How long did they make movies together? I guess I'll never know that stuff.

I felt bad for Gramps when he was having a bad time. He sounds so pitiful when he cries like he does. I wonder what was wrong with him. That little Timmy was sort of whining too when Gramps was in trouble. I've heard that before, Timmy getting upset when Gramps is weirded out about something. When Dino rips Gramps's sheets and stuff from his crib and Gramps yells at him, Timmy freaks out too. That's okay. And then Arnie must have sympathized with Gramps too because he pounded his tray and grunted real loud when poor Gramps was crying.

At least they have these nurses here to help him and all of us. It makes me wonder what life was like for guys like the ones here back before they had places like this. The funny thing is that I *still* don't know exactly what kind of place this is. No one ever told me. I mean, I know it's a place for people who are retarded, like most of these guys are, I guess. I heard talk about that. But why am I here? I'm not like that. I'm just badly hurt because of my accident. I don't think I'm retarded because of my accident. I can't talk or anything, or walk anymore, but I don't think that means I'm like most of these guys, mentally. I just wish someone, the doctor or *someone*, would explain these things to me so I could understand.

On the other hand, sometimes I just don't even care about that stuff anymore. I'm not going to get better, so what's the difference? Really, what's the difference? Really. When I think about it, I know that my life, the way it was, is over. So maybe it's best just not to think about too much. That's why I like to just lie in my bed as much as possible and close my eyes and not think about a lot. I don't have much energy anyway. I hardly have any energy. The best thing for me is to just say my prayers silently, every day, the best I can, and hope they get heard. *Hail Mary, full of grace* ... . That's all I can do. Just pray for the strength to deal with the way I am, the grace I guess. There's nothing else I can do, except concentrate on my breathing.

Except that I'd like it if Billy'd read to me and Buddy more. I like watching those movies, but I think I like it as much, maybe more, when he reads stuff to us. I like his voice. I liked *Treasure Island* a lot. And I really liked *Of Mice and Men*. That was a good story, with Lennie and George and those guys. Curley and Slim and old Candy. I felt bad for Crooks, that stable buck, who had to stay in his room at night and read books because he was black and the other guys wouldn't let him in the bunkhouse. He could play horseshoes outside with the guys, but when it got dark and everyone went to the bunkhouse to play cards and stuff, he had to go to his room in the barn. He said there was a pile of manure under his window. He liked it when Lennie and Candy came into his room when George and all the guys were in town. And I felt bad for Curley's wife, who had no one to talk to and felt lonely. I like to lie in my bed and close my eyes and be read to, or be on that cart they put me on and be in the solarium and be read to there. That's a nice thing. But I hated it when George had to shoot Lennie at the end. I understand why he had to do it. If he didn't, they'd have caught Lennie for killing Curley's wife, even though it was an accident, and would have put him away for the rest of his life in an institution or something. George didn't want that for him. Better to be dead, he thought.

Poor Lennie, though. He seemed like a good guy—just simple-minded. He liked to touch soft things, like velvet and mice. They never got their little farm, never got to "live off the fat of the land," and Lennie never got to tend the rabbits like he wanted. It was a sad ending, but a good book. I felt sorry for George, though, being alone there at the end without Lennie. They'd been together for so long, friends, and George looked out for Lennie all the time, and now George was alone.

When Billy was reading that book, I remember wondering if either of my sisters would like it. I doubt it. I'm not sure what they like these days, but I don't think that book would be to their taste. Maybe Amy. I bet Brandon'd like it, though. He'd like stuff like that. Everyone in the book was a guy except for Curley's wife, so I doubt if a lot of girls would like it. But who knows?

For some reason, I've been thinking of my sisters more lately—wondering what they've been up to. I hope they're doing okay. I like it, usually, when they come to see me here, even though it's hard and really tires me out. Sometimes I have to struggle to remember what they look like, even though they come here to see me when they can. Maybe I don't look at them closely enough when they're here. It's weird. I remember what Stan Laurel looks like with no trouble, but I have to think about what Amy looks like. Or Chelsea. I can't remember whether Chelsea's hair is straight or more curly or frizzy than it was a year ago. I guess it would be nice if I had a picture of them here, next to my bed. A picture of my whole family, maybe. Maybe they think that would make me too sad, and maybe they're right.

Anyway, I hope my sisters are doing fine in school and stuff. I hope they get what they want in their futures. Amy always said she wanted to be an elementary teacher. She'd be good at that, so I hope she can do it.

God, I am *so* tired today. And my back hurts so bad. I wonder if I'd feel better if they gave me vitamins or something. I don't know why I'm so tired anymore since I don't do anything from morning to night, but there it is.

BILLY

I DON'T KNOW if Linc's porking Mary Lou. Whether he is or not, it's not my damned business. What do I care? But I don't think he is. Maybe he is, but I'd be surprised. I don't think he is, but anything's possible. He likes her, that's for sure. Even a clueless nothinghead recluse like me can see that. And it seems she likes him too, though, really, she sort of likes everyone—friendly and social like she is, talks to anyone. Most of the time, anyway. She has her quiet moments. Still, the two of them seem to spend a lot of time these days talking and joking around, and sometimes touching each other a little. I see that during the time between shifts. I saw it today. What I wonder is what the Christ they *talk* about so much? Linc's never talked much to anyone all the time I've known him, which is since I started working here, but he sure seems to have a lot to say to her. I don't get it. What loosened his tongue? What do they find to talk about so much? I don't guess it's sports or the weather. I wish I were invisible so I could get close and hear them.

I wonder if Boyd could carry on a conversation with Mary Lou. He can talk to girls better than me—hell, practically *anyone* can—but still not that well. I doubt she'd find him too interesting anyway. I don't even find him too interesting, even though he's my best friend. I remember one time when we were in the losers' corner in the Jefferson cafeteria at lunch and he was talking trash about the guys on the football team—what "moron behemoths" they were—and this magnificent frizzy-haired blonde came over and asked him if he'd finished his American history homework and could she maybe borrow it, and he said, in a real smart-ass way, "Yeah, baby, but it'll cost ya." She just gave him a bad look and walked away. He turned to me and shrugged. "Hey, man," he said, "what'd *I* say?" Talk about clueless.

Stan's asleep in my lap now and it's good to stroke the top of his furry head with the pads of my index and middle fingers. I like to softly bend back his pointy little ears, one at a time, too. Sometimes an ear'll stay bent, sort of folded over, and then I gently flick it back into place. I wonder if Stan dreams. He doesn't twitch or shake or anything while he sleeps, so I don't think he has bad dreams. He's content. I'm glad he's happy living here with me, that he has a good little life with me. A quiet little life. He couldn't care less about Christmas or Easter or the Fourth of July or whatever. They mean nothing to him. Of course, it's not just a one-way deal. I get a lot out of his being here too. It calms me to stroke his head like this, and I just feel content with my sleepy orange boy on my lap and on my bed, particularly in the morning when I wake up and there he is.

Nick Adams should've had a cat. The poor guy was a wreck. Last night I couldn't sleep and finally said the hell with it and turned on the light and read some of Hemingway's Nick stories—"Fathers and Sons" and "A Way You'll Never Be" and "Big Two-Hearted River," parts one and two. Hemingway's father killed himself in real life, and so did Nick's in the stories. Nick was in the war and saw horrible shit and then came home and went fishing by himself in Michigan to settle his nerves. "Nothing could touch him" in his canvas tent in the camp he made. That's what he wanted. I can relate. But he didn't want to fish in the swamp yet. Fishing there was "a tragic adventure." There'd be other days to do that. I wonder what "tragic adventure" means.

And that deaf old man in "A Clean, Well-Lighted Place" who tried to commit suicide because he "was in despair." At least the older waiter understood the old man.

Then Hemingway blew his head off in Idaho with a shotgun. Both father and son, suicides. Silly Romeo and Juliet, suicides. They weren't real, but still. It's stupid, but it still pisses me off to think about that foolish, careless pair. "Thus with a kiss I die," Romeo said. *Oh, puke!* Fourteen years old Juliet was, or not even, her comfortable life ahead of her, and she offs herself, forfeits her life, over some horny, hot-tempered, smooth-tongued, pimple-faced adolescent idiot. "O happy dagger!" she squealed. "This is thy sheath; there rest, and let me die." Jesus *Christ!* That damned Friar Laurence set the whole deal up. He was just trying to be helpful, I guess, but what was the result? Corpses. I have no sympathy for the lot of them. They mucked themselves.

Okay, that's silly. It is. Very silly. It's stupid. I know that. I do. You should have sympathy for people, even if they mucked themselves some-how. Mucking happens. I'm just tired from not sleeping well last night. You think stupid stuff when you're tired. I do, anyway. Others too, probably. Really, I don't want to see anyone do themselves in, whether they're some desperate dentist or silly lovestruck teenagers or a mean prince. Or me. I don't know what Hemingway's problem was. Maybe he was in despair, like the old man in that clean, well-lighted place. Maybe he'd just seen too much horrible stuff in his life. Or maybe he was bonkers.

Well, I don't want to think about that any more now. I'm done with that for now. Maybe I'll read to my Stanley sometime soon, but definitely no Hemingway stuff. The hell with all that. Maybe *Huck Finn*. I'll read Stan the part about the feud between the Grangerfords and Sheperdsons, but not the part where the king and the duke do The Royal Nonesuch and the crowd's onto them for their flim-flam and on the third night of the play everyone brings in stuff, vegetables and the like, to throw at the king and the duke. Huck says, "And if I know the smell of a dead cat being around, and I bet I do, there was sixty-four of them went in." Stan wouldn't like that.

And I don't want to think about Linc and Mary Lou, either. The hell with them too, for now. I got a kick out of Linc this afternoon, though. He was watching some game on TV and all of a sudden throws his arms in the air and rolls his eyes and looks pleadingly heavenward and slaps the top of his head with one big black hand, pretty hard, and sort of yells, "WHAT? Are you freakin' *kidding* me? I cannot *believe* what I just witnessed. That's gotta be some kind of a twisted damn *joke!* Oh, sweet Jesus, have MER-CY!" I've never seen him so agitated.

When Linc did that, Ricky smiled and even tittered a little but then had a coughing fit. He couldn't stop, and even got red in the face. I went over and sat him up straight in his bed and patted his back, and, when he stopped hacking, got him a little drink of water. He looked scared.

He's going downhill. I can see that. He's losing weight—lighter to pick up each day, it seems—and doesn't seem to have any energy. Not much, anyway. He can't sit up in his chair for long any more. And not much appetite. I wish I knew stuff about sports so I could talk to him about that, but I'm ignorant. I know he likes sports, but I'm not sure which ones he likes best. Maybe football. That's what he was playing when he got hurt. I guess I could see if Boyd could come and talk trash about "moron behemoth" football players to Ricky, but probably that wouldn't fly. The kid might get a kick out of it, since Boyd's basically a twelve-year-old himself, mentally, but I doubt sourpuss Hanson would approve.

I wish I could do more for Ricky, help him, but I don't know what I can do more than I'm doing—reading to him and Buddy when I can, showing funny movies, maybe tell a knock-knock joke here and there.

Except that now when he laughs, a lot of the time, he goes into a coughing spell too. I try to be there for him the best I can, but it isn't enough. It can't be enough. What could be enough? He's going downhill and it seems like there's not a damned thing I can do, or anyone can do. I doubt if anything's enough.

I don't have any bright ideas, and neither does Mary Lou. We still talk about Ricky between shifts, before or after report. Just today I asked her if she could think of anything we could do to make him more comfortable, maybe cheer him up a little. She was wearing a tight yellow T-shirt with a picture of a big pink flower on it—a rose I think, or maybe a tulip—and her boobs were right there, saying hello, with that pleasant cleavage. But I kept eye contact, at least for the most part. "I don't know what to do," she said, and I noticed her dark eyes were moist. "I really don't. He likes those videos you show."

Anyways.

After report, I put Buddy in his chair and then sat on his bed for a bit. I felt very tired. He looked at me with those watery blue eyes, a little string of saliva dribbling from the lower left corner of his mouth. "How ya doin' today, old man?" I asked. He nodded, just a little, and I noticed he wasn't looking at me any more but at Mary Lou and Randi, who were standing by the front desk, talking. Little Randi looked good, too, in a thin pair of aqua pants that came nearly to her mid-calves and clung nicely. Her black curly hair looked fluffier than usual, bigger and springier somehow, and it occurred to me that it'd be good to touch it, to rub my hands over it, to see how it felt. "You're an unrepentant lech, old man," I told Buddy. "I take my hat off to you."

BUDDY

THAT IDIOT LARRY tossed his tray after dinner last night and it damn near clunked poor Davey in the head. It missed him by maybe six inches. Davey screamed and scooted away from Larry, on his back like he does and pushing off with his foot. It's a weird way to get around, but it works for him. I'll say this, that little guy works hard—always moving around the ward and getting underfoot of the aides and all and carrying around a white washcloth to dust off and polish stuff that he can reach from the floor, the bottom parts of crib legs and chairs and like that. It maybe ain't a major profession or nothing, but, damn it anyway, it's *something*. What am *I* doing with my life?

One thing I notice is that the back of Davey's head is getting kinda wore out from scooting all over hell on his back, rubbing on the hard floor. There's a little spot right on the back there where his hair's gone and it looks a little red and sore. But that don't stop him. He just keeps going. So good for him.

I like it now when Billy sets Davey next to me and Ricky in the solarium. This morning we're all out here together, Ricky in his cart and me and Davey in our chairs. It must be getting close to lunch time. Billy covered Ricky with one of them white blankets and tucked it up under his chin. I guess he figured Ricky was cold, and I shouldn't wonder since he's so skinny anymore, and the color of his face is so bad, so kinda pasty. It is a little cool in the solarium. It's a wonder every damn one of us don't catch his death from cold. That's what Amanda always said to my brother when we were sitting in the living room watching TV. "Oh, Donald, you oughta cover Albert up with a blanket. This old place is so drafty it's a wonder we don't *all* catch our deaths from cold." Anyway, Billy put Ricky right between me and Davey, our chairs near touching the edges of his cart. Gramps and Timmy are out here too, and other guys, and the old geezer is looking particularly cross-eyed today.

Gramps was funny at breakfast when Destini and that other one, Cassie, brought in the food cart. Billy'd gotten Gramps dressed and up in his chair for breakfast and set him right near where they put the cart and plug it in to keep the crappy food hot. Destini, for some reason, looked over at Gramps sitting there, and he noticed her looking, and of course he stuck his tongue right up that ugly nose. He's got this pimple now on the right side of his nose. Well, she got just the biggest kick out of that and commenced to giggling like ... well, like a girl. He kept that old tongue in there for I don't know how long and all the while Destini kept staring at him and laughing and after a while that tongue slithered out and he took to singing his song, that bizarre version of "Old McDonald" that he does, holding on to them little cloth dolls in the crooks of his arms. Timmy got a big kick out of it too, tittering and all sort of twisted-up and spazzing out in his little chair.

It's good to be here with the guys, even major feebs like Zach and Jimmy. Dino's here in his new cart, and that damn Larry's here too. Even old Gilbert's out today, poor guy, with his arms and legs bent up and his eyes all crazy. Sometimes he breaks out in a sweat and just stares out wide-eyed into space, at what I don't know. Maybe he's seeing something that the rest of us can't. Maybe he sees God. Who knows? We're mostly quiet except for the little sounds some make, little groans and such, and Larry's stupid "Heek, heek" and Davey's little "O-o-o-h." Arnie's in the corner by himself, going over one of his catalogs for probably the thousandth time. Today I see he's checking out pictures of ladies in their underwear, bras and panties and such. The sun keeps going in and out of the clouds, and when it's out it feels good—warm and very good.

Rita and them even put some Halloween decorations out here, cardboard things of witches on broomsticks, wearing them black pointy hats like they do, and a couple ghosts and some pictures of orange pumpkins. They even got a big plastic pumpkin on the shelf near the nurses' station, and it's got a face on it that looks like one of them faces you carve on a real pumpkin, with weird eyes and a big crooked grin. I remember my Aunt Irene used to make a pretty good pumpkin pie now and again, and she'd squirt whipped cream on it more often than not. Damn, that was good. I wish we'd get some of that kind of pie here, but for some reason we don't.

I think the thing Rita likes best about Halloween, aside from decorating the walls with shit, is eating them little pieces of orange and white candy corn. She carries a bunch of 'em in her pocket, and so far today I bet she ate at least fifty. That's okay, except I heard her complain now and again that she thinks her butt is too big and I don't imagine eating them candies is gonna make it smaller .

The squirrels are busy today. When Billy first put me out here today I noticed there was this one, kind of a dark gray guy, just lying totally still on this thick branch, right where it joined up with the trunk of the big tree outside the window. His eyes were closed and his fur was kinda blowing in the breeze. It looked like the little shit was dead. *Too bad*, I thought. But then, after a while, he woke up and looked around with them beady little black eyes squirrels got and scampered down the tree. It's amazing how they do that, just zipping down a tree trunk headfirst like it was nothing. It makes me jealous. Sometimes I see them squirrels chasing each other around on the ground or in the trees. You wonder if they're just playing or if they got grudges, some kind of little squirrel snits. Today most of them are pretty serious, digging little holes in the ground, I guess to store nuts in for the winter, and zooming up and down them trees, sometimes one of them with a nut, it must be, in his mouth.

I think Ricky'd like to watch them squirrels too. Maybe he would. He's right between me and Davey, the three of us close, but he ain't watching the squirrels or, really, nothing. Mostly his eyes are closed and he's just lyin' there all quiet and still. They always set him up in that cart now so his head's propped up on pillows, and he's tied in so he don't fall out. Sometimes he opens his eyes for a little bit and looks around and then closes them again. Just once he woke up and looked right into my eyes for a little bit, just for a few moments, before he fell asleep again. I don't know what he was thinking about, but I can't say he looked too happy or nothin' like that. I hope he's warm enough. Maybe he needs another blanket. He's so skinny now, he worries me. He must get cold pretty easy.

A little earlier this morning I started to nod off myself, but just then Dino let out with a loud, "YEAH! Hey-kay-kay!" followed by his big belly laugh. I don't know what he heard to set him off, but his "YEAH!" kinda startled Ricky awake. He looked scared for a moment and looked like he might start crying. But he didn't. Instead, he looked first at me again, and then at little Davey, and then over at Gramps and Timmy, holding hands like they do, and then over to the corner where Arnie was still studying them pictures of almost-naked ladies. Then he looked out the window for a little bit and then closed his eyes again. When he first opened his eyes, all startled, the sun was shining bright and Ricky had to squint a little while looking around at everyone. But just that quick, the stupid sun went behind a big cloud and the whole solarium darkened. I was looking right at Ricky's face then and it went from all white, so pale, to gray. Just like that. It was scary, somehow. I had to look away.

Billy came into the solarium a little after that to check on us. "Gentlemen!" he said, kinda loud. "You happy *few*. You band of brothers." Ricky did start crying then, looking up at Billy. I don't know why. Billy rubbed the top of his head. "What's the matter, kiddo?" he asked. Ricky kept crying, so Billy rolled his cart out of the solarium. He was gone for a while, I don't know how long, and then Billy brought him back and stuck his cart right back between me and Davey. I noticed he'd cleaned Ricky up a little, washed his face and combed his hair and covered him with an extra blanket. "Keep an eye on him, old man," he said before he left. "And don't corrupt him with your wicked ways."

I imagine it'll be time for lunch pretty quick now. I ain't in no hurry. Right now, I'm just liking being out here with Ricky and the rest of the guys. Right now, I'm liking it that Ricky's in his cart between me and Davey, and the rest of the guys are nearby. His eyes are closed again. I don't know if he's really asleep or just sort of resting. I guess it don't matter. I hope he's warm enough. This is good. But I'm scared.

RICKY

I CAN'T BELIEVE how bad my back hurts. It hurts all the time now, day and night. Every time I take a breath now, as much as I can do that, it hurts. Yesterday that physical therapist lady came and moved me around and massaged my back, but it didn't help. It hurt just as bad after she was done. Plus, I had a horrible headache earlier today, and I have those almost every day now, too.

I just wish I could sleep all the time now so I wouldn't have to feel so crappy. But, at the same time, I'm scared to sleep because I have bad dreams. Scary dreams. Jeez! Last night—I think it was last night, but not even sure of that—I dreamt I was back in school. It was lunchtime and I was sitting at a table in the cafeteria with a bunch of the guys. We were all laughing and joking around and eating our lunches and stuff. I was eating one of those mock chicken leg things. Then all of a sudden I fell off my chair onto the floor and when I tried to get up again, I couldn't get off the floor. "C'mon," the guys were yelling. "Get up! Get up! You can't just *stay* there all day. Get your stupid butt up." But I couldn't. Just laid there and in a while, I don't know how long, the guys had to leave to go to class. Some seemed like they were disgusted with me, or mad for some reason. A teacher came along and tried to pick me up, but he couldn't. "Ah, the hell with him," he said, and walked away.

I remember that I had another dream sometime recently, too. I think it was a dream. It must have been. I remember in it I was in my bed here, maybe lying quietly and watching TV, and then I was high up looking down at the ward, sort of floating or soaring. I didn't actually *see* myself up there, my body, but I know it was me and I was looking down from high up and seeing the whole ward, all the beds and cribs and all the guys, a lot of them in bed sleeping or whatever—it must have been naptime—and I could see all three groups at the same time and all the carts and the laundry bags, and the tub room, too, and also the solarium. The only aide I could make out was Billy, and he was folding diaper pads and putting them in a neat pile on the bottom shelf of his cart. He didn't look up to see me. I wish he would've. It was a neat feeling, to be that high up and see everything at the same time like that. But it was scary too, like being stuck at the top of a Ferris wheel or something, and you can't control what's happening.

When I was out in the solarium this morning with Buddy and Davey and a bunch of the other guys, I was still kind of upset over that dream about being in school and falling. I had my headache then, too. I feel better now with that, a little better, but my back still hurts horribly. Sheesh! It was okay to be in the solarium with everyone. That was good. The sun felt good, except it kept going behind the clouds and it was cold when it did. Then I think I fell asleep for a minute and was startled awake by some noise, I don't remember what it was anymore. It might have been Dino laughing at something, that big laugh he does. I like that. I remember I saw Arnie by himself in one corner of the room doing his catalogs. I remember I felt okay to be out there with the guys. *That's okay*, I thought. That's fine now. At least it's something. Then I had to close my eyes and try to sleep again.

I was *so* embarrassed, though, when I started crying when Billy came in the solarium. I don't know why I did that. It just happened. I remember I had to pee real bad and my back hurt so bad and then I got cold and maybe was shivering and just all of a sudden there I felt so bad, and just began weeping. I couldn't help myself. Billy took me to the bathroom and sat me on the toilet and held me up straight, and when I was done he lifted me and put me back on the cart and washed my face and hands with a warm washcloth. That felt good. Then he combed my hair and brushed my teeth and gave me some water. "You okay, kid?" he asked. I remember I nodded. "Wanna go back to the solarium?" I nodded again. He put another of those white blankets over me first.

Now it's night again, and I hate it. Someone's snoring a few beds away, maybe Buddy. I can't sleep. I want to sleep. That's all I want to do any more. If I could just sleep all night through, maybe I'd feel a little better. Maybe. But now I can't. I guess I must have slept too much during the day, and now I'm awake. My back hurts *so* bad, and I wish Bernie'd come and turn me on my right side for a while. Plus, my face feels kinda flushed and I'm having trouble breathing through my nose. I'm stuffed up or something, I guess. Maybe I got a cold out in that solarium. I don't know.

Bernie was funny earlier when he mumbled to himself, "Well, boys, spring ain't *that* far off." What did that mean? Winter hasn't even started yet, so what's he talking about? Spring? That seems like a *very* long time away.

One thing I've been doing at night lately is thinking back about stuff. I lie there in bed and try to remember, starting when I was little before my sisters were born. It's funny what a person thinks about. I remember, sort of anyway, being excited when Mom was pregnant with Amy. I was going to have a brother or sister! But then after she was born I remember being upset because she was getting all the attention. Three years old I was, and jealous of a stupid baby. Then later, after Chelsea was a couple years old and she and Amy shared a room, I was partly glad to have my own room that I didn't have to share and partly jealous because they got to be together. Lots of times I heard them in there giggling. Later, though, I was happy to have my own room and my own stuff in it, and I could put up my own posters on the wall and stuff. Then I remember how, when I was eight or nine, Mom and Dad gave me an alarm clock radio and I had to get myself up and ready for school every day. I liked that, but I missed my mother knocking on my bedroom door every morning and telling me it was time to get up. I missed her voice doing that, and could hear her getting the girls up.

Sometimes at night I think about school, too. Just dumb stuff a lot. I remember Sister Maureen telling about the Civil War and the terrible battles they had. I remember she told about how Clara Barton helped so many poor guys who'd been wounded and started the Red Cross, and stuff like that. I wonder if Randi and those other nurses studied about her. I wish Randi was on tonight. I like her more than most of the other nurses. I think I'd feel better if she was here. I like Dawn, too, when she's working some nights. She sometimes feels my forehead, I guess to see if I have a fever or whatever, and it seems like she pretty much knows what she's doing.

I've been thinking now and again about football, too, and how I always wanted to be a running back. I think I was pretty fast, and I could see holes pretty good. I remember thinking that when I got to Jefferson, if I made varsity, I'd have to play offense and defense. Both ways. That's what most guys have to do in high school. So if I got to be a running back I'd probably have to also be a cornerback or a safety, unless I got big enough to be a linebacker. It seems like that'd be tiring, because you don't get to rest much. But in college and the pros, you only have to play one way, or some guys just play on special teams. Maybe I would've had a chance to return kicks or punts, too. Maybe. Well, that's all done now.

I wish I had Rosary beads to hold. I just want the beads to hold on to in bed at night. I don't need to say all the Rosary prayers, most of which I can't remember anyway, I just want to have it in my hands. It'd be a comfort. Or at least it'd be good if they'd hang one on the head of my bed somewhere, so I could at least see it a little bit. Something. I know the Our Father and the Hail Mary, of course, but all I can remember of the Glory Be is that part at the end about " *... ever shall be, world without end. Amen.*"

And the other thing is I want to be okay with God for my sins. I think about that every night. The nurses and aides get together for report and I can hear them talking, though can't make out all they say, and then I hear our aides go out in the corridor and open their lockers and get their coats and stuff and then hear their lockers slam shut and then it's quiet and I start worrying about my sins. Mary Lou was on a p.m. tonight and she was sneezing and coughing all evening long and during report too. She kept blowing her nose into this big red-and-black handkerchief she keeps in her back jeans pocket, and every now and again she'd go, "Oh, *yuck*-a-doodle anyway."

Right after she and the other aides left after the report, I started thinking again. I silently said a Hail Mary and an Our Father and then thought I should maybe say that Act of Contrition, just to cover the bases. I wish I could remember all of it. *Oh my God, I'm heartily sorry for having offended Thee, and I detest all my sins, because I fear ... the loss of heaven and ... the pains of hell.* I remember that part, but I can't remember all the rest. I used to know it by heart. I sort of remember something about that I promise to confess my sins and amend my life, but I don't remember the rest. I wish I did. I hope God can understand that and cut me some slack here. I'm sure He will. I hope that prayer's the right thing to say. I don't know what else to do. I just don't know what else.

I can't think of any specific sins I've done lately that I should confess about, but I'm sure I've done some and I definitely detest them. I'll gladly amend my life, but how? I mean, I've been saying my prayers the best I can and I've honored my parents and haven't taken the Lord's name in vain or anything like that. I haven't had any bad thoughts about anyone, and tried not to feel too sorry for myself because of my situation. I've felt a *little* sorry for myself, but I've tried not to too much. I don't know how much is too much. I don't know if that's a sin or not, but it seems like it could be. Maybe a venial sin.

I don't know what else I can do, except say the usual prayers as penances. I really don't. Just sleep, I wish. Just sleep.

BILLY

DESTINI SAID she's trying to find a home for a cat, a fat black guy named Allan with a piece missing from his right ear due to a fight in his misspent youth. It's her mother's cat and the deal is that her parents are splitting up and her mother's moving out and going to an apartment where she can't have animals and her father hates Allan, and Destini can't take the cat because she's developed an allergy to fur. She said her parents had an ugly argument and her mother screamed, "Why don't you go back to that bitch *DESTINI*, you self-centered *bastard!*" She said that confused her at first, but then she understood. She puddled up a little. "Do you know anyone who might want a cat?" she asked between sniffles. "He's kind of a wimp, but sweet." It was the most she'd ever said to me, except when she told me how she got her name, and I have no idea why she asked *me* about the cat. But I told her I'd think about it. "Thanks," she mouthed silently and flashed that crooked little smile.

"Think I oughta get another cat?" I asked Ricky and Buddy right after lunch. "Think Stan'd like a friend?" Buddy nodded and even giggled a little. I wiped some drool from his chin. Ricky, in bed, didn't do anything. I don't know if he even heard. He looked terrible. I don't know if I've ever seen him so pale. It seemed like he was barely breathing, and he kept closing his eyes and then opening them just for a moment. He hardly ate anything today. I was scared. I told Randi I was worried. She said she knew, that they were keeping an eye on him. "Maybe he needs to be in the hospital," I said. She nodded and said Doctor Winters was on top of it. Somehow I didn't find that reassuring.

I think Stan'd like Allan. He'd probably appreciate one of his own to hang around with, particularly while I'm at work. Being alone probably isn't good. It's what I do as much as possible, but that's my choice. I like alone. That's my life, pathetic as it might be. I'm sure it is pathetic. I know that. But I don't want anything different. If Stan had a choice, though, I imagine he'd like a friend. Who knows? But *Allan?*

150

What kind of name is *that* for a self-respecting feline? It's not as bad as Twinkle, but almost. I wonder how he's a wimp.

Poor Destini.

Poor Ricky. I'm off for a couple days, but if some doofus calls in sick and they need someone to work, I'll do it. Why not? I think I should be here now, with Ricky.

Arnie surprised me this morning. I had to put him on the potty and expected the usual fussing and struggling, but no. I wheeled his chair into the bathroom and damned if he didn't scoot himself right onto the throne and then let me pull his pants down. He looked up at my face for approval. "Good boy, Arnie," I told him. "Good man. Maybe there's hope for you yet. Now just keep those hands off Mary Lou's boobs."

Larry surprised me too. As usual after lunch, he commenced spanking the monkey as soon as I got him out of his chair and onto his bed, employing his usual hapless technique. He commenced, too, his usual "Wah-GOO! Wah-GOO!" and tossed in a "Heek" here and there, and suddenly he was silent for maybe thirty seconds and then practically screamed, in a higher-pitched voice than I'd ever heard from him, "ZORCH!"

It'll be Ricky's birthday soon. I should get him something. He'll be thirteen, a teenager. I'm thinking he'd like a hooded sweatshirt, maybe one of those thicker, quilted ones to keep him warm when his skinny ass is out in the solarium. I can put the hood on and tie it nicely under his chin, and at least it'll keep his head warm a little. That'll be a good thing, what with the colder weather coming on, the chill and so forth. They say most of your heat escapes from your head. Maybe a red sweatshirt or a bright blue one. Something a little more exciting than *my* usual boring gray.

I think it was for my eleventh birthday that my mother gave me my first hoodie. I remember the old man was out of town for some reason, probably screwing around, and she took me out to breakfast to Pancake Palace on a Sunday morning. That was good. I recall I had french toast and bacon and hot chocolate. She had blueberry pancakes and scrambled eggs. I don't know why I remember that. I recall that we didn't talk much, but it was good to be there. There were a lot of people dressed nicely, who must have come there before or after church, I imagine. The sweatshirt was dark-green. I wore it practically every day for the next two years until I outgrew it. After that I bought myself a gray hooded deal every year on my birthday and then another for a Christmas present for myself. Boyd likes them too, but he always gets them in black.

Boyd. He called me the other night all excited because his brother got nine months in county for possession and dealing and now he gets to use his brother's truck for that time—a black Ford with a big dent in the right rear fender. I was asleep in my chair with Stan on my lap when the phone rang. It startled me. My phone hardly ever rings, except when work calls to see if I want to pick up a shift when someone calls in sick or something. I generally decline, but not always. I asked Boyd if he was upset that his brother was in jail. "Hell, no," he said. "He deserved it. Plus, he never even gave me no freebies—no family discount. I got no respect for a person like that."

I should probably call my mother one of these days. That birthday breakfast is a nice memory.

That poor goose. Tomorrow I'm going to go to that park to see him, maybe in the afternoon. It haunts me that the poor guy is always in that same spot by the north side of the pond, always alone. I don't know if he's still in mourning or just incompetent at getting another mate, or whatever. Fall's here now and it's getting colder, the nights are colder, and this poor guy's always by himself there in that damn park, by that pond, by himself. The nights are darker and getting longer, too. That's probably tough for him. It'd be good if some female goose would take pity on him. I'm sure he'd be a good companion, and grateful. Or maybe a whole flock of geese could get him to join up somehow, maybe by telling him how great it'd be to fly south for the winter and hang around the beaches in Florida or Mexico, or wherever geese like to go.

Linc was nice to Ricky today. He was in a good mood, singing show tunes—"Old Man River" and "You Can't Get a Man with a Gun" and "On the Street Where You Live"—and just before shift change came over to Ricky's bed and sang to him, in that deep bass voice:

> *Summertime, and the livin' is easy.*
> *Fish are jumpin' and the cotton is high.*
> *Oh, your daddy's rich, and your mom is good-lookin',*
> *So hush, little baby, do-o-o-n't you cry.*

Just then Mary Lou came into the ward for her p.m. shift and came over to stand next to Linc. He looked over at her for a moment and continued his serenade.

One of these mornings you're gonna ri-i-se up singin'
Then you'll spread your wings, and you'll take to the sky-y-y.
Oh, but till that morning, there's a-nothing can harm you,

He put his arm around Mary Lou's shoulder and turned to look down at her face.

With Mommy and Daddy sta-a-a-ndin' by.

Ricky looked up at both their faces and smiled a little, not much. A weak smile, at best. He's way too pale.

I doubt I'll sleep well tonight. I came home right from work, changed into my sweatshirt and pajama bottoms, made my tea, and fell asleep in my chair, Stan on my lap, before I'd finished three pages of the "All Full of Tears and Flapdoodle" chapter in *Huckleberry Finn*. I must have slept for almost two hours.

It's dark out now, and raining. It's comforting to be here in my little place, secure and warm, and outside it's dark and wet. I'm hungry though. I'll heat up a can of Campbell's Chicken Noodle soup and maybe a Swanson turkey TV dinner. I like the little section of mashed potatoes they have in it, and the other little section of cranberry sauce. I like to mix a little of that cranberry sauce and some of the cheap gravy with the mashed potatoes. It *looks* horrible, but tastes okay.

BUDDY

THEY TOOK RICKY to that hospital in Building One again, damn it anyway. Sometime after breakfast Doc Winters and two nurses, Randi and some other one I don't know, went over to his bed and were looking him over and I don't know what-all they was doing. They took his temperature, I saw that. Then they left and a while later, before lunch, that same bald black guy from before came in with that one big cart, and him and Randi lifted Ricky onto it and covered him with one of them white sheets, and the black guy rolled him out and he was gone. Just that quick, Ricky was gone. Billy ain't on today, but Mary Lou's working a day so she told me where he went when she was feeding me lunch. She looked kinda upset too.

I feel crappy about him being gone, like I felt that one other time he went to the hospital. And scared, too. He came back to the ward here that time, but I remember I was scared and worried for him pretty much the whole time till he got back. Damn it anyway! This shit worries me. Why can't it be me instead of him? It ain't fair. Well, hell, *life* ain't fair. If I know anything, I know that.

The thing is, I didn't get to say goodbye. I can't *say* goodbye, of course, but it might have been nice just to have had a minute with Ricky, just him and me, before he left. But no one thought about that. I don't blame no one. I mean, I ain't special here. No one owes me nothin'. I'm only drooling old Buddy, just taking up space in this stupid world and not doing a damn thing that makes any difference from one stupid empty day to the next. So them aides and nurses, they don't owe me nothin' special. I know that. Still, it would have been good to have a little time with Ricky, just him and me, before they carted him off to that damn hospital. Oh, well.

And I don't know when I'll see him again. I hope he'll just have to be there for a few days, like the last time, and then he'll be back here to B Ward. Maybe they can do something to make him feel a little better over there. I sure as hell hope so, on account of he sure ain't looked good lately.

Then when he gets back we can do the stuff we like, like being in the solarium with the guys and watching Laurel and Hardy and Billy reading stories to us. Myself, I'd like to hear more stories about them nasty pirates, like Black Dog and Long John and them guys.

But what if he don't come back? That's what I worried about the last time he went to that hospital, and now that's what I'm thinking about again. Now it's naptime and I'm in my bed and the ward's pretty quiet. Larry's quiet for a change, thank God. Poor Gilbert's having a tough time, though. All day long he's been doing that little moaning sound he now and again does and that crazy noise that sounds like a laugh but it ain't a laugh, and now he's just lying in his crib covered up to his chin with a blanket but just sweating like anything. His eyes are wild, poor guy, and his forehead is soaking wet. I don't know why they can't do something for him, Doc Winters and them. Maybe there's nothing they can do. Or maybe they just don't care that much about a nobody feeb like Gilbert.

Anyway, what if I never see Ricky again in this life? Well, then I'll see him in heaven. I'll miss him till I get there. And if he don't get to go to heaven, then something's wrong. Then *nobody* deserves to go there, damn it anyway, including me, and I wouldn't want to go there anyhow. How could God *not* let Ricky get into heaven? That just ain't right. Well, if there's any justice, they'll let him in and he can be at peace. I hope he's got some kin up there that he can see. If he don't, maybe my Aunt Irene'll keep an eye on him.

But I'd rather he came back here. Eternity's a long time and down the road I hope Ricky and me'll get to spend that time together in heaven, and Donald and Amanda'll be there too, sooner or later, and then still down the road all the other guys here, Gramps and Timmy and Dino and all them. And then sometime Billy, too, and Mary Lou, though probably that'll be a long time away, young and healthy like she is, and pretty too. I've gotta think she'll have a long life yet.

I'm sure Father Callahan'll get there too, but I hope he's in some other part, some special section they got for priests and guys like that, because I don't wanna have to listen to him no more when this life is over. I've had enough of his stupid poems and all the stuff he keeps saying that I don't know what the hell he's talking about, like that time he said, "The kingdom of God is within." And that crap about us feebs bearing our cross.

Billy, he'll be sad when he hears they took Ricky to that hospital. He was kinda upset that last time, I remember. He likes Ricky, I know that, and

155

he likes it when it's just the three of us watching movies or when he's reading to us, and, lately, Davey, too. He's been off for two days. I think he's back tomorrow, but not sure. I wish he was here.

Maybe I'm wrong, but I notice that Billy's weird sometimes lately about Linc and Mary Lou. Them two spend a lot of time together, talking and laughing and all, and I seen Billy looking over at them now and again and he don't look all that happy. I don't know if he's jealous or what. Maybe he really likes Mary Lou his own self. If so, I can understand that. I wish he'd talk about that kinda stuff, but he don't. He's not much of a talker.

Davey was hanging around my bed most of the morning, and I was glad he did. As usual, he was squirtin' around on his back, polishing and dusting stuff with his washcloth like he does. I felt glad he was there today. I don't know why. He's a pain in the ass sometimes, always underfoot and all, but today I was just glad he was here. I hope after naptime, when Mary Lou gets him up, that he'll come back some more. I don't know why, and I guess I ain't gonna think about it. Maybe this afternoon me and Davey'll watch some of them soap operas. Maybe we'll see some kissing and stuff.

Well, who cares about that stuff anyway? It's interesting now and again, but it don't have nothing to do with me. Now that I think of it, though, I guess I'd just as soon stay here in my bed today. I don't feel like doin' much.

Mary Lou and Randi are sitting by the nurses' station talking. I heard Mary Lou say that Duane, her boyfriend, fell off his motorcycle and cracked his head a little and sprained his right wrist, and the whole deal put him in a bad mood, and he's been kinda mean to her. But, she said, she's trying to be a good girlfriend anyway and be nice to him, but it ain't easy. She said she got him a rack of ribs last night. I don't understand that. How do you get ribs for a guy? I know that word *rack*, 'cause I heard some aide a while back say that word when he meant about some lady's boobs, but I don't know what Mary Lou meant when she said it about ribs.

I understand about her bad mood, though. I'm in a bad mood too, on account of Ricky. It's interesting how quick a person's mood can change sometimes. Before that bald guy came and hauled Ricky to that goddamn hospital in Building One, I was in an okay mood today. I was feeling okay. I wasn't exactly singin' in the rain or nothing, but okay. Now, though, I feel like shit. Now I feel, I don't know, just sad and like I don't wanna do anything, just lie in bed and not be bothered. I feel kinda sorry for myself, and I'm having them thoughts that I wish I could just get this life over with and be done with all the indignities because of being like I am, and not have to put up with all the stupid shit of my stupid useless life, and just get to go up there to heaven, where things'll be different. I hope things'll be different. They better be.

Poor Ricky, though. He sure don't deserve *this* crap.

RICKY

HAIL MARY, full of grace. Blessed art thou among women, and blessed is the fruit of thy womb, Jesus. Holy Mary, mother of God, pray for us sinners ...

BILLY

RICKY DIED just after midnight. I'm okay with that. I am. It's okay. His suffering's over now. The way he was is no way for someone like him to live. What he thought I don't know, but maybe this is what he wanted anyway. Maybe. I don't know. How could I?

I feel terrible just the same. Horrible! It's not like I never thought he might go, but it hit me hard anyway. Randi told me as soon as I came in this morning. She was all red-eyed and blotchy-faced. She told me and then gave me this little hug and laid her head on my chest and sniffled, depositing a little wet snot on my shirt—not much, just a little. "Well," she whimpered, "at least he's at peace now." I was surprised at the hug since I'm not exactly close to her, and, of course, don't know if I reacted right. I patted the back of her head three times and said, "There, there," and held her a little bit. Just a little. I don't know. At least I got to touch her springy hair. The feel of those pert little bazooms pressing against my puny chest wasn't horrible either.

I told Buddy right away. But he knew. He must have overheard people talking. I've never seen him look the way he did when I went over to his bed. His face was paler than ever and his skin sort of drawn tight. His blue eyes were soft and watery. I stayed with him for as long as I could before report, and just patted his bony shoulder—that pathetic clavicle. I didn't know what to say.

At report, that weird Dawn said they'd taken Ricky from Building One to the regular hospital downtown around eleven yesterday morning because they were worried about him and couldn't help him, and his parents came to that hospital, and he lost consciousness around ten last night and his parents called a priest who gave him the Last Rites and he died peacefully enough, though he had "labored breathing." Bad pneumonia, his system was worn down, antibiotics weren't working, couldn't fight it off, blah blah. I wanted her to get done talking so I could go get the kids ready for breakfast.

I got Buddy up and dressed him in his brightest Hawaiian shirt. I think he wanted to stay in bed, but I made him get up and into his chair. I got

159

Arnie and Larry and Davey up and dressed and into their chairs and wheeled them over near to Buddy. I cranked up Gramps and Timmy and Dino and Jimmy in their beds. Gramps looked at me funny, real serious, cross-eyed like he is, his forehead all furrowed, almost like he knew something was up. Maybe he knows more than we think. Gilbert was fast asleep, his face paler than usual and forehead shiny with sweat and mouth open. He must've had another bad night. I just let him sleep.

Destini and Cassie were quiet when they brought the food cart in. Destini looked over at me with those big eyes behind her gold-rimmed glasses while I was setting Davey up near Buddy and whispered, "I'm so sorry." I just nodded. Someone must have told them about Ricky when they brought breakfast to A Ward.

Buddy wasn't hungry. "Listen, old man," I told him, "you gotta keep your strength up. I know this oatmeal tastes like crap, but it's all there is. If I had some Crêpes Suzette, I'd give you some. I'd call up Christy and tell her to bring you some lovely scrambled eggs with cheddar cheese mixed in, sprinkled with chives, and a side of bacon, but I imagine she's busy on a Sunday—probably sleeping in with that ugly greaseball shitbird." He looked at me funny for a moment and then smiled, just a little, and accepted four bites of the crappy oatmeal. "Good enough," I told him.

After breakfast I got the other guys cleaned up and dressed and out to the solarium. I took as much time as I could with each one, changing their diapers and washing them off and brushing their teeth and putting on clean T-shirts and, on some, pants. That's what I needed to do, for myself and them—the routine of the day, keep the guys clean and dry and comfortable. That's what I need to do. That's what I can do okay. I know I can do that okay—okay enough, anyway. I put Gramps and Timmy next to each other as usual in the solarium, and made sure his dolls were secure in the crooks of his arms. Even Timmy was quieter than usual, less spastic and squirrely.

I only had to do one bath, Davey. It would have been Ricky's bath day. I did Davey in the tub, not that stupid slab. I always did Ricky in the tub, never that damn slab where you rinse off some helpless human being with a humiliating spray hose! At least I think I did *that* right.

I didn't go on break. I didn't want to. I didn't want to sit in that break room with those whining women talking about Ricky. I just wanted to deal with the kids in my group. That's what I'm okay at. That's what I want to do. It's maybe the only thing I *can* do okay. What do I have to say to people anyway? I don't have anything to offer. What do I have to offer? Nothing. I never know what to say. It's just awkward, anyway. And today I don't want to hear anyone's grousing. I'm good enough, I hope, at taking care of these kids, maybe making their tedious lives a bit more comfortable while they're still breathing, for however long that is.

Longer for some. Gramps is seventy-two. Ricky was twelve. He would've been thirteen in two months. Two months. I was going to get him a quilted hooded sweatshirt. They're basically babies, most of these guys, and always will be. That's something to think about. They'll live and die as babies, mentally anyway, and just need to be fed and cleaned up and made comfortable and cared for each tedious day until they croak. That's all. That's okay to do.

Now it's after lunch on a quiet Sunday afternoon, nap time The guys are asleep, most of them. Not Buddy, though. This is a tough day for him. I can see that. I'll do what I can. I'm sitting with him near his bed, and we're watching *Rio Bravo*. The two of us. It's an all-John Wayne day on some channel. I'm glad it's on—a nice piece of luck. I can be quiet and not talk to anyone and Bud and I can just watch Sheriff John T. Chance do his thing: be in charge and prevail in his world, be a man, not be scared. It's interesting that everyone except Chance has a nickname, not a real one: Dude, Stumpy, Feathers, Colorado. I remember thinking about that when I first saw it. I remember once when I watched it and the old man was with me. Maybe it was my birthday. I think it was. He made us popcorn, I recall that, and then ate most of it himself, scooping up huge handfuls, the self-centered asshole.

Walter Brennan, old Stumpy, is limping around cackling to Chance. "Jumpin' *Jehosophat*," he's griping, "why don't nobody never *tell* me nothin'?" Dean Martin as Dude's a drunk with the shakes, but he gets better when the nasty bad guy, Nathan Burdette, tries to intimidate him and Chance and Stumpy by having the greasers in his bar play a particular somehow-ominous tune. They said the name of it, but I forget. Feathers—Angie Dickinson, with those legs—has a crush on potbellied John Wayne. He looks old enough to be her father, but she likes it that he's manly and confident, capable, in control. He barks out orders to everyone, including her. Maybe women just like self-confidence in men, being in control of life and not having doubts, even if their disgusting fat gut's hanging over their belt and they walk like they have a gerbil up their ass. What do I know?

Even Ricky Nelson, the sultry teenage heartthrob, has a part in the movie, as Colorado.

I wish Linc were here today. I wouldn't mind Linc being here today. It wouldn't be bad to talk with him a little. He liked Ricky. I'd feel better, I think, if he were here. He seems to have confidence, like John T. Chance. Today I'd sort of like to hear him commenting on some stupid game on TV, cussing out a referee maybe, or doing one of his songs. Maybe one of these days he'll sing that one Ricky Nelson song:

> *Hello Mary Lou, goodbye heart.*
> *Sweet Mary Lou, I'm so in love with you.*
> *I knew, Mary Lou, we'd never part...*
> *So hello Mary Lou, goodbye heart.*

"At peace now," huh? Well, that's a lovely thing to think. It must be. I wish I believed it. I don't. He's not at peace, he's just history. He's a memory. He's not in heaven, finally happy after his sufferings and with God at last and enjoying his reward for being good and living by the rules. His life's just over, before it should've been. That's all. Nothing more. I'd *like* to believe Ricky's soul's in heaven now, and forever, out of pain and in bliss and enjoying some beautiful reward. At peace now. But I don't. That'd be comforting to believe, but either you believe that sort of thing or you don't. Hell, I'd like to believe that if you cast your bread upon the water it'll come back tenfold. But I don't. I believe I'll just get soggy bread. I'd like to believe that if I put my tooth under the pillow the Tooth Fairy'll bring me a few bucks. I'd *like* to believe I'll see Ricky again down the road, up there in a lovely peaceful place somewhere over the rainbow, and Grandma too, and we could all spend eternity together in great happiness and contentment enjoying each other's company and watching the angels playing their harps or whatever it is they do. I wish that'd be the way it is. But it isn't. At least I don't think it is. Maybe it is. So if sweet Randi wants to believe he's at peace, fine. More power to her. It doesn't cost me anything if that's what she thinks, does it? If that fairy tale comforts that randy little registered nurse, fine.

Still, Ricky's bad times are over now. There's that. Maybe that's a lot. Maybe that's good enough. Maybe that's all you can expect. He had a good run for a while until he got mucked and then his good run ended. Abruptly. Now his run's over. Good, bad or mediocre, it's over. Probably he would've had a long good run if he hadn't gotten mucked in that football game. Maybe he'd have discovered a cure for cancer or hemorrhoids or

Down syndrome or even just the common cold, with all that sniffling and sore throat and hacking and stuffed-up head. Or pneumonia. Goddamned pneumonia. Maybe he'd have been a wonderful dentist or a plumbing contractor. A great father. Maybe an athlete. Not now though. No chance now though. Now, Randi says, he's at peace. How nice.

Anyways.

Davey liked his bath in the tub. I'll do that from now on. It takes a little more time. So what? Maybe once in a while, on weekends anyway, I'll put a little bubble bath stuff in his tub. He'd like that, I think. I believe he'd like that. Maybe he'd like playing with the bubbles. We'll see.

Well, I hope Ricky liked the movies. I think he did. It seemed he did. He smiled or even laughed a little at a lot of parts. He liked it when Stan screwed up his great face and cried. *Swiss Miss*, I think, was his favorite, the part with Stan and the dog and the brandy. I liked it when he and Buddy, and later Davey, too, would sit around watching in the afternoons, particularly on the weekends when the big shots weren't around. I remember how he laughed when Ollie, in some movies, would turn to Stan, all exasperated, and say, "Why don't you do something to *help* me?" or "Well, here's *another* nice mess you've gotten me into."

I remember, too, how he got a kick from the part in *Pardon Us* where the boys decide to go on a hunger strike in the prison and one of the guards says, "What? You're not going to eat that nice big roast *turkey* with chestnut dressing and sweet potatoes Southern style, *great big* pans of hot biscuits, and strawberry shortcake *smothered* in whipped cream, sprinkled with powdered sugar, with a nice big maraschino cherry on top, followed by a nice *big* slice of ice-cold watermelon, and a big black cigar?" Stan asks, "Any nuts?" and the guard says, *"All* you can eat of them." Ricky liked that.

I'd watch with them when I could. Now and again I got the other guys gathered around—Gramps and Timmy, even Arnie. That was nice, a bunch of my Group One guys together. I hope they got a laugh here and there. But toward the end, Ricky'd get to coughing when he laughed and a couple times couldn't catch his breath. That was scary for him. I could see in his face how scared he was.

He must have been scared to go to the hospital this last time again, to leave the ward and go there. This is where his friends were. This is where I could watch out for him a little, and Mary Lou, too, try to make him comfortable, maybe a little less scared. This is where I read to him and

Buddy, and would've more. I'll still read to Buddy, and maybe Davey. I wish I could've figured out how to read *Huck Finn* to them without being crude. I know they'd have liked it. I know Ricky would've. He would've liked the part where Jim grouses to Huck about King Solomon wanting to chop the disputed baby in two. Oh, well. I just hope to Christ I did *something* right.

Tonight I'm going to plop my pathetic ass in my beige recliner and be with Stanley. I'll heat a can of cream of tomato soup and make a grilled cheese on rye, probably with Swiss, maybe just American, and Stan and I'll watch one of my videos. It'll be a tribute to Ricky. I'll think of him. Maybe *Blockheads*. Or maybe *A Chump at Oxford*. I like the part where Stan gets clunked on the head by a window and reverts to his identity as Lord Paddington, the greatest scholar and athlete in Oxford history. Ollie becomes His Lordship's valet and Stan orders him around and criticizes him. "Fatty," he exclaims in a nasally aristocratic voice, "you don't seem to have the *dignity* becoming of a lackey ... no, uh, *poise*." I never got around to showing that one to Ricky and Buddy. They would've liked it. Ricky would've laughed at the part where Stan, as Paddington, wiggles his ears when he gets angry and the parts where Ollie looks right into the camera and sighs, pleading for our sympathy. Well, someday soon I'll set up Buddy and Davey to watch that one. I'll maybe bring Gramps and Timmy over too, and Arnie. Maybe even Dino, so he can hear the sounds, especially the theme song that's at the start of each movie, "Dance of the Cuckoos." Dino likes that cuckoo sound at the end.

I'll cut my sandwich diagonally so I can dip the pointed ends in my soup. That's fine, the tomato soup and bread and cheese flavors mixed together. I remember I did that once at school and Boyd guffawed at me. He said the way I shook the excess soup off my sandwich before eating it was "like a wimpo namby-pamby." Maybe he was right.

It'll be good to be with Stan tonight, him sleeping on my afghan-covered lap. I'll rub the top of his head and scratch gently behind each ear, maybe bend his ears a little like I do, and scratch under his chin and stroke the fur on his orange back while he sleeps—long slow strokes. He likes that. Me too. It's calming somehow. When I see Destini this week, I think I'll talk to her about that fat black cat she's looking to find a home for. I asked Stan if he'd like a friend and he didn't say no, so I think it'd be okay. Allan's not a good name though. After the movie I'll read some and then probably fall asleep, hopefully with Stan still on my pathetic lap.

Destini. She's one of those people where the more you see them, the more you sort of like them.

What do I do during *my* run, assuming it lasts for a while? I'll never discover a cure for anything, not even the common damn cold, and I'll definitely never be some desperate suicidal dentist. It wouldn't be bad to keep being here, though, with these guys—Buddy and Arnie and Dino and all, and even that whack-job Larry. Taking care of these guys is certainly better than poking around into people's miserable stinking mouths day after dreary day and then slumping home, soul-weary, to guzzle martinis and contemplate doing yourself in—that temptation of sweet oblivion.

Poor Mary Lou. She'll be broken up about Ricky. I'll tell her when she gets in. Maybe I should even call her at home first. Maybe I'll get to hug her and feel her bazooms, which aren't little and pert, mashed against my puny loser's chest. That wouldn't be horrible.

BUDDY

I AIN'T FELT SO LOW since I don't know when. I can't believe Ricky's gone. Somehow it don't seem real. It don't seem right. I keep looking over to his bed and kinda expect to see him there, lying there like he did, maybe with his eyes closed and just being so quiet and still like lately.

Hell of a life!

I wish it'd been me. I do. I just wish I could've died and he could've stayed living, and even got better. If I could've made a deal like that with God, I would've done it. I don't know if things work like that. I don't know nothing. I'm just a useless no-good-to-nobody nothinghead taking up space. Now I've lost my best friend, and he was just a kid. A kid.

I feel dumb for feeling sorry for myself. It's Ricky who ran out of luck here, not me. I'm still alive. I don't know for how long, but right now I'm still alive. I lived longer than he did, and I'm still here. I maybe ain't all that happy, but I'm here. So why should I feel sorry for myself? It don't make sense. But that's how I feel.

Mrs. Hanson said to Rita that "God needed him." I wonder why? Did He need Ricky to be one of them choirboys up in heaven? Maybe to carry messages back and forth between some of them angels? Maybe to be an angel himself? I don't know. How does Mrs. Hanson know that stuff anyway? So God says, "I need me a twelve-year-old kid. Okay, let's see. I'll take ... *him*—that skinny little blue-eyed guy down there in B Ward, the one next to that drooling old fool all slumped over in that there ugly brown wheelchair." Who knows how that sort of thing works? I wonder if God'll ever need me for something. I can't imagine what though. It ain't like I got any talents or skills or nothing.

I hope Ricky's in heaven now, and doing okay. I hope he's happy there. Maybe by now he's met my Aunt Irene up there, and she's introduced him around a little and is kinda watchin' over him for the first week or so, showing him around and telling him the rules and all like that. Father Callahan said in heaven we get to sit at Jesus's feet. I guess that's okay, but I imagine Ricky's tired of sittin' around, like he had to down here, and he'd just as soon move around a little, and maybe even dance or run around or just take a long walk in them clouds. That's what I'm gonna do when I get there, and it'll be great to take a walk with him, with all four of our legs working just fine, thank you very damn much. I got nothin' against Jesus, and I'm sure he's kind and warm and concerned and all like that, but just sitting around at his feet for eternity ain't my idea of heaven.

I don't know if you eat in heaven. I don't imagine you do 'cause you're dead and done with your body and all, but I don't know. If you do eat up there, I hope you can have as much bread as you want—all different stuff, like rolls and muffins and toast and everything—and that you get to dip it in gravy. That sounds like a good heaven to me.

I don't know if they have movies and shows and stuff like that in heaven, but I hope so. Me, I'd like to see some movies about pirates. I been thinking about that now and again since Billy read *Treasure Island* to me and Ricky. I liked that movie me and Billy watched yesterday afternoon, that cowboy movie. I liked that Stumpy. He was funny, cranky like he was and always buttin' into everyone's business. I liked it when that mean rich guy came to visit his brother in jail and the sheriff told him that if anyone tried a jailbreak his brother'd get "accidentally shot." Stumpy did that weird high-pitched laugh he did a lot and said, "I can practical *guarantee* that!" That was good. But I wish I could see some movies or TV shows about pirates and the stuff they did. When Billy was reading that story, I could picture Long John Silver and George Merry and them guys. I still wonder why Captain Flint's face was blue, like Silver said. I never understood that. Was he just cold? And then Silver's parrot who was always squawking, "Pieces of eight! Pieces of eight!" That was neat. I wonder what a piece of eight is.

I'd like it if they'd have a parrot here in B Ward, some green thing in a cage near the front desk or, better yet, flyin' around and perching on the rails of guys' cribs and screaming out cuss words and stuff. Dino'd get a kick out of that. I bet a parrot'd like being in the solarium with us guys and looking out the window and seeing all them other birds, the sparrows and hawks and whatnot.

That's one thing I'm gonna miss, being in the solarium with Ricky. That was something I'll always think of, always remember. Toward the end there, Ricky wasn't in such good shape. He seemed cold out there pretty much, and sometimes he could barely stay awake. I'll never forget how he looked when he was out there the last few weeks. Bad. I remember how pale his face was, and how sometimes he just lay there so still in his cart, covered up, not moving hardly at all. But there were good times before then, when a bunch of us would be out there, even guys like Dino and Jimmy, and old Arnie hunched over lookin' at his catalogs, and Gramps with them two ugly dolls he's always tonguing, and Timmy, and Davey too, and Ricky could be there sitting up in his chair then, and it was nicest in the summer with the sun shining and the leaves on the trees and we could see the cornstalks green and shiny in the sun. That was good. Now Ricky'll never be out there with us guys ever again. Not ever.

I guess I wouldn't mind if they'd take me to his funeral to say good-bye. They most likely ain't gonna let me do that though.

Sometimes I wonder if that Doc Winters did a good enough job of looking after Ricky. I don't know. I always liked him okay, but it seems like he never gets too worried about stuff. Every time he comes into the ward he just kinda shuffles in, same blank expression on his face, his gray crewcut head sorta leaning to one side, and looks over the charts and when he comes to check on any of us he hardly ever says a word. He'll maybe say "Hello, Buddy," to me but that's about it. I noticed when he'd look in on Ricky, a lot lately, he hardly ever said anything to him. He musta known that Ricky could understand stuff, but he never said much—just poked at him and looked at his eyes and ears and stuff and listened to his chest with that black thing that hangs on his neck. He'd talk to them nurses who always hang around with him when he's in the ward, Randi and them, but not much to us guys. I never even seen him smile, now that I think of it. Maybe he's one of the greatest doctors in the history of the world, but he don't inspire confidence somehow. If I get sick, I ain't all that sure Doc Winters would do so great taking care of me.

But what the hell's the difference? I'd just as soon be done with this life as quick as I can anyway, so I can get my stupid feeb ass up to heaven and see Ricky again and be done with all these damned indignities.

This morning, for instance. Before the day shift started, the aide who was working nights—Andrea I think her name is, usually works on C Ward—was helping me pee. She held that metal urinal for me and I peed and she was shaking my thing off, getting the last drops, and accidentally banged my dingus against the side of the urinal. *Damn,* that hurt! Bernie's a lot more careful. Maybe she had something on her mind, I don't know, but she shoulda been more careful. It still kinda hurts. That there's a delicate little thing. Plus, she had this ring on her finger with a big red stone of some damn kind, and I was afraid she'd scratch me down there. Well, when I get to heaven I won't have worries like *that* no more.

I'm glad today's Monday and the weekend's over. They don't show them soap operas on weekends, and I miss that. Today Billy put me and Davey in front of the TV after lunch and right now we're watching *All My Children*. Erica's all pissed off about something, I don't know what, but she's ranting and raving to some poor blue-eyed blond lady in a pretty yellow dress. "I will not be *treated* that way," she's saying. "Who can you think you *are* to speak to me in *that* tone of voice?" Seems like she's pissed off a lot, pitching fits and all, but maybe she got good reasons. Maybe people are mean to her a lot. Billy even talks mean about her. Every now and again he stops to watch the show for a minute, and one time when she was on he shook his head and said, "Jesus Christ, what a little bitch. Glad I don't have to put up with *her* bullshit."

Billy's sad about Ricky, too. I can see that. Yesterday he was more down than I ever seen him. A couple times there I thought he might cry. He was better, though, when we watched that movie with old Stumpy. When Mary Lou came in for the p.m. shift the two of 'em fussed and hugged and Billy pulled her against him, sort of, and a few minutes later she took to sniffling and got all wet-eyed so he pulled her to him again and kinda held her tight for a little bit, pressing his open hand hard against her back. I guess he felt sorry for her.

Davey's quiet today. A couple times while we been sitting here I thought I seen him have them little seizures like he does, where his mouth opens and his head droops and one arm kinda jerks up a little bit and then he's okay, though I notice his eyes look funny then for a few moments, sorta blank. Once he fell asleep there in his chair, with his mouth hanging open and drooling a bit, like me, but then that kid Christopher did that cat sound he does and Dino busted out laughing and startled Davey awake. I'm glad Billy put Davey with me. Crappy as I feel about Ricky, I'm glad to have his company. I wonder if he knows about Ricky, and if he does know I wonder if he's sad too. I wish him and me could talk to each other. That'd be okay.

And I wish that after naptime Billy sets up Gramps and Timmy and them guys by me and Davey, either here by the TV or maybe out in the solarium. Arnie, too, and Dino in his cart maybe. Maybe even Jimmy and some of them guys from other groups, like Zach and Matthew. I don't know. For some reason I just feel like it'd be good today for us feebs to hang around together. That'd be okay. Not Larry, though. He's a pain in the ass.

Gramps was funny this morning. Mrs. Hanson came into the ward a little while after breakfast with some tall, thin redhead lady carrying a black notebook. I never seen her before. Gramps and Timmy were sitting together in their chairs near the tub room, and when Gramps saw Mrs. Hanson he screwed up his face and gave her one of them mean looks like he always does when he sees her or Doc Winters and some other of them important people. But then he looked over at the redhead lady and his bad look left and he just looked at her for a little bit and then his tongue come out of his old mouth and went right up his ugly nose. I don't even think she noticed him, because she was looking around at all the guys. But Timmy saw it and laughed, that weird little tinny laugh he does. Billy noticed it too. "Hey," he said to Gramps when Mrs. Hanson and the lady were at the other end of the ward, "cool it with that stupid tongue thing, you wrinkled old reprobate. You're never gonna get a girlfriend with *that* move." A minute later Hanson and the redhead walked past us again, heading outta the ward, and Billy stopped and watched 'em walking away and then turned to Gramps again and shrugged. "Then again," he said, "what do *I* know?"

Billy gave me Ricky's clock. Just before breakfast, right after he got me up and dressed, he went and unplugged it from the shelf near Ricky's bed and brought it over and put it on the little metal stand near my bed and plugged it in and set the right time. It has red numbers on it. "He would've wanted you to have this," Billy said. I'm glad he did that. I'm gonna think of Ricky every time I look at that thing.

Hell of a life!

BILLY

WHAT A DORK I am! I'm sitting here at the food court eating my pizza and studying the fluffheads in their tight jeans who've flocked to the mall after school and thinking about the funeral when all of a sudden, *BOOM!*, a piece of sausage slides down the wrong way and I panic. I coughed and hacked but couldn't dislodge the damned thing, and I imagine I was all bug-eyed and white-faced, and had a brief image of myself expiring right there and then, slumped over my table with my face in the cheese and tomato sauce. But I gulped down the rest of my big Cherry Coke and, thank God, that washed the damn thing down. The worst thing though was that three chickie-poos a few tables down noticed and stared and, when I ceased choking, commenced to tittering and chattering. I could imagine what they were saying: "Did you see *that* weirdo? Oh ... my ... God! *What* a loser! Can't even handle a slice of pizza. I've seen him here before, always *alone.* My God, how *pathetic!"*

One thing I liked, though, was that there was this couple parked in front of the Taco Bell a few minutes ago—a tall good-looking guy in a maroon sweater and gray pants and a pretty woman with long dark hair dressed in a blue-and-white-checked skirt and a jacket over a sort of ruffled white blouse, and high heels—and they stood there just facing each other with their arms around each other's waists, foreheads touching, eyes closed, for maybe two minutes. Now and again one of them would open their eyes and look in the other's face for a moment. She was wearing a name tag on her jacket, so probably she's a clerk at some silly store in the mall. People stared at them while they were hugging. They didn't care. Then, after a bit, they unclasped and kissed gently and rubbed the tips of their noses and he turned to walk out of the food court, and she watched him go, and after he was out of sight she turned and walked slowly back into the mall.

But the nice thing was that she was smiling, this mysterious kind of Mona Lisa smile, the whole time she walked away. Then just before she got out of sight, she let go this absolutely *huge* disgusting sneeze that everyone in the mall, not just the food court, probably heard. Old Dino would've loved it.

The funeral was okay, I guess. The whole thing at the church first was tough, though interesting in a way since I wasn't familiar with the ritual and didn't know what to do. I just sort of followed the lead of the people there who knew what they were doing, standing up and sitting down and standing up again and going up to the front to get a wafer from the priest and all like that. I didn't do the wafer thing. Mary Lou's boyfriend seemed pretty familiar with the whole deal. One part I liked was when the priest, who looked like Ichabod Crane, would raise one hand, fingers spread, and sing out, "The Lord be with you," and everyone would sing back, "And also with *you*." I liked that. It just seemed friendly for the crowd to throw that back to him like that. It's nice.

I liked the part, too, where the priest was telling about the Last Supper that Jesus had with the disciples, Peter and Paul and those guys, not long before the Romans croaked him, and he told his friends about the bread being his body and the wine being his blood and all that and the priest said at one point, "Again he gave thanks," referring to Jesus. I thought that was nice. *Again* he gave thanks. It just seemed very polite and humble, considering the guy's desperate plight.

The only thing is I wish it'd been more personal about Ricky. The big theme was that he'd been baptized and had Communion and so was in the everlasting glory of heaven with his Lord and enjoying eternal life in Christ Jesus and so, supposedly, all was hunky-dory. Everyone was sad he was dead, of course, but somehow I got the message from the whole deal that his death was ... a *victory* or something. It wasn't. It *wasn't!* The priest, toward the end, said a few nice things about him—he was a dutiful son and brother and grandson, he liked sports, he had many friends, he went to church regularly, blah blah—but it felt somehow like all that didn't have much to do with the kid I knew in B Ward. Then again, the kid I knew was probably just a shadow of the kid all these people knew, before he got mucked. Still.

The burial was the tough part. Watching Ricky get carried from that ugly black hearse to the gravesite was bad enough, but what was tougher was watching the casket hovering above that terrible hole in the ground on that contraption with the straps while the priest led the family and the others of us in prayer and a couple times sprinkled holy water, it must have been, on the thing, and then his parents and sisters did that too. For a moment I felt like Laertes in *Hamlet*, wanting to jump into Ophelia's grave. But that passed and I just wanted to get it over with and come here to the food court for a while and then get back to my apartment, to Stan, and away from the gloom, the tears, the stream of empty words, words, words. When the blather and prayers were finally done and the mourners gone from the gravesite and the cemetery guys had lowered Ricky into the ground, I left as quickly as possible.

They had a thing at the family's house afterward, with food and, I imagine, more blather, but I didn't go.

Poor Mary Lou. She'd sobbed a little bit there at the church and again at the cemetery, and Duane did his best to be kind to her. He'd cut his hair and sliced off that ugly goatee since the one time I'd seen him, and wore a nice blue suit to the funeral, but I'm not sure his tie was all that tasteful for the event. It had cartoon drawings on it of Donald Duck and his three nephews—Huey, Dewey and Louie. But whenever Mary Lou blubbered, he at least threw a skinny arm around her, with an elastic bandage wrapped around one wrist, or held her hand or touched her some way or another, which seemed nice. Once I saw him pull a white handkerchief from his back pocket and dab at her eyes when the priest was telling how Ricky was enjoying his great reward or some such. That sentiment got her all misty.

I wonder if Mary Lou would rather Linc'd been there with her instead of Duane.

Earlier in the week, I'd mentioned to her that maybe it'd be good for Buddy to be able to come to Ricky's funeral. I didn't ask him, and maybe I should've, but I think he'd have wanted to go. Mary Lou asked Mrs. Hanson if that could happen, but, of course, the witch said no. "I don't believe that would be *appro*priate," she'd said, her long nose pointed north. Mary Lou argued with the hag a little, bless her heart, but to no avail. I wish I had her balls.

I wonder why I didn't cry. I felt like it. When I was staring at that dark -brown casket and then at the hole it was soon going into, and knowing that Ricky—what was left of him—was inside that box, and thinking that he'd be in that damned thing tonight, covered with dirt, alone and cold, instead of in his bed in B Ward, covered with his orange comforter, I felt like crying. Maybe I can do that tonight, at home. I'll be warm there, in my chair, covered with Grandma's afghan, behind our locked door. It'll just be Stan and me.

I told Destini I'd take her cat. I'm thinking I'll change Allan's name to *Ollie*. It sounds close enough that he hopefully won't know the difference. The thing I'm thinking about, though, is what if he wants to sleep in my lap too? I don't know if that'll work. Stan pretty much spreads himself out when he's there, so I don't believe there'd be room even for a little cat. And Destini said Allan weighs close to twenty pounds. Maybe he can just sit *next* to me in the chair. I'll have to maybe put him on a diet. Maybe I'll call that Sheila at the shelter, with the high-pitched voice, and see what she recommends.

That little Destini seemed glad I agreed to take the cat. She gave me a nice smile, that nice crooked one she does, and her eyes were warm.

So now I'll feel better about going to Junior's before work or the mall once in a while after work, when I feel like it, and not have to worry so much about Stanley being lonely.

Next week sometime, I'll maybe go see Christy before work. That'll be okay. That'll be fine. I'll sit there on my usual red-plastic-covered stool and order my usual eggs over easy and white toast and bacon and just sit there with the regulars, even that corned beef hash asshole, and shlurp my coffee and eyeball that pockmarked little waitress, her sweet little butt swishing around so pleasantly in that tight green uniform, kidding around with the guys and refilling coffee. *"More, hon?"* I wonder what Christy'd think of my little home and my feline companions. I guess I'll never know.

I wonder what my mother'd think of all that. My life. Thanksgiving's soon. I'd like to see her. The old man, the hell with him. But I'd like to see her. I should, anyway. I've been thinking that I should reach out, some way or another. I should do that. I will. Maybe I'll call her before Thanksgiving. I hope she's okay.

Thanksgiving. Christ almighty! Now Rita and the rest will no doubt be decorating the ward with pilgrims and Indians and cornstalks and silly cardboard things of the various bounties, pumpkins and squash and ears of corn and roast beef and the like. Gramps and Timmy always enjoy that holiday festivities stuff, and even Arnie gets a kick out of it now and again. For some reason, Arnie liked it when they put up those green shamrock cutouts for Saint Patrick's Day. He did his little girl giggle. Davey squealed last year when they put up the Christmas tree. Larry, he could care less about Thanksgiving. The main thing he'd be thankful for is if his incessant whacking paid dividends once in a while, like I think it did the other day when he yelled "ZORCH!"

I'll have to think hard about what I'm thankful for when that day rolls around. Probably there's a lot.

I don't know what Buddy thinks of the holiday decorations. I never paid attention. I wish he could've come to the funeral. I wish he was here with me now at the mall. The lech might like seeing the chickie-poo fluffheads.

Maybe this weekend I'll get the guys together, Buddy and Davey and Arnie and others, and we'll watch *Sons of the Desert*, with Stan Laurel eating Mrs. Hardy's wax fruit. Or maybe *A Chump at Oxford*. All us chumps together.

Anyways.

About the Author

Now and at the Hour is Martin Drapkin's first work of fiction, followed by *Ten Nobodies (and their somebodies)*, *The Cat Tender*, and *Poor Tom*—all available through www.HenschelHAUSbooks.com.

Marty is also a photographer, specializing in black-and-white street photographs and portraits of mothers and daughters. He and his wife, Erica, live in rural Cross Plains, Wisconsin, with several mildly neurotic rescue dogs.

For more information, please visit Marty's website,
www.drapkinbooks.com

Printed in the USA
CPSIA information can be obtained
at www.ICGtesting.com
CBHW062247020924
14006CB00028BB/729